Jenni,

May God

Bless You

Always.

Love,
D. A. Rhodes
7-22-13

This book is a work of fiction. Names, characters, places, and incidents are products of the author's imagination or are used fictitiously. Any resemblance to actual events or locales or persons, living or dead, is entirely coincidental.

For information regarding special discounts for bulk purchases, please contact D.A. Rhodes at dasrho@yahoo.com

Cover and layout design by Delaney-Designs
Manufactured in the United States of America

ISBN - 13: 978-0-615-31900-1
ISBN - 10:   0-615-31900-1

WHY?

D.A. Rhodes

A Note From The Author

I began the journey of writing this book over eight years ago. I asked the question, why would God allow little girls to be molested by the very men who claim to love them . . . their fathers, uncles, brothers, and even close family friends? That simple, yet profound, question turned into the work of fiction you hold in your hands. While this is not my story, it is a story that needs to be told. It is my prayer that you will walk away from this reading experience more enlightened, having a deeper sense of compassion for victims of child molestation, and healing if you are one of the millions of people who have had to endure such pain and suffering.

There are so many people to thank for helping to make this dream a reality. Thank you, Jesus, for strength and endurance throughout this entire process. Thanks for listening to me in the midnight hour as I cried, laughed and just asked for guidance and wisdom as I put the words you gave me to paper. Mom, thanks for your continued support and for being the first to recognize that I lived in a dream world and helping me to develop my daydreams into stories that others would actually want to read. I love you with everything I have and ever hope to have. To my brothers, Lewis and Stevo, your never ending support and encouragement has meant the world to me. Just knowing that I can depend on the two of you in my time of need has made my journey a little smoother. I love you both.

Unfortunately, my dad, Wendell Sockwell, did not live to see this day, but his love, memory and legacy will live forever. Dad supported me in everything I did. No matter how big or small, good or bad, he was there to cheer me on. I know without a shadow of a doubt he loved me with everything he had to give. Thank you, Dad, for your love and for being a constant force in my life.

My true motivation for not only completing this book, but for everything else I do in my life, is my daughter, Imani Marie. She is the true light of my life. May God's blessings, mercies, peace and favor follow you all the days of your life.

A million and one thanks to everyone on my "team." Although we never had one team meeting, it took an entire team to pull this project together. Each person on my team was truly a Godsend, and I wouldn't have made it without them. The team consisted of; my editors, Velda Love and Alifa Omar. Diane Wilson, my friend, my cousin and my marketing director. Thanks for your support over the years and always telling me I could make it. Stephanie Jackson, most importantly, my prayer partner, and one of the many people who helped to keep me organized when things got a bit hectic. DeWayne Glover, when asked what you would do on the team you boldly said, "I'm here to advise you on your book." You didn't realize you were really sent to be my spiritual advisor. Thank you for keeping me grounded, always applying the word of God to every situation and sharing your wisdom with me. Janel Reliford, thank you, girl, for putting together an awesome website. I almost cried tears of joy when I pulled up **www.darhodes.com** for the first time. It exceeded all of my expectations. I still smile every time

I look at the site, and can't wait for others to check it out. Stephanie Dunn, the woman who wrote and produced my very first radio spot for this book, and who also produced the first chapter of the audio book. Your talent is unmatched. Your commercial made me want to buy my own book. Thank you for believing in me and the book. Jock Hardy, thank you, for your love and support along this journey. Your creative ideas, ability to see everything in a positive light, always pushing me towards excellence, not allowing me to give up, has meant more to me than you'll ever know. Kim Walton. Thank you, thank you, thank you. You have been my stylist, my mentor and my sister. You are the one with whom I share all of my crazy thoughts, ideas and dreams, the one who sees everything way bigger than I could ever imagine and yet, somehow, convince me that it really is attainable. Thank you for being my midwife in the birthing of "Why?" Knowing that this baby was well overdue, you stepped in and held me accountable for pushing this baby to life. I can't thank you enough for your vision, love and support.

Finally, thank you After Eight Book Club - My book club. Toni Hall, Jutta Browder, Dawn Chambliss, Tracie Tyson, Crystal Mitchell, Stephanie Jackson, Bridgette Thomas, Al Oneal, Vertreasa Hunt and Peggy Salmon. Thank you, guys for your support over the years. You have been with me during my ups and downs, have read rough drafts of not only this book but other stories as well. Thanks for your honest feedback and continued encouragement. I love you guys.

D. A. Rhodes

CHAPTER 1

ELLA

Sunday, May 5, 1963, life as my family knew it changed forever. At 6 p.m. my father walked into *"The Corner Bar"* on 55th and South Park in search of his baby brother, Do-Man. *"The Corner Bar"* was Do-Man's favorite spot. Making his way through the smoke laden room that was unusually crowded for a Sunday evening, and the sounds of B.B. King soulfully telling yet another story of how his woman was cheating on him, my father found Do-Man perched on his usual bar stool in the corner, by the big plate glass window at the front of the bar. When Daddy walked in and saw Do-man sipping his Gin and Tonic, taking long slow drags from his Kool 100's, laughing and talking with the other regulars, he froze. The rage that he had been carrying around for the past two days made him crazy.

Juanita, one of the pretty barmaids that Do-Man liked to flirt with, had just freshened up his drink when she looked in my father's direction and knew that something was wrong. She stopped laughing and quickly turned back to Do-Man and said, "Do Baby, ain't that yo' brother standing over there by the door looking like he 'bout to kill somebody?"

Before Do-Man could put his drink down and tell my father to join him, my father was standing two feet in front of him with a 38 Smith and Wesson pointed at Do-Man's head. After about ten seconds of silence, someone yelled, "Damn! Dat nigga got a gun!" Feet started shuffling, tables were turned over, and people started screaming and running for cover. Then, BANG! BANG! BANG! BANG! BANG! BANG! Daddy unloaded his 38 on Do-Man. Do-Man fell back on his stool crashing into the wall. Blood shot from his chest, mouth and forehead. My father stood over his brother's body, a hot gun dangling from his curled fingers as his hands dropped to his sides. Silence was the only sound allowed until the biting screams of the ambulance sirens broke the spell. The police were the first to enter the bar with their guns drawn. They stood at the end of the bar and yelled at my father, "Drop the gun, nigger!" Daddy did as he was told and put his hands up. The police put the metal bracelets around my father's wrists and the paramedics rushed in to take Do-Man's vitals. They discovered what everyone else in the joint already knew. Do-Man was dead.

At the trial, Daddy showed no remorse, no emotion what-so-ever. Not once did he even look at the jury of his peers: nine white men, two white women and one old, black woman. At the end of the three day trial, Daddy was found guilty of pre-meditated murder. But the judge went easy on him and gave him twenty years.

"Will the defendant please rise?" the bailiff ordered.

"Mr. Boxx," the Judge began, "you have been found guilty by a jury of your peers. Is there anything that you would like to say before I pronounce sentencing?" My father slowly raised his head, stared the judge in the eyes and said, "My only regret is that I could only kill him once." Surprised, but not shocked by my father's response, the judge replied, "Lee Otis Boxx, I do hereby sentence you to 20 years in the state prison. Not becoming eligible for parole before serving at least ten years."

My mother let out a loud scream. My sisters and I wept in silence as we watched our father walk out of our lives. Right before he crossed the threshold that would take him away for the next ten to twenty years, he stopped, turned around and looked at his family, as he knew it, for the last time. The moment was stolen when everyone's attention was drawn to the back of the courtroom, to the loud voice of a very small woman shouting, "Fear thou not, for I am with thee: Be not dismayed; for I am thy God; I will strengthen thee; yea, I will help thee: yea, I will uphold thee with the right hand of my righteousness!"

It was that crazy woman from East St. Louis, the one who stood on the street corners screaming Bible verses to all the sinners passing by. What was she doing here? How did she get here?! The entire courtroom was stunned. The judge struck his gavel and screamed, "Order! Order in the courtroom! Order in the courtroom! Bailiff, get that woman out of here!" Before the bailiff could reach the woman, she turned around, walked out and disappeared. We turned back to my father only to hear the steel door slam shut.

My family and I rode the CTA (Chicago Transit Authority) bus home in complete silence. I wondered what would happen to us now that Daddy was gone. With her face firmly pressed against the window, my mother blankly watched the outside world creep by as the bus took its sweet time going from stop to stop. She closed her eyes and a single tear rolled down her cheek. Opening her eyes, she caught me looking at her. Ashamed, I lowered my head. A part of me blamed my mother for what was happening. She insisted on working even after Daddy told her he wanted her to stay home to be with me and my sisters. Her only concern was having brand new furniture and a new television set for the holidays. That way, she could show off in good fashion for our relatives coming from East St. Louis. Instead of working, my mother should have been home to protect me from Do-Man.

Had I never told my father about Do-Man sneaking down to our apartment and into my bedroom while my parents were at work, none of this would have happened, and my father would still be with his family instead of locked up in some prison.

CHAPTER 2

LEE OTIS

Yeah, my only regret is that I killed him once. Every time that bastard touched my baby, he killed her over and over. Hell, I did his ass a favor by only shooting him six times. But my baby...my baby...my baby...She'll always be haunted by the memories of what Do-Man did to her, day after day.

My brother was propped up on that bar stool staring at me with that stupid ass grin on his face. The same grin he used on Mama, when we were kids, to stop her from beating his behind. Well, that shit wasn't working on me. Here this nigga was, my own damn brother, and he go and do this to my baby girl. The thought of it makes me want to kill him again.

CHAPTER 3

ELLA

How does one begin to tell a story of such pain, anguish and shame? My Grandma Babe would say, "From the beginning." Well, my name is Ella Mae Boxx and I have two older sisters, Mattie, who is four years my senior, and Cora, who is two years older than me. My mother named me Ella after one of her dead aunts on her father's side. I don't know why she would name me after someone dead, but she did. Anyway, I was born in East St. Louis, Illinois in 1955 during the time when the stock yards were booming. My family moved to Chicago when I was seven years old because my father, who had been out of work for three months, got a job as an insurance man for the Unified Insurance Company in Chicago. His baby brother, Cleofis, a.k.a. Do-Man, who had moved to Chicago a year earlier, had been trying to convince my dad to move to the big city for months. Do-Man had been run out of East St. Louis in 1959 because he was suspected of molesting the five year old daughter of his live-in girl friend. The woman's family tried to make her press charges against Do-Man, but she wouldn't. Our family believes she wouldn't have him arrested because she thought Do-

Man would marry her, and if she pressed charges, her chances of marrying a half way decent man would be over. See, she was one of those really pretty women that had the worst luck with men.

One night, the woman's father and three brothers cornered Do-Man coming out of a local joint. The oldest brother put a switch blade to Do-Man's throat, another brother stuck a knife in his ribs. The third brother held a pistol tightly against Do-Man's groin, while the father stood nose to nose with Do-Man and whispered, "Death would be too good for a nigga' like you. But I tell you what. I'm gon' give you something to remember my grandbaby by." The grandfather stepped back and spat a wad of tobacco juice in Do-Man's face. Just as the slimy brown liquid crept down his face and hit the top of his eel skin shoe, the brother holding the knife slowly slid the blade from the right side of Do-Man's neck to the bottom of his left ear, leaving a trail of blood in its path. That night, Do-Man gassed up his 1950 Fleetwood, Cadillac and hit the highway heading North – north to Chicago, where he stayed until his untimely death.

No one knows for sure if Do-Man molested that little girl, but after that incident the family secretly looked at Do-Man with a suspicious eye. They didn't have the courage to openly say anything. Truth be told, no one wanted to believe such a thing about the man everyone loved to see coming. It wasn't a party in our family until Uncle Do-Man arrived. He always had a funny story to tell, a compliment to dole out, a drink in his hand, and the prettiest woman in East St. Louis on his arm. Everyone loved Do-Man, except for me. My gut told me that Uncle Do-Man wasn't right.

He was one of those men, who hung out in joints, had lots of women, drank lots of whiskey and was nickel slick. A real cool cat. Always dressed in some colorful, outlandish, would be pimp suit. The fact that he was extremely handsome with "good hair," and a brilliant smile that showed off that gold tooth in the front of his mouth, made people overlook a lot of the mess and trouble that he so often found himself in. Being the youngest of ten brothers and sisters, known for protecting what belonged to them, didn't hurt.

After the accusations came, people began to question why he would always have the woman's little girl with him, even when the mother was not around.

Once, I overheard my Grandma Babe telling her youngest daughter, Sally, "Something just ain't right 'bout Do-Man and that little girl." They didn't realize that I was in the next room so they spoke freely as they snapped green beans in the kitchen. Aunt Sally was Grandma Babe's favorite child, so Grandma would talk to her about anything and everybody.

"Mama, why you say something ain't right with Do-Man and that little girl? It seem okay to me. Everybody knows how much Do-Man love kids."

"Listen at what I tell you. Do-Man is my son, and I know him better'n anyone. And I'm tellin' you, something ain't right there. 'Sides that, why would that woman of his leave her girl child with some man all the time like she do anyhow? Now do that make any kinda good sense to you Sally?"

Before Aunt Sally could answer, Grandma Babe huffed out, "Naw, it don't make no sense!" Just as Sally was about to respond I dropped my silver jax and ball on the floor.

"Who's der!" Grandma shouted.

"Uh, it's just me, Grandma. I was coming in to git some water." I lied.

"Um-hmm. Well, git yo' nosy self on in here and git yo' water and git on back outside fo' I make you come in and stay. Then you can help me and Sally wit dese here beans."

I sheepishly went in to the kitchen, got my water and drank it slowly, hoping they would resume their conversation despite me being there. No such luck.

"If you not gon' drink that there water, give it to me and I'll finish it fo' you," Grandma said as she snapped her green bean. I knew that was my cue to hurry up and get out. I gulped the last of my water and put the glass in the sink, not bothering to rinse it out. I turned to walk out of the kitchen and Grandma said, "Gone on out the back door. And if you keeps running in and out of my house, I'm gon' keep you in here. Now git on out there!"

As the screen door slammed behind me, I heard Grandma say, "That there the nosiest grandchild I's got. Bet she know mo' family secrets than the skeletons themselves." They both laughed and went back to snapping green beans.

I didn't hear anything else about Do-Man and the little girl until her mother paid him a visit in Chicago.

CHAPTER 4

LEE OTIS

My 3:30 P.M. appointment with Mr. and Mrs. Jones turned out to be waste of time, or so I thought. Mr. Jones didn't come home until 4 o'clock. Old Grand-Dad was his cologne of choice. The fragrance hit me as soon as he walked in the door and stumbled over to the couch where Mrs. Jones and I sat going over the insurance papers they were to sign that evening. Mr. Jones stood right above his wife, with his crouch in her face, and said, "What the hell is this nigga doing in my house and I ain't here?" Mrs. Jones looked up at her husband and said, "Calvin, you better sit yo' drunk ass down somewhere, and git the hell out of my face!"

That was my cue to get my things and get out of there. Everyone in the neighborhood knew that whenever Calvin Jones went home drunk, which was every other day, there was going to be a fight at the Jones' house that night. We also knew that when Mr. Jones woke up the next day his hangover would be accompanied with two or three hickies on his head, compliments of Mrs. Jones.

I told her that I would reschedule our appointment once things calmed down. As I was about to walk out of the door, Calvin Jones slurred my name, "Hey Boxx!" I slowly turned around and said, "Yeah, what is it, man?"

Swaying from side to side he muttered, "Uh, I heard that Do-Man uh…"

"You heard that Do-Man what?"

Before he could finish his sentence his wife interrupted and said, "Don't pay Calvin no mind, Mr. Boxx. He drunk out of his head and don't hardly know what he talkin' 'bout."

"The hell I don't! I knows exactly what" he let out a burp, "I'm talkin' 'bout." Mr. Jones said still swaying from side to side.

"Well spit it out, man. What you got to say about my brother?" For some reason Calvin Jones thought it would be better if he stood directly in front of me when he said what he had to say. So he attempted to lift one leg and put it in front of the other, but the alcohol rushing through his body wouldn't allow him to lift his leg fast enough. So he drug it around and tried to put his weight on it, causing him to crash to the floor. I stood in place watching the pathetic Mr. Jones try and pull himself up from the floor. His wife bent down and tried to help him up but he shooed her away.

After several failed attempts, he finally pulled himself up and let the poisonous words fall from his mouth. "Word on the street is, Do-Man like young, tender meat. And he like to keep it real close to home."

"Man, what in the hell are you talking about?"

The whiskey told Calvin Jones that I didn't understand what he was trying to say, because he was standing too far away. So he got right in my face and said, "I mean Do-Man likes young gals."

"So what that got to do with me?"

"One of dem young gals is yours."

Before I realized it, Calvin Jones was on the floor again, this time holding his jaw. I was standing over him and his wife was kneeling by his side holding his head in her lap. I turned around and stormed out of their basement apartment and ran the entire four blocks to my own home.

When I got there, my two oldest daughters were outside talking with some friends. I immediately knew they were not the ones in danger; it was my baby, Ella. I ran up the three flights of stairs to our apartment and saw my wife standing over the stove cooking dinner. The minute she saw me she knew something was wrong and asked, "What you doin' home so early? Is everything alright?"

"Where is Ella?" I said, as I began to look around the apartment. She put her cooking spoon down and followed me through the apartment. "Ella is in her room. Why? What's going on?" she said.

I opened the door to Ella's room and found her in the bed under the covers. I rushed over to her and realized that she was asleep. As I stood there looking at my baby girl everything started making sense. For the past couple of weeks, she seemed withdrawn around others. After dinner she would go right back to her room. Whenever I tried to get her to stay up front with the rest of us and watch television, she would always come up with some excuse. Her mother and I thought she was just upset because we told her she would only be spending three weeks of her summer vacation in East St. Louis instead of the whole summer like we had planned. Come to think of it, Ella didn't look sick at all, she looked dead.

Her eyes were vacant, and she barely talked. She never went outside to play, didn't even want to sit on my lap and complain about how she hated Chicago, and couldn't wait to get back to East St. Louis and her Grandma Babe.

I looked at her mother and asked, "Has she said anything to you about Do-Man or anybody looking at her or touching her in any way!?" My wife looked at me with horror in her eyes. "No! She hasn't said anything to me about Do-Man or anybody else! Why?

What's going on!?"

If Calvin Jones was telling the truth, somebody was going to die that night.

CHAPTER 5

DO-MAN

I can't believe my own brother shot me! Shot me in a bar; the bar where I hung out; in front of all my friends. He shot me dead! What kind of shit is that?! Yeah, yeah, I know y'all saying I deserved to die, but before you become judge and jury, hear me out. I got a story to tell just like everybody else.

See, you don't understand the pain and turmoil I had to endure growing up. My life wasn't easy. Coming up the youngest of ten kids wasn't no picnic. It was every man for himself. Only the strong survived, and damn it, I was gon' survive. Those niggers wasn't gon' leave me behind. We even had to fight for Mama's attention and affection. With all those kids it was easy to get lost in the shuffle. And if you didn't make any noise, you was forgotten about like last Sunday's sermon. So I did whatever I had to do to make sure Mama and everybody else noticed me. I even tried to get my Daddy to show me some love, but he always dismissed me like I didn't count. That hurt like hell; nothing worse than a man's Daddy not taking any real interest in him. Fucks with a boy's self esteem, makes him wonder where he fits in in the whole scheme of things; makes him question his self-worth. I know Mama noticed how he made a difference between me and the other kids, but she tried to ignore it and told me that Daddy was just tired all the time, and that's why he didn't have no time for me when he came home from work. The old man never would spend time with me just for the hell of it. Oddly enough, the man always found time to give me a good beating whenever he thought I was out of line about something. Never could understand why he treated me so bad, that is, until my aunt called herself giving me a little family history lesson.

One day, Mama's oldest sister, Aunt Europa, was having a barbecue at her house. I must have been about six or seven at the time. Aunt Europa liked to drink, and by the time nightfall came, she was good and drunk. She, and all of the adults, had been inside the house dancing, drinking and playing cards. Drinking and playing cards always led to arguing and sometimes fighting. This particular night, it led to my mother and Aunt Europa arguing. Europa accused my mother of cheating during the card game. Well, my mother wasn't going to stand for anybody calling her a cheater. The argument almost ended up in a fight until Aunt Europa's boyfriend stepped in the middle of the two sisters and told Europa to go outside on the porch and cool off.

Reluctantly, Europa stepped out on the porch. Still mad because she couldn't finish the argument with my mother, Europa decided she'd settle the score by ruining my life. She spotted me running across the yard and came to the edge of the porch and yelled, "Lil' Do, git your narrow behind up here on dis porch! I got's something I want to tell you!" I ran up on the porch as ordered.

She sat down on her homemade porch swing and asked me, "Who you think you looks more like, yo Mama or yo Daddy?" she said it with a frightening smirk on her face. I shrugged my shoulders up and down and said, "I dunno. Mama say I just look like me." Aunt Europa started laughing and said, "Boy, let yo' auntie tell you a little story." She patted the empty space next to her and told me to sit down.

According to Aunt Europa, the man I called "Daddy" all my life wasn't even my Daddy. She claims that my real Daddy is some cat who was in the Navy, stationed at Great Lakes Naval Base and went down to East St. Louis to visit some of his people one weekend before he was shipped off to the war. As the story goes, Mama and Daddy had been separated for about six months, and Mama started hanging out at some juke joint with Aunt Europa and Europa's boyfriend, Woody. Well, one night they were all at the joint when this Navy cat strolled in with a few of his kin folk. Aunt Europa said the man was about 6'2" tall, had jet black wavy hair with skin to match, and funny colored eyes. Supposedly, my mother thought he was the best looking man she ever saw. After three or four drinks, the Navy cat and my mother ended up getting a room in the motel in back of the joint, which was nothing more than a couple of shacks thrown together with some old beds that barely had clean sheets on them. After their night together, the Navy cat went back to Great Lakes and Mama went back to her nine kids and eventually her husband. I don't think she even knew his last name. Aunt Europa couldn't remember his first name so I always thought of him as "that Navy cat."

Some years later, I asked Aunt Europa why she bothered to tell me about some man that people suspected of being my Daddy. She said, "People can suspect all they want, but yo' auntie know the truth – just like yo' Mama knows. And I thinks you had a right to the truth. Since yo' Mama wouldn't tell you, I did. Now whether you believes me or not is up to you. But I'm telling you the cold hard facts, boy. That man you been calling Daddy all these years ain't none a yo' Daddy. Yo' Daddy was some man in the Navy that Babe laid up wit one night and got pregnant by, and that's that!" Now how you think news like that made me feel? Like a damn fool!

After my aunt and I had our little heart to heart, things at home just got worse. Not only did I despise my father, but I slowly began to hate my brothers and sisters for having and knowing their father, and he actually loved them. He must have sensed that I knew something was wrong, because things really got bad between the two us. The beatings got worse, along with other things.

CHAPTER 6

GRANDMA BABE

That boy always talking about something that happened a hundred years ago. Yeah, me and my brothers and sisters used to get together and have some real parties. And yeah, we used to get drunk, argue, fuss and sometimes fight, but we all loved each other. And we always made up for it the next day, so wasn't no love lost 'tween any of us. 'Sides that, all of that took place way 'fore any of us was saved, especially me.

Far as his Daddy being some man I laid up wit one night, who was in the Navy...well...that's the truth. Europa and her big ass mouth, pardon my French, but the heifer always did have a big mouth. Always telling something she ain't got no business telling. See, back then, Europa was jealous of me. Jealous because me and my husband, Cleveland, had a pretty good thang going. You know, he loved me and I loved him. We got married and had a bunch of kids. Europa was mad 'cause she felt Cleveland should have asked her to marry him instead of me. After all, she met him first and he had come by the house to see her. But when I answered the door, the man changed his mind and decided that I was the one he wanted to court. The rest is history. She never did forgive me for that. Can't say I blame her. He was a good looking man. Cleveland's father was blue black and his mother was a red-brown Indian woman. Cleveland took the best features from both of them. He was a beautiful chocolate mix. When you looked at him, you didn't know if you wanted to eat him, hold him like there was no tomorrow, make love to him as if it were going to be your last time, or just stare at him and try to figure out how God made such a beautiful specimen. The first day I saw him, I knew I would be loving and making love to him for the rest of my life. And when I looked down and saw those size 14's tapping on the porch, just waiting to cross the threshold, I knew this man would be mine. Well, no matter how hard Europa tried to act like she didn't care about me and Cleveland, the hatred she carried for me always came out in some vindictive way.

I always meant to tell the boy about his real Daddy, but how do you tell your baby something like that without him being hurt? And I certainly wouldn't have told him at some barbecue with all the other kids around. But what's did is did. Nothing I can do 'bout that now.

I never did tell Do-Man if what Europa said was true or not. All I could tell him at that very moment was that his auntie was drunk and she ain't knowed what the hell she was talking about. He know he can't listen to what a drunk say, 'cause any and everythang is subject to come up and out they mouth at any given time. I thought that maybe I had calmed him down and that he would eventually forget about that whole thing, seeing as how he wasn't nothing but about six or seven at the time. But I should have known that my secrets would come back to haunt me, as well as my family. I know I can't make no excuses for what Do-Man did to Ella, but I can't stop thinking that if I had never gone into that juke joint that night, all of our lives would have turned out differently.

When Europa asked me to go to the juke joint with her and her boyfriend, Woody, that night, I initially told her "No." My gut was telling me to just stay home. See, my husband and I had been separated for about six months at that time, and were talking about patching things up and getting back together. He said that he might even stop by later on that night and we could talk about it some more. Well, when Europa and Woody came by to pick me up, I told them that I wasn't going because Cleveland was coming over. Now, most people would have been happy about a man and woman getting back together, especially a colored man and woman wit nine childrens, but not those two. All they cared about was partying and getting drunk. And the more, the merrier. So Woody says to me, "Aw Babe, I don't know what the hell you waitin' on that nigger fo'. I just saw him down at Minnie's house not more'n a half hour ago. You know they still foolin' 'round, and she ain't 'bout to let him go, 'specially since you knows about that baby they done had."

See, me and Cleveland split up 'cause he kept sneaking 'round over there to Minnie's house behind my back, and I got fed up wit it and put his ass out. That's when he ended up staying with her. Well, all hell broke loose when I found out that she had his child. Miss Babe wasn't 'bout to put up with that! So, I did my fussing and then I tried to kill him. But you know how it is when you really loves yo' man, and you loves making love to him; it's real hard to keep him away for too long. So I was getting weak and was gon' let him come on back home. Hell, you know I must've loved making love to him, we had nine kids together. But when Woody reminded me that Cleveland and Minnie had a child it just did something to me. Anger and pain rose up in me and I just couldn't take it anymore. I marched right in my house, put on my good, juke-joint dress, (the low cut red one that hugged my body in all the right places and hung just above my knee), and shoes to match. I put on my good smelling perfume, fixed my hair and makeup, and was ready in 20 minutes. When I stepped out on that porch, Europa and Woody didn't hardly know who I was. Woody started making cat calls and Europa hit him upside his head with her pocket book. "Ouch! Ropa, that hurt." Woody wined. "Oh shut up, Woody, acting all crazy like you ain't never seen a woman before! That ain't nobody but Babe standing up there on that porch wit a clean dress on. Hell, she don't look no better'n than me, and I'm standing right next to you, and don't you forget it!" We all started laughing.

I had pushed that little voice in mind that was telling me to stay home, all the way out of my head. I was headed straight for the joint that night to party like nobody's business.

Even after having nine children, I still had a pretty good shape. All that hard work out in the fields made sure of that. No sense in letting it go to waste. I prided myself on my big pretty legs, my wide solid hips and butt to match, my small waist line and nice size breasts.

We walked down to *Junior's Juke Joint* on Center

Street, and the place was jumping. *Junior's* was the one place in town where black folk could go and have a good time and not worry about the cares of the outside world. One foot into *Junior's* was like taking a leap into a world where all things were even, equal, happy and most of all, COLORED. The only time you ever saw a white person in *Junior's* was when the police were called to bust up a fight - and that's if they bothered to show up while the fight was in full swing. They usually came once the guns had gone off, the knives stuck and the fists connected to some poor soul's jaw, mouth or eye. It was a sure bet that there would be at least one fight every Friday and Saturday night, and two or three arguments on Sunday evening. One of the reasons they had so many fights in *Junior's,* besides all the drinking, is because, by law, *Junior's* should have held seventy-five to one hundred people, max. But on any given weekend, you was bound to find twice that, and then some, in that joint. They might have had 15 to 20 tables in the whole place. You couldn't seat more than four people at a table. So the mixture of liquor, cigarette smoke, body heat and bad breath was enough to make anybody fight.

It was only 9 o'clock p.m., and already the place was darn near packed. Come to find out, the Bohanna's had kin folk in from out of town and they was all going down to *Junior's* to party. This was big news because some of they kin was in the service and World War II had just began. Now even though segregation was the way it was throughout the country and in the military during that time, our boys were still willing to go to war for this country. So we was gon' do whatever we could to support 'em.

Most of the colored folks made their way down to *Junior's* to wish the GI's well. That included the boys from right there in East St. Louis. I knew as soon as I walked into the joint that something big was going to happen that very night. I inhaled anticipation and let out excitement. It was intoxicating to the senses. You could see it on their faces. They were glowing despite the dimness of the joint. It looked as if people were dancing on air and the laughter was coming from somewhere beyond their souls. The ugly people looked pretty and the pretty ones were beautiful. A good time was going to be had by everyone.

The three of us went on in and grabbed a little table by the band. After a few drinks and a couple of dances, everybody was feeling real good. We was just sittin' there mindin' our own business when in walks this big handsome man with a Navy uniform on. He walked right up to our table and said, "Excuse me, pretty lady, but would you like to dance?" He was looking me dead in my eyes when he asked. It felt like I was under a spell, or like he had some kind of hold on me, cuz befo' I knew it, I was out on the floor with this big, black man, and all I could see was him. We never took our eyes off one another the whole time we was dancing. We must have danced for thirty minutes straight before Europa decided she was gon' cut in. Must have looked like I was having too good of a time so she figured she'd put a stop to it. She always was jealous of me. There she was sitting wit a man and still gon' try and mess up somethin' I got goin' on. Anyway, after they danced for one song, he escorted her back to our table and asked if he could join us. Well, we know Europa didn't mind, and Woody was so drunk by that time he wouldn't have cared if the Germans themselves came and sat down. I just sat there trying to look cool and cute and not too eager.

Turns out his name was Wesley. I never did know his last name. We laughed and talked and had a few more drinks, even danced a couple more times. Next thing I know, me and Wesley is making our way up the back steps of the joint that led to the motel. I kept reaching out in front of me trying to catch hold of the back of his jacket so I wouldn't trip up that dark stairway.

Once we finally made it inside the room, I screamed out, "Ouch!!" I had bumped my knee on the corner of the night stand. Wesley was trying to find a match to light the little lantern sitting on the night stand. He finally gave up and started taking off his clothes. Time wasn't wasted on small talk and pleasantries. I was being pulled into the big strong arms of a total stranger, and I liked it. Damn, did I like it. Felt like those arms had been pulling me all my life. At that moment drunkenness became my best friend. It told me that no man had ever made me feel this good. It also told me that this adultery I was committing wasn't no sin. After all, it couldn't be that bad, 'cause the wetness in my cotton panties told me it was okay. Then the drunkenness said; If Cleveland could have a baby wit' that damn Minnie, then surely I could have at least one night wit' a handsome stranger.

When it was all said and done, ole' Wesley went on back to wherever it was he was from, and a few weeks later, me and Cleveland decided to patch thangs up for good. Nine months later I had a baby boy that I naturally thought was my husband's until the midwife put the baby in my arms and I looked down at my grey eyed boy and knew, without a shadow of a doubt, that that was Wesley's baby. When Cleveland came into the room he also knew right away that the baby wasn't his. I gotta give it to him though, he tried real hard to accept the boy as his. But the boy looked more and more like his real Daddy as each day turned to night. And that's got to be hard on any man. Not only did he look like his Daddy, but he acted just like his Daddy's people – the Bohannans. A bunch of wild animals that had been let loose on society. No matter how much we whipped that boy, he just couldn't be calmed down. He was just wild, stayed in trouble. But nobody could stay mad at Do-Man for too long. The little boy could charm the pants off anything walking and pretty much talk his way in or out of any situation that came up.

That charm didn't go over to well with Cleveland, especially after Do-Man got older. Cleve was real hard on him. I knowed he was really trying to punish me for getting pregnant by somebody else. But it wasn't too much he could say – seeing as how he had done the exact same thang to me.

I never did hear from Wesley after that night at the juke joint. Never saw him in East St. Louis with his relatives or nothing. For all I know, he could have been killed in the war, or shot to death by some other woman's husband. I just don't know, and I was too ashamed to ask any of his people about him because, that would have given legs to the rumors that were flying around town about me being pregnant by some stranger from out of town. It didn't make me no never mind, seeing as how Cleveland was taking good care of me and all my children – including Do-Man.

CHAPTER 7

ELLA

By the summer of 1962, my dad hadn't worked a steady job in three months and money was tight. Daddy had worked in the stock yards for over ten years and was considered an excellent employee by all of his bosses, which is why we were shocked the night Daddy got fired. It was the craziest thing. He left for work that afternoon and everything was fine. By the time he finished his three to eleven p.m. shift, he was out of a job - "A good job with benefits," as my Grandma Babe would say. My sisters and I woke up the next morning and made our way to the kitchen for breakfast. We were surprised to see Daddy up so early, drinking coffee with Mama and a swollen black and blue eye popping out from his handsome face. The three of us noticed everything at the same time. We stood at the table staring at Daddy, not knowing what to say. He looked at the three of us and didn't utter a word. Mama nervously wiped her hands on her apron, cleared her throat and said, "Breakfast ain't ready yet. Y'all gon' back upstairs and wait for me to call y'all when the food is done." We filed out of the kitchen in a single line. Cora and Mattie headed straight for the stairs. I took a detour to Daddy's favorite chair, strategically located in the living room within ear shot of the kitchen, which is how I heard Mama and Daddy discussing the fight between Daddy and the Bohannan brothers.

The Bohannan brothers, known for being rowdy drunks, worked the 11:30 evening shift. For some reason they would always try and pick fights with my dad. They went to work drunk - five out of six nights. Everyone figured that the only reason they didn't get fired is because there were so many of them that the bosses were all afraid of them. The Bohannans were the only colored people in town that the police didn't bother just for being colored.

This particular night, the Bohannan boys decided that Daddy should be their entertainment for the evening. Even though Daddy wasn't a punk to anyone, he was no match for the four of those animals. A fight broke out, and when it was all said and done, Daddy was fired and the Bohannan boys were given a warning. No matter how many bosses Daddy spoke to, or how much he begged, not one would give him back his job.

After Daddy had been out of work for so long, Mama finally went out and got a job working for the Cranwells, a rich white family that lived on the edge of town. She cooked, cleaned and cared for their two, spoiled-rotten kids, Gracie and Albert. Mama worked Monday through Saturday, and some Sundays if Mrs. Cranwell was having one of her Ladies of Elegance lunches, or some other high society brunch.

Daddy couldn't stand it. His pride told him it was wrong for his wife to help out when the family was in need. It was his job to take care of and provide for his household, not his wife's. So every morning at 5 o'clock, he would wake up and give Mama a hard time about going to work for those "Ugly white folk." He would say, "They so damn ugly they got to live on the outskirts of town, not fit to live up on the hill with the other rich white folk." His comments would always lead to an argument, which would end with Mama storming out of the house and slamming the door behind her. Daddy would take his sweet time walking out after her, making Mama even angrier because she had to wait on him to drive her to work.

It meant a lot to him that for as long as he and Mama had been married, she never had to work outside the home. He liked home cooked meals, a clean house, well cared for children and a woman who's only job in life was to take care of her man and her kids.

Mama didn't seem to have a problem with that mentality until Daddy was no longer bringing in the money to keep the house running the way she liked. That's when she went out and got a job. That's when all hell broke loose. That's when Daddy decided we were moving to Chicago with Uncle Do-Man. My uncle had promised to get my father a job with the same insurance company he worked for. According to Do-Man, it was the easiest job for a Negro to get where he could wear a shirt and tie to work everyday and get a little respect from the people in his community at the same time.

One Sunday after church, Daddy called a family meeting to discuss the possibility of us moving to Chicago. All important decisions were discussed with the family before anyone did anything or made any kind of move – with the exception of Do-Man of course.

"Good, we're finally all here," Daddy began. "Now y'all all know that I've been out of work for some time now, and thangs don't look to be getting much better." Everyone nodded in agreement. Daddy continued. "So me and Sadie has decided that we gon' go on up to Chicago where Do-Man is and see's if we can make a go of it. Now we done already discussed this with Mama and the girls and just wanted to let the rest of you know what's going on. We gon' take a bus to Chicago next week and leave the girls here with Mama until we can get ourselves situated." Daddy's five brothers and three sisters along with their husbands, wives and children were all nodding their heads in agreement with him. They knew if Daddy made it in Chicago, then one by one they, too, would go to the big city and make a new life for themselves and their families.

Since it was a done deal, there was no sense in belaboring the point. When Daddy asked if there were any questions, they all shook their heads no and the meeting was over. I wanted to raise my hand and ask, "What if I don't want to go?" But I knew better than to question a decision that my parents had already made for the family, even if I did think it was the wrong decision, especially for my life.

After the meeting, everyone gathered around Grandma Babe's dining room table and began to eat like there was no tomorrow. Eating was always the best part of those family meetings. Grandma Babe was the best cook in East St. Louis. No one ever missed a chance to eat Sunday dinner at her house.

After dinner, we all said our goodbyes and went to our respective homes. Once we were settled in, my mother made us girls go over our 'things-to-do-and-don't-do' list while she and Daddy were in Chicago again. We would be staying with Grandma Babe of course, and since school had just let out for the summer, we had a whole laundry list of things to do so we wouldn't be in Grandma's way. My parents figured it would take two to three months for them to get situated and then they would send for my sisters and me. I had mixed emotions about moving to Chicago. I didn't want to leave my familiar surroundings, my family, my friends and my school. So I was glad that Mom and Dad were going without us. It gave me a chance to enjoy my last summer of peace.

I dreaded moving to Chicago so much, that I began to have recurring nightmares about a strange man chasing me down the street wearing long johns and combat boots. He had no facial features but large hands and feet. His torso and his legs were each 6 feet tall. His legs were slightly in front of his torso. Even though his legs were the same length, he ran with a limp and a grotesque sound came from his face when he ran. His arms and hands were outstretched trying to grab the back of my head and pull my pony tail. Just before he could grab my hair, I would wake up in a cold sweat. Grandma Babe said, "You keep having those nightmares 'cause you eat so much candy before bed and yo' stomach is full of worms. If I catch you eatin' anymore candy, I'ma beat the candy, the worms, and the living hell out of you!" From that point on, all candy consumption was done in secrecy.

The second week of August in 1962, at 6 a.m., my sisters and I boarded a hot Greyhound Bus in East

St. Louis to begin our nine hour ride to Chicago. We were finally moving to the big city. Grandma Babe made sure we each had our own brown paper bag with ham sandwiches, potato salad, two slices of her homemade pound cake and a bottle of Coca-Cola. She also gave each of my sisters $0.25 cents for emergency purposes.

We must have made about ten stops before we pulled into the downtown bus station in Chicago. Mama and Daddy were right there when we walked off the bus. As we waited for the driver to unload our luggage, my mother put her arms around my sisters and asked them about the trip. My father grabbed my hand and said, "Hey Miss Molly, how was your trip?"

I leaned my head into my dad's side and mumbled, "It was okay." He gently rubbed my head and said, "Aw, Miss Molly, you mean to tell me that nothing exciting happened on that long bus ride to Chicago?"

"No. The only thing that happened was that Grandma said we all had to sit together. So we sat in the last row right across from that stinky bathroom on the bus. They made me sit on the outside seat so the smell would hit me before it got to them." Daddy just shook his head and let out a little chuckle. The driver finally placed the last of our bags on the sidewalk, we grabbed them and headed for Uncle Do-Man's car that Daddy had borrowed and drove to the three bedroom apartment that my parents were renting on 54th and Indiana, on the south side of Chicago. Uncle Do-Man was renting a one bedroom apartment upstairs from my parents in the same building.

I hated the place as soon as I walked in. Because we were on the third floor, you could smell the breakfast, lunch and dinner cooking in the other apartments as you made your way to the third floor. The different scents made me sick. On any given day, the rancid smell of chitterlings would hit you in your face on one floor, the sweet aroma of chocolate cake invaded the second floor and the mouth watering smell of hot fried cat fish would greet you on the third floor. It was almost too much to bear. I was used to living in a house where I could run, jump and play at will; my mother had already made it clear that we were not to behave as wild heathens in our new apartment. The biggest reason I didn't like apartment living is because from the moment I stepped into the place, I could feel the bad spirits lurking throughout. Bad things were destined to happen in that apartment.

Cora and Mattie were excited about moving to the big city. They were tired of living in a small country town where everyone knew all of your business. I, on the other hand, loved it. Knowing other people's secrets gave me a crazy sense of empowerment. I was intimately connected to people that I had never even said hello to. My grandma Babe always did call me her nosy grandchild. She was absolutely right. Since I was so young, innocent looking and quiet, people felt at ease around me. They would tell some of the wildest stories in my presence and not even realize that I was there.

I remember how every Saturday evening, Grandma Babe would send me and my sisters out to get our hair done at Ms. Irene's Beauty Shop right down the street from Grandma's house. We were usually her last customers for the day. My sisters would always go first and run right out the door as soon as both of their heads were done. I really didn't mind because I liked having Ms. Irene all to myself. That's when she would tell me all about her daughter and son-in-law who lived in South Carolina and their four year old daughter. I would often fantasize about the little girl's life and what it would be like for me if I were an only child and my parents spoiled me by giving me all the toys and candy my little heart and mind could stand.

Well, one Saturday Ms. Irene was in the middle of pressing my hair when her best friend Natty, came rushing in the shop looking around to see if any customers were there. When she saw that I was the only one there she said, "Good, ain't no-body here. Girl, guess what I just found out!"

Ms. Irene put her pressing comb down and said, "Whatever it is it must be hot as this here straightn' comb the way you come bustin' up in here all in a tizzy! Chile, what is it?" Natty looked around the little shop again just to make sure no one was there. After she was satisfied that the coast was clear she leaned in to Ms. Irene and began to spill the juice.

"Well, you know old white Mr. Cobb?" Natty began.

"Yeah, used to live in Fire Works Station," Ms. Irene said as she put a wad of grease on the next piece of hair to be straightened.

"Um Hmm. Well, you know he and his family moved to Alton a few years ago. Anyway, word is, old man Cobb been coming back to East St. Louis every other weekend, creepin' in to see his girlfriend." Natty said just above a whisper.

"What's the big deal about that? Hell, everybody in town knows he's foolin' round with big butt Sarah with all them kids," Ms. Irene said as she put the straightening comb in my hair.

"Yeah, that is old news. But did you hear that old man Cobb 'bout to become a Daddy? And it ain't with Sarah! Word 'round town is he dun gon' and got Sarah's oldest daughter pregnant. And she ain't but 14 years old!"

Ms. Irene forgot that she had that hot comb in my hair, because instead of her combing it straight through she stopped right before she reached the end of that patch of hair, which was right in the middle of my head. By the time she realized that my hair was burning, it was nothing but a hard crispy piece of hair that fell out as soon as Ms. Irene took the hot comb out of my hair.

"Ooh baby, I'm so sorry! Don't worry, Ms. Irene gon' fix your hair up real nice and nobody will ever be able to tell that we had a little accident." She looked up at Natty and said, "Natty, get on out of here so I can fix this child's hair. Come back in 'bout half hour."

"Alright, I'll be back in exactly one-half hour 'cause I got's even more to tell you 'bout old man Cobb."

"Yeah okay, but right now I need to finish this child's hair."

Natty left, and Ms. Irene went back to pressing my hair. When she finished I gave her the customary $3.00 for a wash and press. She smiled and gave me $1.00 back and said, "Have an ice cream sundae on me, baby." I smiled back and said, "Thanks Ms. Irene." I realized that it was hush money, but the thought of a chocolate sundae pushed the hair burning incident right out of my mind. Besides, she did fix my hair up really nice.

Not five minutes after our things were unpacked, my sisters bolted for the front door to go out and play.

My mother told them that they couldn't go outside without me. I told her I didn't want to play and wanted to stay inside and finish unpacking. My mother wasn't going for that, and said, "Ella Mae, you might as well get on downstairs with your sisters and start making friends like the rest of them." I reluctantly obeyed. The street was filled with children between the ages of two and 14. Cora and Mattie began working the crowd the moment they reached the pavement. I found myself sitting alone on a curb in the midst of all the kids outside. I was actually content to sit back and observe the excitement from my curb side seat. My sisters didn't even notice that I was not by their sides. That is, until the street lights came on and Mama yelled out the window for the three of us to come in for dinner. By that time, the streets had thinned out and there were only six or seven kids left outside.

I was so glad to hear my mother's voice yelling our names out of the third floor window, I didn't know what to do. When we got settled and finally sat down to eat, Cora and Mattie could barely contain their excitement as they talked about the new friendships they were going to forge in the neighborhood. My father noticed how quiet and withdrawn I was during dinner; my mother was too wrapped up in Cora and Mattie's recount of the afternoon and evening to notice.

After dinner, Daddy took me in the living room to talk while my sisters and mother cleaned the kitchen. He sat down in his favorite chair, the one he and his father made just months before my grandfather died. "Come here, Miss Molly, and sit on Daddy's lap." He pat his leg and motioned for me to jump up in his lap; I readily obliged. "Alright Miss Molly, what's going on?

You were awfully quiet during dinner. Did something happen while you girls were outside?" I rested my head on his chest and said,

"No."

"Did you meet any of the new kids?"

"No."

"Why not?"

In my pouttiest voice I said, "I just didn't want to meet any of them. They didn't seem all that nice to me anyway, and besides, Cora and Mattie had everyone's attention. The other kids didn't even know I was there."

"I've told you a million times, sometimes you just have to jump right in and let people know you're there. But I don't think it's the other kids that's bothering you. You really miss East St. Louis, don't you?" I shook my head yes. Somehow, my father always knew exactly what was on my mind.

"Listen, babe, movin' ain't easy for nobody. We all have to make the best of it. It took me a while to get adjusted to living up here, away from most of my family and friends. But now, I'm making more money than I have in my entire life, which is a good thing for the whole family, you know what I mean, jelly bean?" Then he started tickling me. Once he saw a smile on my face he made me get up and start preparing for bed.

Six months of being in Chicago and I was still homesick for East St. Louis, Grandma Babe, and everything else I left behind when they dragged me from the country to the city. Most of my days were spent going back and forth to school. Most of my time after school was spent alone because my mother had started working during the Christmas holiday to have extra money since our relatives were coming up from East St. Louis, and she wanted everything in the apartment to be perfect. Too bad it wasn't.

Two months after Christmas, Mama was still working. Daddy and I tried to tell her that she should quit, but she liked that independent feeling a woman gets once she starts making her own money. My sisters were too busy hanging out with their newfound friends to care that mom wasn't around as much, and as long as I wasn't tagging along behind them, all was well with the world.

The end of May came and the school year was finally over. My friend count was exactly the same as it was in the beginning of the school year. Zero. Fortunately for me, my sisters were so popular that no-one dared to touch or tease their little sister.

Aside from my father, uncle Do-Man was the only other person in my family to notice that I was a loner. He would watch me when I came home from school everyday. He should have been at work but because he sold insurance he would often come home in the middle of the day and frolic with one of his women. We found out later that Do-Man had actually lost his job right before Christmas but never said anything; and he made Daddy promise not to say a word until he got back on his feet. Daddy agreed, thinking that Do-Man could look out for us girls when we came home from school and make sure that we got in safely.

Do-Man noticed that I would normally get home at least 15 minutes before my sisters. Once the weather broke and the time changed, he noticed that my sisters were more like thirty and sometimes 45 minutes behind me. My sisters knew that my mother didn't get home until 4:45 p.m. so they had from 3:15 to 4:30 to get home and at least start on their chores before my mother got in. Apparently, Do-Man had been watching our schedule long enough to figure it out as well.

One day as I was letting myself into our apartment, I heard Do-Man and one of his "women" arguing outside of his apartment door, which was directly above ours. I couldn't see her face but I knew that voice from somewhere. I heard her yell, "I know you did it Do-Man!"

"Bitch, you don't know what the fuck you talkin' 'bout. I'm a grown man; I don't have to go 'round screwing little girls to get my kicks!" Do-Man shouted from his apartment door.

"My baby said it was **_you_** who laid her on your bed, spread her legs and stuck yo' damn dick in her, but when she started screaming and you looked down and saw blood you jumped up and told her to go take a bath. I know you did it Do-Man! I know you did it!"

The next sound I heard was a loud slap and my uncle shouting, "Get the hell out of here with all that crazy talking! I done told you and everybody else that I ain't never touched that little girl! And if you come around here again talking that shit I'm gon' beat the hell out of you!" The woman was crying by now and trying to make her way down the stairs at the same time. I was so frightened that I couldn't move from in front of my door. In a fit of rage, Do-Man kicked the woman in the back. She rolled down the stairs and stopped right at my feet. I stood frozen as fear held my legs and feet captive. I recognized the woman lying at my feet as Do-Man's live-in girlfriend from East St. Louis whose five year old daughter had accused him of molesting her.

CHAPTER 8

DO-MAN'S FUNERAL

The piercing sounds of sirens ripped through the entire community of Fire Works Station as the ambulance rushed to Grandma Babe's house early one Sunday morning responding to an emergency call placed by Aunt Sally. Grandma was rushed to Baker's Memorial Hospital in East St. Louis, where doctors determined she had had a massive heart attack, brought on by the tragic news of one of her sons killing the other. They kept Grandma in the hospital for ten days, while at the same time, Do-Man laid on a cold slab at the local funeral home. No-one knew what to do about Do-Man. Should they leave him at the funeral home and wait for Grandma Babe to recover before they started making arrangements, or should they just have his body cremated and call it a day? No-one wanted to make that decision. They knew if the wrong decision was made they would have to deal with Grandma's wrath. So they waited, and waited, and waited, until Mr. Happy, the owner of the funeral home finally called and demanded that a decision be made within the next 24 hours, otherwise, Do-Man's body would be dumped in Potter's Field.

There was a general consensus amongst the siblings that they should let Mr. Happy dump Do-Man's body in Potter's Field. As far as they were concerned, he was an embarrassment and disgrace to the family. It would be easier to just wash their hands of him and let everyone move on with living. Aunt Sally was the only one who felt they should wait and let Grandma Babe make that decision. She took a lot of heat for that way of thinking. Uncle Butch led the charge in calling Mr. Happy instructing him not to do anything until Grandma Babe could make the final decision. Aunt Sally stood her ground, and fortunately, for the rest of them she did. Had they told their mother that they allowed Mr. Happy to throw their brother away in some field she would have killed each and every one of them.

The day Grandma was to be released from the hospital, the eight siblings were forced to tell her what was going on and that something needed to be done right away. As soon as Grandma heard the news she immediately got dressed and tried to check herself out of the hospital. My aunts and uncles made her wait until the doctor made his rounds and officially released her. Dr. Boyd's parting words to my Grandmother were, "Mrs. Boxx, I'm going to let you go home today, but I want you to promise me that you'll go home and take it easy."

Grandma Babe huffed out, "Didn't I tell you that my baby boy is laying up there at Happy's funeral parlor?"

"Yes, Mrs. Boxx, you did, but I…"

"Then how in the hell do you pro - pose I go home and take it easy?!"

Dr. Boyd knew he had lost this battle so he looked

at my Aunt Sally and said, "Listen, Sally, if you could at least get her to take her medicine and not let her do too much, that would be a tremendous help within itself."

Before Sally could answer, Grandma snapped, "Listen, Doc, I'm Sally's Mama, not the other-way-around…"

"Mama, he's only trying to help." Aunt Sally quietly said.

"Look here, the only help I need is getting' out of here and on down to Happy's, so I can take care of, or at least make some arrangements for Cleophis." And with that Grandma Babe stood up from the bed, grabbed her suitcase and coat, and proceeded down the hall to the hospital elevators. All eight of her children followed behind her. Aunt Sally turned around to Dr. Boyd and said, "Don't worry, we'll take care of her, and I promise we won't let her do too much." The doctor shook his head and said, "Good luck, Sally. Call me if you need anything," and continued with his rounds.

The car hadn't come to a complete stop in front of the huge brick building that had been converted from a single family home owned by white folks to one of the first black owned businesses in East St. Louis, before my grandmother was trying to get out and make her way to the front entrance with the double glass doors. The blond brick building proudly held a white sign with black letters which read, "Happy's Funeral Home, We Share, We Serve, We Care." LeRoy Happy, Sr. was just making his way to the front of the funeral home when he spotted a small caravan pulling into his parking lot. Immediately he recognized the Boxx family. Happy's Funeral Home had been the only black owned and operated funeral home in East St. Louis for the last

25 years. Before then, the white morticians handled all of the black bodies. Sometimes the family would recognize their loved one, most times they would not. Not only did the white morticians not know what to do to or for the black bodies, they didn't care. Their main concern was to get as much from the families as they could, which is the one thing that the Happy family did take from their predecessors; the art of fleecing their clients for as much money as they possibly could. Sometimes they would mark up the cost of the funeral so high just to see how far the family would go to get the money, which is what Mr. Happy was banking on with the Boxx family.

All eight siblings and Grandma Babe filed into the funeral home, and Mr. Happy escorted them to his small office in the back. Grandma Babe, Aunt Sally and Uncle Butch took the three empty chairs that sat in front of Mr. Happy's desk. The other siblings decided to wait in the hallway until all of the arrangements were made.

A simple service was finally decided on. Mr. Happy tried like hell to convince Grandma to spend the entire five hundred dollars from the burial policy on the funeral. Mr. Happy didn't realize that even though Grandma was sick and grief stricken, she still had all of her wits about her. She was as shrewd as any man when it came to business and financial matters. No way would she spend all of her money on a funeral for Do-Man, the one who brought shame and humiliation on the family with his wild and wicked ways. The only reason she was so adamant about having a service of any kind is because it was the decent and proper thing to do for your own child, regardless of the circumstances.

The funeral services for Uncle Do-Man went according to plan. The immediate family and a few of my grandmother's neighbors were the only ones to attend the services. There was no real program prepared. Grandma hired the minister on staff, and instructed him to say a few brief words about Do-Man and to end the service as quickly as possible.

The service lasted 20 minutes and the minister was leading the family back down the aisle to the front door and out to their cars. Not a song was sung, nor a tear shed for the man who molested his own niece, for the man who was shot down by his own brother, for the man who caused so much pain in the lives of all he touched, for the man who lived with his own unspeakable demons that he could no more control than a ravenous dog let loose in a school yard full of children. No one felt sorry for him. No one missed him, not even his own mother. Even in death, Do-Man looked like he was having the last laugh. He lay in his casket adorned in a purple suit, gold shirt and a purple tie. It was the only thing that Grandma Babe had that belonged to Do-Man. She didn't bother asking his brothers if they had something their brother could wear and she certainly was not going to spend any money on a brand new suit to bury him in, so she went with what she had. The suit made him look like he had just come from the juke joint doing what he did best - partying like there was no tomorrow, and for him, it had finally come to an end.

On the way to the cemetery, Uncle Butch noticed a strange car in his rearview mirror following the procession. He knew the car didn't belong in the funeral line because there were only four cars in their procession and, this car didn't have a funeral sticker on the windshield, yet the car was running all the lights and making every turn they made. The woman behind the wheel was wearing dark sunglasses with a cigarette hanging from her mouth. Her hair was jet black and wild. It looked as if it hadn't been combed in months. Uncle butch couldn't make out the woman's face, but he felt he knew her, or had at least seen her before. He kept watching as the short line of cars made their way to Washington Cemetery and finally to Do-Man's grave site. As the family filed out of their cars, Uncle Butch saw the strange car sitting close to the entrance of the cemetery. He was about to approach the car to find out who the driver was and why she had followed them when Aunt Sally called out to him to help Grandma out of the car. Uncle Butch stopped just before he got to the unknown vehicle, and turned around to go and help his mother to his brother's new home.

Do-Man was to be buried in the family plot, which up until that day, was home only to Grandpa Cleveland, Grandma's husband of 45 years. The family gathered around the casket sitting beside the open hole that would soon be its final resting place. There were no real tears of sorrow shed for Do-Man. Each of his siblings had their own thoughts about the timing and the circumstances surrounding his death. One sister couldn't believe it took this long for him to be murdered. Uncle Butch couldn't believe they were having a service for someone who had raped their niece and granddaughter, and God only knew how many other little girls had their innocence snatched away by Do-Man. The second youngest brother, Jimmy, couldn't wait for the whole thing to be over so he could go home and make love to his new bride. They all knew in their heart of hearts that Do-Man would die a tragic death; they just didn't think it would be at the hands of their own brother.

The minister was finishing the committal rights when a half-crazed woman, dragging a frightened little girl behind her, pushed her way through the small group and stood directly over the casket. The woman grabbed the little girl by the hand and began pointing and screaming at the casket, "That's the son-of-a-bitch that did those God awful things to you and gave you that nasty disease! But that's alright, Shug, 'cause his ass is gon' rot in hell for all eternity for what he did to you!" She opened a huge black cloth sack and emptied its contents on top of Do-Man's casket. Everyone screamed when the snakes began slithering on top and down the sides of the casket. The minister who was standing right over the hole clutched his chest and fell in the grave. Grandma Babe fainted in Uncle Butch's arms, Aunt Sally started running and the rest of the siblings and grandchildren followed suit.

Uncle Butch laid Grandma on the ground and ran over to the woman who was now chanting over Do-Man's casket. He snatched her by the arm and spent her around to face him. Once face-to-face, he recognized her as Do-Man's last live-in-girlfriend, the one whose daughter had accused him of molesting her before Do-Man high-tailed it to Chicago. The crazed woman, a.k.a. Hattie Mae, spat in Uncle Butch's face and yanked away from his grip. She returned to the casket and began chanting once again. Uncle Butch wiped the spit from his face with the sleeve of his suit coat and quickly grabbed Hattie Mae's arms from behind and pulled her away from the casket, practically throwing her into her car. She went kicking and screaming all the way, the little girl following behind them, crying as she went.

After Uncle Butch forced Hattie Mae into her car and made sure she drove off, he headed back to the grave where he had laid Grandma on the ground. He heard a loud scream coming from Do-Man's grave. Before he tried to revive Grandma, he looked over into the hole and saw the minister tying to claw his way out of the muddy grave. Two of the snakes had made their way into the watery grave as well. Just as uncle Butch was about to bend down and help the minister he spotted the two grave diggers making their way back to the site. The three of them pulled the minister out of the grave and escorted him to his car where he sat with both hands at 10 and 2 on the steering wheel, staring out the windshield for over and hour trying to regain his composure.

By the time Uncle Butch went back to the grave site to revive Grandma, she had already begun to come around. "What the hell am I doing on the ground, Butch!" she said, as she made several futile attempts to get up.

"Let me help you Mama."

"I asked you a question boy. What the hell am I doing on the ground!? And where is everybody?" Grandma demanded.

"They all gone home, Mama. You was on the ground 'cause you fainted when that crazy ex-woman of Do-Man's come here and put all them snakes on Do-man's casket. You fainted and everybody else took off running. The preacher tried to run but he fell in the hole. Me and the grave diggers had to pull him out."

Grandma tried to keep a straight face as she dusted herself off. She looked at Uncle Butch and said, "Well, I guess that nigga's got the last laugh anyway." She and Uncle Butch walked up to Do-Man's casket to see if the snakes were still there. They were not. Looking down at the casket, Grandma said, "Well, Do, this is it. You raised all kinda hell while you was livin' and you still causing all kinds of hell in death. I sho' pray that the Lawd had mercy on yo' soul."

"Amen." said Uncle Butch, then he and grandma walked hand in hand to the car.

CHAPTER 9

SADIE

I kept trying to figure out how in the world I missed all of the signs that something was going on with Ella. Maybe I really did see the signs but it was just too painful to deal with. She began to act just like I did after I had been raped. Nobody held my hand and told me everything was going to be alright. I just had to deal with it the best way I could, and that mean stepmother of mine didn't make things any better. Heck, I think she was glad that I was raped. Not once did she ever hold my hand or pat me on the back and say that everything was going to be okay. The day I came home after being raped by those sons of Satan, the only thing my stepmother said to me was, "Gal, what took you so long to git back here? I been waitin' on yo' tail for near 'bout a hour. Where da hell you been?!" she snapped.

I was shaking so bad that I could barely talk. So I just stood there in the middle of the kitchen floor holding what was left of my dress with my head hanging down, staring at my bare feet. She didn't notice me right away. She was so busy stirring her pots and fussing about my laziness that she didn't notice the tears streaming down my face and the blood running down my legs were compelling me to make a puddle on her freshly waxed floor. She finally turned around from her pots when I didn't answer. I couldn't see her face but I clearly heard her faint gasp.

She ran over to me and said, "Gal, what's done happened to you?!" For that brief moment, my stepmother showed some compassion - towards me. But that moment was fleeting. She hugged me and said that everything would be okay. Standing there, being held by a woman who hated me, and hearing those words, "Everything's going to be okay" made me lose it. My knees buckled and I dropped to the floor. She helped me up and walked me to my room, the back porch, where they had put my bed. As she began to give me a sponge bath she said, "Lot's a gal chillun go through dis everyday, especially colored gals. But you be okay. Dis just prove to make ya stronger. I know you gon' be alright 'cause you ain't dead." I looked at her through the tears rolling down my face and all kinds of questions were dancing in my head, just trying to make their way down to my tongue, but they kept getting tripped up somewhere between pain, shame and anger. Those three emotions did such a dance with my questions that finally my questions just went on somewhere else and sat down. They were just taking a break. They'd be back, just as soon as they gathered their strength. At that moment, I thought weakness would be my friend forever. Strength at that point had walked out on me like an inconsiderate lover.

Her words did nothing to comfort me. What did she mean, "Lot's of colored gals go through dis everyday?" Had it happened to her? The questions were starting to come. Here comes the strength. I'm opening my mouth. Nothing comes out. But wait, I have questions. Once again they decide now is not the time.

My stepmother allowed me to lie down after she cleaned me up. She told me to rest for a minute and that she would call me if she needed me to do anything. Surprisingly, she didn't call me for the rest of the evening. I don't think I could have gotten out of bed even if she had screamed my name, like she normally did when she wanted something. I laid there in my bed trying hard not to think. But every time I closed my eyes I would see those men taunting me, telling their dogs to get me. I saw myself standing in the middle of that circle they formed, feeling like I was going to pass out at any minute. Between the dogs barking, and those fools jeering at me with their sticks, and pouring beer and moonshine on me, I know I threw up at least three times. But that didn't stop them from having their way with me. The first one grabbed me and pulled me to the ground. He ripped my dress and tore off my panties. The others were standing around cheering him on. I was too afraid to even scream. I just laid there silently crying. I remember him holding me down with one hand and pulling his suspenders down and undoing his pants with the other. I blacked out from the pain coming from in between my legs. I remember waking up a couple of times and seeing a different man on top of me each time. The last time I woke up I was all alone on the ground wearing remnants of what used to be my clothes. I looked around hoping to see something familiar. The only thing I saw was an empty moonshine bottle and a bunch of beer bottles on the ground. Somehow I was able to stand myself up. It must have been 90 degrees that day, but I was cold. Making it all the way back to my house is a blur. Walking up the steps to the back porch and entering the kitchen, looking at my stepmother's back and hearing her words cut me like a knife, didn't have the usual sting that afternoon.

I finally drifted off to sleep. By the time I woke up from my little nap I heard my father in the kitchen talking to my stepmother as she prepared his supper plate. They did their usual small talk about nothing. I was secretly hoping that she would tell him about what happened to me, and that he would run into my room and tell me that everything would be okay, and that he was going to kill each one of those low-life dogs for hurting his baby. I laid there in my bed just waiting for my Daddy to bust through that door. I waited and waited, and waited. I waited so long that the next thing I knew, my stepmother was yelling my name telling me it was time to get up and start on my chores.

I looked down towards the foot of my bed, where the one and only window in the room was, and saw that the sun was making its morning climb. The same place it stood the day before as it shone down on those animals that raped me. I wiped my eyes and realized that my Daddy had never even come into my room. Didn't she tell him? She had to have told him. But why didn't he come to see about me? I heard my stepmother making her way to my room. I knew I was in trouble because that's the only time she ever bothered to come to my room. I figured I better hop out of bed and start getting my clothes together. She walked right into my room, and said, "Listen, I didn't tell yo' Daddy what happened to you 'cause it don't make no sense in him gittin' all riled up goin' down der to dem boy's house accusing dem of something we don't know all the facts to no how. What good is it gon' do anyhow? He go down der messin' wit those fools, he liable to end up on some chain gang for the next 40 to 50 years, or worse yet, we find him swangin' back and forth from some tree limb. So you makes sure you keeps yo' lil' filthy mouth shut! Don't you tell yo' Daddy nuthin', you hear me gal?" I stood there on the side of my bed and nodded my head up and down. She looked at me long and hard before saying, "You bet not tell yo' Daddy nutin', 'cause if you do, you be the death of yo' Daddy and the death of dis family. And I be damned if I let the daughter of some two-bit whore come up in here and destroy myze family. Now git yo clothes on so you can gon' out der and start feedin' dem chickens." And with that she turned and walked out of my room. I was so frightened I couldn't move, that is, until I heard her spit out my name as if it were laced with poison. "Sadie, git on out der to dem chickens!"

So my Daddy wasn't gon' help me, thanks to his ugly wife. That's when I realized that nobody in this world gave a damn about me. So I put on my clothes, walked out the back door and started feeding the chickens. I could barely walk when I went out there to feed my friends. I was sore in places that I had never felt before. I wanted to get back in my bed and die.

I usually found comfort in feeding those chickens. They were my only friends. But even they seemed to shun me that morning. Not one of those dumb chickens got close enough to peck my legs or hands while trying to get their feed. From the ground, they chose to eat.

I wanted to cry. No one cared about me. I was all alone, wishing for my mother. Where was she? Who was she? Did she know that I was alive? Was she ever coming to get me? From the looks of things, the answer was no. I found out years later that my mother was a white prostitute who secretly slept with Negro men in town. My father was one of them. By the time my mother found out that she was pregnant by my father, it was too late to see the old woman in town who took care of such matters. The old woman also served as midwife to the colored women in town and agreed to help my mother with the birth of her colored bastard. Story has it that, immediately after I was born, the woman wrapped me up, handed me to her daughter and told her to take me to my grandmother's house. My mother demanded that they let her hold me at least once before they took me away. "Hush, chile. No need in you getting' hooked on a baby you cant's keep," the old woman hissed at my mother. The daughter took me away without me ever having felt my mother's arms around me or inhaling her breath through my tiny nostrils.

I lived with my grandmother until she died. I must have been about ten years old when that happened, that's when I went to live with my father and his wife. A few times I overheard my stepmother telling my father that she never would have married him had she known she would be raising the child of some two bit whore, and a white one on top of that.

I must have been standing there day dreaming about my mother for a while because I heard my stepmother yell from the back door, "Gal, you better stop all dat driftin' off and git to feedin dem chickens, 'cause when you done wit dat, I needs you to brang dat wood up here to da back porch! You hear me, gal?!" I snapped out of my daydream and did as I was told. My stepmother never talked about what happened to me that horrible Sunday afternoon. I never told a soul, not even my chickens.

CHAPTER 10

LEE OTIS

I tried not to blame Sadie for what happened to Ella. Sadie was still trying to battle her own demons. Some people can be so hurt by situations in their lives that they become damaged goods. So damaged that they don't even realize how deep the bruises go. That's how it was with my wife.

Oh, she tries to carry on a normal life, but it's hard. I will say this: she did seem to breathe a little easier once all the crackers who raped her were gone – even if for a little while. On the other hand, once the crackers were gone, she started breathing with a new heaviness. She was convinced that the whites would start a riot, sho' nuff. There was no need to worry about that. Me and my brothers took care of everything.

CHAPTER 11

SADIE

One spring evening a few months after Lee Otis and I got married, we were walking through town and decided to stop at Johnny C's soda shop before heading home. Well, just as we were approaching the door to the soda shop, the group of white men sitting outside the shop decided to block the entrance. Lee Otis, being the brave and outspoken young man that he was, grabbed my hand real tight and said, "Ain't no cracker gon' keep me and my wife from going into dis here soda shop." I was terrified, especially when we got closer to the door and I recognized one of the white men as one of the ones who raped me when I was just a girl. I began shaking uncontrollably and couldn't move another inch. I looked that white man right in his lifeless eyes and wanted to scream but nothing would come out. I just stood there with my mouth hanging open. I heard one of the men say, "Oh, that nigger ain't gon' 'cause no trouble. That's one of Aunt Babe's boys. Let em' on in." The little group at the front door parted so we could make our way in. Lee Otis tried to start walking, but couldn't get anywhere because I couldn't move. He yanked my arm and somehow my feet became unglued to the pavement beneath me. When we got inside the shop he turned around and looked at me and said, "What the hells wrong with you?! I'm trying to make my way from 'tween all dem crackers and you just standing there. You tryin' to git us both lynched?" I couldn't even respond. I just stood there shaking like a leaf.

When Lee Otis realized that I was terrified he grabbed my hand and we went rushing out of the store like we had been caught up in a hurricane. We didn't stop walking until we were well out of eye-shot of those crackers. Lee Otis stopped all of a sudden, grabbed my shoulders and said, "What in the world has got you so upset? I ain't never seen you acting so scared over some no count crackers." I stood their just looking at him as the tears rolled down my face. I wanted to tell him what happened to me all those years ago, but my stepmother's words kept ringing in my head, "*You bet not ever tell yo' Daddy. If you do, you be the death of him and dis family.*" Well, I certainly didn't want my husband to go off and do something crazy to get himself locked up or killed. So I stood there shaking my head saying, "I can't tell you." With a desperate plea in his eye and a frantic cry in his voice he said, "Why not?!"

"Because, it'll be the death of you." I mumbled. With a puzzled look in his eyes he said, "What could you possible say that's gon kill me?"

Something inside of me broke and I could no longer hide the secret that held me hostage for all those years. If I didn't tell somebody soon, that whole ordeal was going to be the death of me. Through the tears and snot running down my nose, I told my husband of four months, that one of the white men standing in front of the soda shop had raped me when I was a little girl. I told him all about my stepmother forcing me into silence. All Lee Otis said was, "Which one of them crackers raped you?" I saw the anger and the pain well up in his eyes. My own fear returned. "I'll kill him," is what I heard Lee Otis say as he started walking back towards the soda shop. I quickly ran behind him, begging and pleading for him not to go back there and do something crazy. I went running behind him trying to talk some sense into him, but he wouldn't listen. He was determined to make his way back to Johnny C's. I had to do something , and quick. I yelled out, "Lee Otis, stop! I'm pregnant!" He came to a dead halt. He turned around and said, "What did you say?"

"I'm pregnant." I said looking up at him.

His face softened just a little. I told him, "That's why I didn't want you going back there messing with those grey boys. I can't have you running off gettin' hurt or worse yet, killed when we got us a baby on the way." I tried to sound calm but he could tell that I was still upset. I knew that he still wanted to go back there and take care of not just one cracker, but every last one of them devils sitting out there on the porch. He kept looking in that direction like he was going to make a mad dash for the soda shop at any minute. I kept talking to him, trying to calm him down. After about five minutes of begging and pleading, Lee Otis decided that it was time to go home. That meant, he would deal with the situation later. He made me swear that I would tell him everything once we got home.

I tried to tell him all about the rape but the words kept getting stuck in my throat. How in the world could

I tell this man that five white men had their way with me and nobody bothered to protect me after they found out? He kept telling me that it was okay for me to just let it out and that he was there for me, but it was hard to speak the words. The tears started flowing after the first two words. After a whole sentence I was sobbing so bad that he could barely understand what I was trying to say. I was able to tell him how my stepmother told me not to ever tell my Daddy, and how I would still have nightmares about the whole thing. I told him that that's why it was difficult for me to make love to him sometimes, but I was trying real hard to be a good wife to him. He asked me if I thought I would feel comfortable talking to his mother about what happened to me. I immediately said, "No! I don't want to talk to your mother or anyone else about this. I'm trying real hard to put his whole thing behind me. The last thing I need is for your Mama to be all up in my head. Naw, let's just leave it alone." At first Lee Otis looked helpless. That helplessness turned into something strange. I didn't know that type of strange.

Not too long after that night, that white boy's family reported him missing. At first I thought it was just him getting his just deserts, but then, one by one, all five of the men that raped me were found dead or came up missing. That's when the anxiety and tension began to set in. I couldn't ask, but my gut was telling me that Lee Otis was involved. Whoever was doing the killing, sure was cunning. They didn't kill those crackers right behind the other. Oh no, it took them years to finish the job. Every year or year and a half, you would hear about one of those devils being brutally murdered. The second of the five was found on the patch of land I was raped on. He was cut up into small pieces and spelled out the words, nigger lover, and the body pieces were painted black. Nobody in town, including the Sheriff, knew what to make of such a horrible thing. They didn't know if they should start killing niggers on the spot or run for their own lives.

No more bodies were found after that second one, but the other three men who raped me all disappeared. Not a trace of them anywhere. The only reason the sheriff and the rest of the people in the town didn't go crazy and start an all out war against the Negroes is, they hated those five white men more than they did any Negro in town. Rumor has it that, those five crackers were so mean and cruel that none of the women in town would bother with them, so they would have sex with their sisters and their own sheep. I even heard that they raped a little white girl and said that some nigger drifting through the woods had done it. The little girl survived, and told her parents that those white men had raped her. They lied and said they were the ones who found her in the woods and that they were the first ones she saw when she woke up after that nigger left her for dead. Now, because the girl was only seven and her parents were rock bottom poor, they didn't have much of a voice in the community; they had to take their lumps just like all the colored folks in town had to do. Unfortunately, a 15 year old black boy from New Orleans, visiting some of his kin folk for the summer, was found swinging from a tree a couple of days after the little girl had been raped. Somebody had to pay.

The colored folk were outraged. They went down to the sheriff's office demanding justice for the boy's death. A mob of white folk had formed outside of the sheriff's office as soon as they saw the coloreds making their way up the stairs to the sheriff's office. They stood in front of the court house shouting, "Go home niggers, or you're next!" The colored folk tried to show their strength and unity by ignoring the threats and holding their ground, but soon scattered when gun shots rang through the air. The pastor leading the charge told them that it didn't make sense to have anymore killings in their communities and that maybe it would be best if they went to see the sheriff on a one on one basis. They agreed it was best to leave well enough alone.

The last one of them white boys to disappear was the meanest of them all. I think his Mama must have been drinking moonshine when she was pregnant with him 'cause they say when he was born he came out with a dark film over his face. They called him, *The White Terror.* He was mean to the white people, the Indians and especially the colored. He didn't care if you were young, old, boy, girl, man or woman. If you got in his way after he had been out drinking with the good 'ole boys, God help you. No telling what he might do to you.

When his trashy wife called the Sheriff to report him missing, there was no real sense of urgency on the part of the Sheriff, or anybody else in the town for that matter, to try and find him.   It was a relief to the entire town that he was gone.

CHAPTER 12

DO-MAN

Everybody thought Daddy was such a good man. He wasn't shit! And when I tell you the whole story you gon' be in total agreement with me.

Yeah, Daddy used to beat me for breakfast, lunch and dinner. Don't worry, I ain't trying to get no sympathy, just telling my story like everybody else. Eventually, I got used to the beatings. I knew they would only last for so long and then I would be back to running and jumping with my brothers and sisters. What I couldn't understand was why Daddy would take me on those long ass "drives" in the evenings. Sometimes they would be after one of his near death beatings when Mama would come out the house and start yelling for him to stop 'cause he was gon' kill me for sho'. So he would stop knocking the hell out of me and say, "Get in the car, boy." Then, other times I could be outside doing my chores, minding my own business, and out of no-where, Daddy would show up and say, "Come on, boy, we goin' for a ride." Mama thought those rides were a good sign, like Daddy was trying to bond with me or something. Yeah right.

The first "ride" he took me on was down by Dead

Man's River. I couldn't have been no more than six or seven years old at the time. For the life of me, I didn't know why Daddy would bring me down there and it was almost dark. We weren't going fishing 'cause we didn't have no fishing poles, no live bait, and it was too late in the day. I was too afraid to ask what we were doing there so I just sat there looking and feeling like the deaf and dumb boy all the kids would tease at school. We sat in the car not saying a word for what seemed like hours. The old man sat looking straight ahead. Finally, he turned to me and said, "Sometimes, when little boys are bad like you, they got to be punished so they won't be bad no mo'. You understand what I'm sayin' to you?" I just knew another beating was minutes away. I shook my head yes and tried to hold back the tears. My brothers had told me I needed to start being tough, so I didn't want to cry in front of Daddy. Maybe if he saw that I wasn't a cry-baby anymore he would stop beating me. He began to unfasten his belt buckle. The beating was coming for sure. My heart starting racing. Daddy said we were just going for a ride. I looked over at him unfastening his belt but he didn't take it off. Maybe he was simply adjusting it. He did that sometimes when he had eaten too much of Mama's good cooking. But we ate almost two hours ago. He couldn't still be full. Then he began to unbutton the top of his work pants. What was Daddy doing? He unzipped his pants and began to feel on his dick. Is this man crazy? I was scared. I didn't know what to do. So I asked him, "Daddy, does your wee-wee hurt?" He looked at me and said, "Naw, it don't hurt, it just needs to be rubbed a little. Here, put yo' hand on it and feel it." He pulled it out of his pants and took my little hand and placed it on his filthy, black dick. Why was he making me touch him like that? I knew it wasn't right, but what could I do? This was the man that beat me whenever he got a notion. I stopped resisting when I realized that at least he wasn't mad at me. Maybe if I rubbed his dick he wouldn't beat me anymore.

The beatings kept coming just like the days of the week. It got to the point when I knew he was going to beat me. He would come home with this look in his eyes that said, "I'm just looking to kick a nigga's ass today." And of course, my nigga ass was always the one getting kicked. The rides began to happen more frequently. We would go down to the river bank and stay for hours. He would say the same thing each time, "Bad little boys need to be punished, and you is a bad little boy. Now do what you do to make things better." I would grab his sorry dick and start rubbing. Then it got to the place where rubbing him wasn't good enough. Naw, this dirty bastard told me that if I really wanted to make things right I had to actually kiss it. The first time he said it, I cried. The old man turned to me and said, "Crying ain't gon' make thangs better. So you might as well kiss it and prove to me that you really do want to be a good boy." Then he pulled my arm towards him, forcing my whole body to move closer to his side. He put his big, dirty, calloused hand on top of my head and forced it down to the top of his dick. He must have just taken a leak, because I remember the smell of piss.

That's when the hate set in. I wish he would have beat me ten times more instead of doing those filthy things to me. The only good thing about our "rides" is that usually, he wouldn't beat me for at lest a week. And if I kissed it real good I could go for maybe a week and a half. So I learned how to do it just the way he liked - as best I could.

At one point, Mama must have gotten suspicious about our rides because she questioned the old man about our little trips one day. I heard her say, "Cleve, what you and lil' Do be doing down there by the river bank all the time?" He looked at her and said, "Listen, woman, don't question a grown man 'bout his business. I'm trying to teach the boy a few thangs. That *is* what a 'Daddy' do wit his *sons* ain't it?" No response from Mama. Daddy looked at her and said, "Yeah, that's what I thought." Mama never questioned Daddy about those rides again. Guess she fixed her mind to believe that he was really trying to take an interest in her little bastard child. Mama lived in such denial. She wanted to believe any and everything that Daddy told her.

I didn't understand my mother when it came to the old man. She always buckled down to him, even when it came to her own children. What kind of hold did he have on her? Whatever it was it was strong and tight. She even knew about that damn Minnie woman and Daddy's outside kids and still found some way to love him and stay with him. Yeah, there was some resentment towards Mama, too. Daddy didn't get all of my hatred. Even my brothers and sisters got some. They all trying to figure out why I'm so crazy. They just don't know the hell I went through growing up with *their* Daddy. I guess you could say that I made it my business to make everybody else's life a living hell, just like the one I tried to pull myself out of.

Ella described me as being a ladies man, one of those real slick talking Negros, always the life of the party, real sharp dresser. Yeah, that was me. But that was just a front. I had become a predator, always stalking out my next victim. It didn't matter to me who he or she was. Somebody was gon' pay for all the shit I had been through. I made it my business to make sure that someone felt the pain I had trapped inside of me for all those years. Me being the life of the party, was to make people feel safe around me. Nobody ever suspected that I had actually molested five girls and two little boys - nobody except Mama. Mama knew something wasn't right. She just couldn't put her finger on it. Although I think she knew full well what was going on, but once again she chose to turn a blind eye on the situation.

Now Ella was a different story. See, I never meant to hurt her. When I really think about it, I think I was feeling her pain. She was a loner. Never had any friends, and her fast ass sisters didn't spend any time with her. So I started hanging around her just to keep her company. The strange thing was, instead of me feeling some type of compassion towards her, I saw her simply as a pathetic little soul, lost with nowhere to turn. Most uncles would have felt sorry for their niece, but not me. That's when my predator traits came out on her. I began to look at her as just another helpless creature in the wild who had wondered away from the protection of the herd: it was the height of hunting season and the lions were on the prowl. My strategy with Ella was slightly different than they do in the wild. Instead of me scoping her out and then begin my attack, I invited her into my world to make her feel comfortable around me.

Even though she had been around me her whole life, she had never been apart of my world. Ella didn't like me when she was a baby. I would stick my arms out to hold her and she would start crying. Everybody in the family thought it was funny, except Mama. When Ella was about two years old, she would scream bloody murder whenever I walked in the room. That child wouldn't let me get near her, let alone touch her. Her mother began to take note and would quietly keep Ella away from me. The rest of the family thought it was funny. Not one of them took Ella's screams for future help seriously. They would say things like, "Do-Man, you must be pinching that baby." Or, "Do, you must have some type of haint on you, that's why that baby gal don't like you." And then they would all start laughing and go back to doing whatever they were doing. No one recognized little Ella's prophetic screams for help.

I doubt if she knew what she was feeling, but her instincts were right about me all along. But me being the slick nigga I was, I wasn't gon' let some little girl stop me from doing what I wanted to do. So I did everything I could to befriend little Ella. I started off by having her go to store and get my cigarettes and let her keep the change. After I lost my job, Lee Otis handed me the key to the promised land. He asked me to keep an eye out for Ella when she came home from school. Handed her to me on a silver platter. So everyday I would make sure that I would be in their apartment when Ella got home. I would talk to her about school and help her with her homework and let her sit on my lap while we watched television. That made her feel real comfortable. Then one day while we were watching television, one of those Chevrolet commercials came on telling you how beautiful and wonderful you would be if you ran out and bought a brand new Chevy. During the commercial, Ella said, "Uncle Do, I bet everybody would like me if I had one of those brand new Chevrolets." I looked at her as she sat on my lap and said with a little laugh, "I bet they would like you even better if they saw you driving a Cadillac." She looked at me with those big green, almond shaped eyes and said, "You the only person I know who drive a Cadillac." Now the wheels were spinning in my head. I said, "That's right, baby girl, and yo' old uncle gon' teach you how to drive his big ole Hawg. How 'bout that, Ella?" That girl was so excited that I think she forgot that she was really afraid of me.

Right after that commercial went off, I told Ella to put on her tennis shoes so we could go driving. She ran like the wind trying to find her shoes. We drove to an empty lot not far from the apartment. I made her promise to keep this between the two of us because her parents would kill me if they knew that I let her drive at such a young age, especially since I wasn't taking her sisters and they were older than her. She bought it hook, line and sinker. All she cared about was having someone who wanted to spend time with her.

On our first ride, I tried to make her feel as comfortable as possible. I put her on my lap so she could see over the dashboard. She was so excited that I almost felt guilty for what I was about to do to her. But the predator in me wouldn't let her get away. So, on the second time out, I moved in for the kill. I put her up on my lap just like we did the day before and told her to put her little hands on the steering wheel at the 10 and 2 positions. Then I positioned her butt right in the middle of my lap so that it was nice and comfortable for me. Then I told her that we were getting ready to take off. I put my foot on the gas pedal and gave the engine just enough gas to rock her little behind right back in the center of my lap. That first little thrust was like a rush to my brain. Damn that felt good. We were on our way. We drove around that parking lot for at least 30 minutes. I made sure we drove over every bump and hit every pothole. By the time we were done, little Ella thought that she had peed on herself. She said she didn't want to go driving anymore. I told her that it was nothing; lots of little girls got that excited when they first learned to drive. She wasn't buying it, but I kept talking to try and calm her down. I eventually convinced Ella to go riding with me a few more times before finally she just flat out refused. I wasn't going to be satisfied until I really hurt that girl. I don't know what it was but, I just couldn't rest until I had her.

So everyday for the next two weeks I would pick Ella up from school and take her driving. One Friday afternoon while taking her lessons, Ella felt something poking her in her behind. She tried to adjust herself in a more comfortable position, but every time she moved, I would put her back in her original spot. Finally, she said, "Something is poking me and it hurts." She said with a little whine. I said, "Oh, it's okay, lil' bit. That's just uncle Do getting excited because you driving so well. See what happens when you make your Uncle Do happy?"

CHAPTER 13

LEE OTIS

Growing up, none of us knew that Do-Man had a different Daddy than the rest of us. We just knew that he didn't act like the rest of us. I noticed how Daddy treated him. It seemed like Daddy was always yelling at Do-Man for the simplest things, and he would beat him like he was a grown man. He beat Do-man for some of the same things the rest of got away with on a daily basis. There would be times when we would be running around in the yard playing like kids do and Daddy would come home and Do-Man might run past him, and before you knew it Daddy would snatch Do-Man up and start beating him, yelling things like, "You know better'n than to be running through this yard like you some kind of animal!" Daddy would beat him so bad that I thought he was trying to kill him. It was years later when I realized that Daddy was trying to kill his spirit. Seemed like the more he tried to kill that boy's spirit, the stronger it got.

Now I don't know what made Do-Man do the terrible things he did to kids, especially little girls. The whole family thinks it was those beatings Daddy used to give him. Seem to me like by the time Do-Man got to be 'round twelve or thirteen, he just started hating girls - just when most boys start to have some kind of liking towards the girls. He would come home every other day talking about how some girl made him beat her up. Mama would go upside his head whenever she would hear him talking crazy like that, but it didn't stop him from fighting with those girls everyday.

CHAPTER 14

DO-MAN

Ella was right, I did know her after school schedule better than anyone else. I had to. If I was going to make my move, I had to know when the right time would be. After our driving lessons Ella tried to keep her distance. So, one day I decided that I would be waiting for her when she got home. I was sitting right there in the living room reading the paper when she opened the door. Startled, she made her way on into the apartment and went straight to her room. Can you believe that? She didn't even say hello. I went and knocked on her door and said, "Ella, you okay in there?" She didn't answer right away so I knocked again, except this time I opened the door and she was just sitting there on her bed looking terrified. As I walked towards her bed I saw her tensing up. She was clutching a pillow. I sat down next to her and put my arm around her shoulder and said, "If I didn't know better, Ella, I'd think you didn't want me in your room." She kept looking at the floor. I put my hand on her knee and said, "Do you mind if I sit here and talk to you for a while?" No answer. I ran my hand across her back and said, "I'll take that as a yes." Tears began to slide down her cheeks. I held her little face in my hand, tilted it up towards me and said, "Tell Uncle Do why you cryin'." She didn't say a word. I could feel her body trembling. Yeah, she was scared. Just like I thought she would be. I ran my hand over her head and whispered, "Ella, your uncle Do-Man don't feel too well. Now you could be a good girl and make him feel a lot better. All you have to do is touch me right here." I took her hand and guided it to the bulge in my pants. She never looked at me. She kept clutching the pillow with her free hand while cryin'. I told her that if she told anyone they would all think that she was lying and just trying to get back to East St. Louis. A small part of me wanted to feel sorry for her but that predator in me was in full control. I forced her hand to stay put on my crouch, she tried to move it but I wouldn't let her. She began to whimper. I held her hand tighter. She began to sob. I finally let her hand go and said, "I guess you made your ole' Uncle Do feel a little better. Maybe you can help me out the next time I'm not feeling well." I got up and left her in her room. Before I closed the door I stopped and said, 'Remember, Ella, this is just between us. You don't want them to think you're making up stories just so you can get back to East St. Louis, right?' She didn't answer. She kept crying and shaking like a little leaf. I closed her bedroom door and went on down the street to *The Corner Bar.*

I waited a whole 24 hours before I went back to my brother's apartment. I needed to see if Ella was going to tell anyone, especially my brother. When I saw my brother in the hallway the following evening and all he said to me was, "Man, where you been?" I knew the coast was clear for me to fully initiate Ella into my world. "I been lookin' for a job, "I lied.

"Any luck?" I could tell he was happy to hear I was doing something productive.

"Naw, not yet. But I got some good leads," I said with all the bullshit I could muster up.

"Alright then, let me know what happens. Oh yeah, you think you could watch Ella tomorrow when she gets out of school? I don't think she's feeling to well and me and Sadie don't want her here by herself when she gets home from school," he said as he made his way down the stairs.

Damn, this was going to be easier than I thought. Here they were handing me this little lamb on a silver platter. I almost hate to admit it, but what the hell, I got excited just thinking about it.

The next day I was waiting in my brother's apartment for little Ella to get home from school. You should have seen the look of terror on her face when she opened the door and saw me sitting in the living room reading the paper. I pretended I didn't notice her at first. Not sure what to do, she stood there frozen. Finally, I got up and said, "Hey lil' bit. How was school?" as I made my way over to her. She stood there with her hand on the door knob not knowing if she should come in or run back down the stairs. I gently took her hand off the knob and helped her inside the apartment. She tripped over her own feet as she tried to resist my pull. Unfortunately, Ella didn't realize that it was too late to resist me. She and her parents had given me complete permission to do whatever I wanted to do with her.

CHAPTER 15

ELLA

The bus ride from 26th and California all the way to the south side was done in complete silence, silence borne out of fear and shock. Once inside the apartment, everyone went to their own room. Time and space was needed to figure things out. I flopped down on my bed and the tears began to flow. My Daddy was gone. I didn't even know for how long. What would happen to us now? I walked over to the window where I had spent countless hours waiting to see my Daddy walking home from the bus stop just a block away. He always tried to be home between five and six so we could have dinner together. He would usually have an appointment after dinner and would come back around 8:30 p.m. I stood at that window staring out at the empty street. I half-way expected my father to turn the corner with his briefcase in hand. I stood there for what seemed like hours before I heard my mother's voice calling me from the kitchen. "Ella? Ella?!" she yelled. I came back from my trance and moved mindlessly down the corridor to the kitchen where my mother stood over the sink washing out her coffee cup and saucer from that morning's breakfast. "Are you hungry?" she said with her back to me. My 'no' was barely audible. I stood there in the kitchen doorway with my chin in my chest trying to hold back the tears.

I knew that if my mother looked up from that sink and saw me crying she would have a fit. Before escaping my mother, Cora and Mattie made their way to the kitchen, each pushing one of my shoulders as they entered. Mama finally turned around to face us. I was half way back to my room when I heard her say, "Where's Ella?" Neither of my sisters bothered to respond. "Ella, get back in this kitchen. I need to talk to all y'all." Shocked that I was being included in a real family discussion, I quickly sat down in my usual kitchen chair. She looked at the three of us with tears in her eyes and said, "Now that Daddy's gone, I'm not sure how we're going to make it. But I know somehow, some way, we gon' make it through. Now y'all know that Daddy would want us to be strong while he's away. So that means that each one of us is gon' have to step up and do her part." She was looking for a response, none was given. I wanted to go back to my room, stare out the window and wait for Daddy to turn the corner on his way home.

Daddy wasn't coming home and Mama wanted us to step up. Step up and do what? That didn't make sense to my nine year old brain. But Mama was serious as she stood over that kitchen table in her best Sunday dress. For the first time during this ordeal, I really looked at my mother. I watched her as her head hung ever so slightly, biting her bottom lip. The dark circles around her eyes, the permanent laugh lines forming around her mouth, the deep lines etching their way into the center of her forehead were her badges of worry and unmistakable signs that she was aging fast. It would only be a few minutes before the tears started to pour. My sisters went to our mother to hug her. I had no desire to hug her. One word kept swirling around in my head. I tried to keep it there, in my head. It wasn't suppose to come out for the others to hear, but the word had a mind of its own. Before I could stop it, it rushed from my head to my mouth and leaped out for fresh air, "Why?" The three of them looked at me like I had three heads. Again that word insisted on doing its own thing. "Why?!"

"Why what?" my mother finally asked, irritation in her voice.

All of a sudden fear wanted to take over, but WHY was on a roll. I cleared my throat so WHY could be heard loud and clear. After all, that's what it wanted anyway. This time WHY brought a few friends along for the ride. "Why did you let this happen to me? Why didn't you stop Uncle Do-Man from doing what he did to me and..." before all of WHY's buddies could make it out, I heard a hand crashing into the side of someone's face. When I finally woke up, I realized that the hand belonged to Mama and *my* face was the crash pad. Deep was the anger and hatred she carried for me.

I crawled out of bed and walked over to the window. It was dark outside and rain poured from the sky, knocking against my window. I could barely see. Through the fog, a figure emerged. Was God really that kind, or was He playing a cruel joke on me? Wiping my eyes to get a clear view, I saw the image sway from one side of the sidewalk to the other, almost crashing into the side of a building. The image tripped over an empty Ne-Hi bottle and fell to the ground. Struggling to get up he fell again. As the image got closer to my window, I realized that it was Mr. Jones, the neighborhood drunk. My heart sank. He was heading home from *The Corner Bar*. I bet his family wished he would go away and never come back; and yet, even in his drunken state, he still managed to find his way home every night. How did they get to be so lucky?

I stood at the window for so long that my shins began to ache. I almost collapsed from the pain. Once in bed, I thought I would sleep for hours - no such luck. Six-thirty the next morning, someone was laying on our doorbell like there was no tomorrow. Who in the world could that be at this time of morning? I heard my mother and sisters scrambling around the apartment. I stayed in my room. I wasn't sure if it was safe for me to come out yet. My mother opened the front door and I heard my dad's oldest brother, Uncle Butch, saying, "Sadie, I came as soon as Mama told me what happened," as he made his way into the apartment. I cracked my door so I could see and hear exactly what was going on.

He drove all the way from East St. Louis to Chicago by himself. He sat down on the couch in the living room and Mama went and made him some coffee. She was still in her night gown and robe. This must be pretty serious because Mama never received company in her night clothes. I stood at the door peering out, afraid to be seen because they wouldn't talk as freely if they saw me. My sisters were sitting in the living room talking to Uncle Butch when Mama brought him his coffee. "Where's Lil' Ella?" he said between sips. Mama looked in the direction of my bedroom and said, "I think she's still sleep. You know this whole thing has really been tough on her." Uncle Butch shook his head in agreement and said, "Girls, I need to talk to your mother for a moment." They looked at Mama and got their cue to leave. Cora and Mattie slowly got up, not wanting to leave, but having no choice, and went back to their room.

My uncle looked up at my mother, who was still standing, and said, "Listen, Sadie, I'ma get straight to the chase. Every since we got the call yesterday afternoon 'bout Lee Otis we been meetin' and talkin', and we think that you and the girls need to come on back home where you got family that can take care of you. Ain't no sense y'all staying up here all by y'all selves and what not." Mama stood there clutching her robe around her neck listening to Uncle Butch go on about what the family back home felt was best for the four of us. When he finally stopped talking, Mama tightened the belt around her pink fluffy robe and sat on the edge of the chair across from the couch. After about a minute of silence, Mama looked at Uncle Butch and said, "I know everybody back home want what's best for me and the girls, but right now I think we need to stay put. Besides, if we move back to East St. Louis, I won't ever get to visit Lee Otis up there in Joliet. It's bad enough he gone be locked up for the next 20 years, now here you come telling me that you don't want me to see him but once a year, if I'm lucky. Naw, me and the girls is gon' stay right here in the home me and Lee Otis was trying to make for all of us."

"What about Ella? You thank she ought to stay in this apartment after everythang that's don' happened to her?! Come on, Sadie, let's be reasonable. That don't make a bit of sense."

A tear rolled down my cheek. Mama sat back in her chair and said, "Yeah, well, Ella ain't the only child I got. And those other two are doing just fine right where they are." I couldn't believe what Mama was saying. Didn't she care about me at all?

"That's all well and good, but what about Ella?" Uncle Butch pleaded.

"Ella gon' be just fine right here with her Mama and sisters. Now, I really appreciate you driving all the way up here, but I'm afraid this was a wasted trip," Mama said, as she stood up.

"Look, Sadie. I didn't want to have to tell you this, but, Lee Otis called down to Mama's and told us that he wants you and the girls to move on back to East St. Louis," Uncle Butch confessed.

My mother looked as if she had seen a ghost. Through clinched teeth she said, "You mean to tell me that he hasn't even had the decency to call here and check on me and the girls, but he can call down there to tell y'all that somebody needs to come and git us?!"

Acknowledging the fury in my mother's eyes, my uncle said, "Listen, Sadie, let's just calm down. I didn't come up here to get you all upset and what not. I just think, I mean, the whole family thinks you need to get Ella out of this place. So much has happened to her up here. Don't you think she deserves a break?"

"I told you, Ella gon' be just fine."

"Come on, Sadie," my uncle begged, "You of all people know how hard something like this can be on a child. You want Ella to go through …" Before Uncle Butch could finish his point, my mother jumped up out of her seat and shouted, "Look Butch, me and my girls is gon' be just fine! So you can git back in your fancy

car and head on back down to East St. Louis and tell
the rest of yo' family that we ain't going nowhere!"

Uncle Butch stood up and said, "I hear you Sadie,
I really do understand where you comin' from. But
this is what Lee Otis wants." He put his hands up to
stop Mama from talking, "Listen, I'm gon' run around
the corner and grab some breakfast real quick. Then
I'm gon' come back and maybe we can talk about this
a little more rationally." Uncle Butch was at the door
before Mama could even start talking. He gently closed
the door behind him and Mama slowly made her way
towards the kitchen, briefly stopping at my bedroom
door, noticing it was slightly cracked. She couldn't see
me because I had eased my way to the other side. I
held my breath as she stood outside my door, releasing
it only after I heard her footsteps shuffling towards
the kitchen.

I couldn't believe Mama was gon' actually make
me stay in that awful apartment after all I had been
through. Why didn't she just send me back to East St.
Louis with Uncle Butch? That way I would have been
out of her hair, no longer a constant reminder of my
Daddy, her husband. I felt the resentment welling up
in her even on the bus ride home from the court house.
It wasn't what she said, it was the way she looked at
me through the corner of her eyes while we rode for
what seemed forever on that slow city bus.

CHAPTER 16

UNCLE BUTCH

I left Sadie's house and drove a couple of blocks to that little soul food restaurant called GiGi's, that they all raved about when they would come home. I had never seen a restaurant in the basement of an apartment building, but they supposed to have the best soul food around. I doubt if it was any better than my Mama's but what the hell, I was hungry so I stopped in to get some breakfast while I gave Sadie a chance to cool off, and give myself time to plan my next move. Somehow I had to convince her to move back home. I never knew that girl could be so stubborn. Before now, she did whatever Lee Otis told her to do. I don't know who that woman was standing in that apartment going toe to toe with me like she was some man.

I found a payphone right outside of GiGi's. I dialed zero for the operator, "Yes, I'd like to make a collect call to Babe from Butch."

"One moment please, while I connect your call." the operator said.

Mama picked up the line on the third ring. "Hello?" she said in her groggy voice.

"I have a collect call from Butch, will you accept

the charges?"

"Yes, I will"

"Okay Sir, go ahead with your call." And just like that the operator was gon'.

I could hear the tiredness and the weight of a heavy heart in Mama's voice. "Hey, Butch, you made it up there alright, huh?"

"Yeah, I made it up here with no problems." I didn't know how I was gon' tell Mama that Sadie was refusing to come back home with me. That was the last thing she wanted, or needed to hear. She had just buried one son and another had been sentenced to 20 years in prison. Maybe I would just call her back after I tried again with Sadie. Somehow I had to convince that woman to come back with me.

"Butch, you there?" Mama said, breaking up my thoughts.

"Uh, yeah Mama, I'm still here."

"Good. So let's make this quick, boy, 'cause you know you running up my phone bill. What time is you, Sadie and the girls gon' be headin' back dis way?"

"Well, I really don't know at this point." I tried to sound like everythang was cool.

"What you mean you don't know at this point?!" she snapped.

"I need to talk to Sadie some more to find out what she wants to do. So, I'll call you later on tonight or in the morning to let you know what we gon' do." I hung up the phone before Mama could respond. I knew that I had just bought myself a good cussin' out the next time I talked to her, but I had also bought myself a little more time in getting Sadie and the girls back home. I went inside the small, drably decorated restaurant and grabbed a stool with a red plastic cushion for a seat, looked over the menu and decided to have the scrambled eggs, grits, pork rind bacon and biscuits with a cup of black coffee.

As I waited for my food, I overheard a couple of women sitting at the opposite end of the counter discussing the latest neighborhood gossip.

"Chile, did you hear what happened to Lee Otis Boxx yesterday?"

"Who?"

"You know Lee Otis Boxx, the insurance man from over there on 54th and Indiana."

"Oh yeah, that fine nigga that killed his brother a little while ago."

"Yeah, that's the one. Well they had his trial yesterday, and honey, I heard the man was sentenced to life in prison."

"Girl, you got to be kidding. I know they didn't give that fine ass man life fo' killing that scoundrel of a brother, even though, the brother was fine too. Didn't the brother rape Lee Otis's three year old daughter?"

"Yeah, something like that. Seems to me like I heard, it was his little boy. Anyway, chile, that shole is a shame what happened to him. But wait, that ain't all of it. Baby, word is, Lee Otis' wife had her new man over there last night and the Negro didn't leave until this morning.

"Baby, don't tell me nothin' bout these low count women. Man ain't been in jail a good minute and her new man done already moved in. No wonder that poor chile of theirs got raped. The mama ain't fit!"

They stopped cackling only to graze over the food that was placed in front of them. But it only kept them quiet for about one and a half minutes before they came up for air and started talking about some other poor soul in the neighborhood. By the time my waitress placed my food in front of me I no longer had an appetite. I told the waitress, "Make this to go."

CHAPTER 17

SIMP

When Do-Man first took the insurance job he didn't realize that it came with such a huge perk. But he knew he was in heaven when his first potential client opened the door and my pretty little grand daughter stood right by her single mother's side. When he laid eyes on little Penny, he knew that he would have to get my daughter to buy a policy. Charm and good looks made it easy to gain people's trust. My poor, unsuspecting daughter would soon fall prey like others before her. After one appointment, Margaret bought a $3,000.00 life insurance policy, just the ticket Do-Man was looking for. Do-Man could see the desperation burning in her eyes when she invited him into her one bedroom apartment. Her sad, begging eyes told Do-Man that she would do anything to have him in her line of vision, even if it was just every now and then. He found her eagerness to please a complete stranger both pathetic and amusing, all of which he would take full advantage. He also knew that my daughter couldn't afford to keep up the policy, but because she wanted him she would scrape up the money every week for as long as she could, anything to get him in her house once a week.

D.A. Rhodes

Unfortunately, for her, Do-Man was not interested
in making her his woman. He only liked pretty women
and pretty little girls. But to satisfy his selfish needs,
he would deal with my ugly daughter to get to the
pretty chile'. He started off by going to Margaret's
house once a week to pick up her premiums. The first
couple of times she offered him coffee, after that, the
savory aroma of her southern cooking would greet him
long before she ever opened the door. How could he
possibly refuse the generous dinner invitations? After
all, it was dinner time and he had been working hard
all day; surely he needed to eat.

So every Wednesday, Do-Man would make his
way up to the third floor apartment, greeted with an
envelope holding the unaffordable premium and a hot
meal. Sometimes Do-Man couldn't remember if he was
an insurance man or the neighborhood pimp. There
were days when he would have as much as $500.00 in
his pocket, all of it belonging to the insurance company.
Sometimes it would make it to the its rightful owner,
sometimes it wouldn't, depending on the day of the week
and how thirsty Do-Man was at the end of his day.

Eventually, my daughter invited Do-Man to her
apartment on days outside of his normal premium
pickup day. Usually he would decline, but every
now and then he would accept her offer. Margaret
was so glad to have a man sitting at her table on a
consistent basis, she let down what few guards she did
have up. She even told her daughter to, "Be nice to
Mr. Boxx." Next thing you knew, my precious grand
baby was sitting on Do-Man's lap hugging his neck,
while he would pretend that his leg was a horse and
give her a horsy ride. Do-Man did such a good job in

102

making Margaret think that he was genuine, that my poor daughter actually thought they were going to be a family, even though she only saw Do-Man a couple of times a week - in her apartment. Sometimes he would make up an excuse to go to the store and offer to take Penny along with him. Pleased that he was taking an interest in her baby, she always allowed my grandbaby to go. The only time she ever became suspicious was when he kept Penny with him for over an hour. When the chile' came home she had a different look on her face. Do-Man could tell that Margaret wanted to ask questions so he started in with his fast, slick talking, to get her mind off of the obvious. The second time it happened I was at the apartment. When Do-Man and Penny came in, I was immediately alarmed when I saw the distraught and frightened look on my grand baby's face. I asked her in front of Do-Man, "Baby, what's done happened to you?" She shyly looked up at Do-man then to her mother. Not a peep out of the child. Do-Man went into his routine, but I shut him down before he could get started. I told him to leave. I needed to talk to my granddaughter in private. Do-Man tried to hug little Penny but I pulled her next to me and said, "Good day, Mr. Boxx." He looked at the three of us and decided it was best that he get to stepping.

Once the door shut behind him, I told my daughter, "Don't let that baby keep goin' off with that man. Ain't no telling' what he might be trying to do to her." Then I turned to Penny and said, "Come here, baby. Did he try to touch you?" She looked scared. She kept looking down at the floor. Her mother didn't say a word, praying the chile' had nothing to say either. I gently took Penny by the hand and led her to the kitchen table, where all serious matters were discussed. I put Penny on my lap and said, "Baby, ain't nothin' for you to be afraid of in this house. Now you know Granny always done told you to tell the truth, 'cause if you tell the truth I can't be mad at you. Now, I wants you to tell Granny where Mr. Boxx took you this afternoon." Penny looked up and said, "He told me not to tell nobody where we went."

"Why did he tell you not to tell?"

"He said that Mama might get mad at him and not let me go places with him no more." I looked over at Margaret, who was standing by the kitchen sink with her arms tightly folded in front of her, unable to control the nervous twitch in her right eye, tapping her right toe on her freshly waxed floor. I looked back at Penny and said, "Don't worry, baby, yo' Mama ain't gon' be mad at you, is you daughter?" Margaret shook her head no. "See, yo' Mama wants you to tell the truth too. Now tell Granny what happened."

She told us that Do-Man took her to the store to buy her some candy and then back to his apartment where he let her watch television and gave her some Kool-Aid. He sat down on the couch next to her and put her on his lap and told her she was beautiful and that he wished she was his little girl. Then he kissed her on her forehead and took her hand and put it on his private and made her rub it for a long time. And he kept telling her that she was a good girl for making Uncle Do feel so good. He told her they would stop at the five and dime store on their way back to her house and buy her something really special. Margaret turned her back to the girl and began to cry over the sink. I held Penny in my arms and gently rocked her back and forth. Finally, I told Penny to go to her room while I talked to her mother. Once she was gone, I spat out, "Okay, gal, what we gon' do bout this nigger you done let come up in here over yo' chile? " She didn't respond. "Did you hear me? I said, what is you gon' do? 'Cause I'ma tell you now, ain't no need in you standing over there crying like a baby. Git yo'self together and let's figure out what we gon' do bout this bastard that's done hurt yo' baby." Still facing the sink, in a barely audible voice Margaret whispered, "Don't sound like he hurt her all that much to me."

Once again my daughter was willing to put a man over her own chile'. Well, I wasn't gon' to stand for it this time. No longer would I quietly sit back and watch her desperately go after some no-good man at the expense of my grandbaby. "What you mean don't seem like he hurt her all that much to you? Didn't you hear what that baby said that fool did to her?" Anger seeping out with each word uttered. I got up and walked over to the sink, grabbed Margaret by the shoulders, forcing her to turn around and face me. "This has got to stop right now! You can't do this to that baby!" Margaret stared me in the eyes and said, "Why not? You did it to me."

"Listen, gal, we ain't even gon' go into all that right now. We need to focus on that baby in there. This madness has got to stop. Now, if you ain't gon' do nothin' to protect yo' chile then I will. And I'm gon' start with that no count man." I stood back waiting for a response. No answer.

It was time for me to take matters into my own hands. I turned around and walked out of the kitchen and into the baby's room. I told her to pack some of her clothes because she was going to stay with Granny for a few days. When she asked why, I said it was because her mother didn't feel well and she needed some time to rest.

Penny stuffed a suit case full of clothes, pajamas and underwear. We walked out the front door without a word to the chile's mother, nor did Margaret say a word to us, nor did she try to stop us. We all knew that would be the last time that child would ever live with her mother.

I took my grandbaby home and tried to comfort her and told her she would be staying with me for a little while. After I got the child settled, my next thought was taking care of Do-Man. Murder or assassination? Naw, killing the Negro might come back to haunt me, like the time I had my first husband's girlfriend shot. It was just by the grace of God that I wasn't convicted of first degree murder.

It was settled. Something bad, really bad was going to happen to Do-Man. I just didn't know what it would be. First thing Monday morning, I was going down to that insurance company he claimed to work for and tell them what type of person they had working for them, and demand that they fire him immediately. If they didn't, me and my granddaughter were going to march around that building day in and day out until something was done. If it took the rest of my life, I was going to destroy that man. Now all I had to do was remember which insurance company he worked for. And why did Margaret have all that life insurance anyway? A simple burial policy was all she needed. Hell, that's all I ever had. Life insurance was for those you leave behind. They might use it to bury you, they might not. With that burial insurance your people don't have a choice but to bury your black behind. But you can't tell Margaret's want-to-be-high-falutin'-tail nothing, no how. Just like you can't tell her nothing about that no-good man she been letting hang around for the past month or so. But that was all about to change. I would fix it like I always did.

Fortunately, we all lived in the same neighborhood and knew all of the same people, which made it easier for me to put my feelers out on Do-Man. I started asking questions around the neighborhood. I started at *The Corner Bar*, and worked my way over to GiGi's, where everybody in the neighborhood went to eat on Saturday nights after they had been out partying all night. I found out exactly where he lived, who his people were, where they went to church, what type of car he drove, who his friends were, and what type of whiskey he drank. Any and everything there was to find out about Do-Man, was found out, and fast. There was no time to waste. I had to put my plan into motion, quickly. After the perfect scheme was hatched, I needed the right person to help execute my secret plot against Do-Man. This individual would have no idea they were helping to get rid of a child molester.

For my plan to work, I had to hang out at that same bar, so I could see Do-Man in action. You wouldn't believe how he had all those people eating out of the palm of his hand. It was as if he had some kind of spell on them. They all laughed at his jokes, the bartender gave him free drinks, the men gathered around to hear what he had to say and the women were tripping over themselves, and each other, just to sit next to him.

I decided that, old drunk, Calvin Jones, would help to free our neighborhood of Do-Man. Calvin Jones was a regular at *The Corner Bar*. He and Do-Man were there every Wednesday, Thursday, Friday, Saturday and Sunday. You could find Do-Man roosting on his usual bar stool, flashing all that insurance money around, like it actually belonged to him. That, too, would come to a screeching halt.

I would get to *The Corner Bar* right before Do-Man and find a little table close to the back so I wouldn't be noticed. While waiting for Do-Man to make his grand entrance into the joint, I realized how lifeless the bar was without him. The music had no real rhyme or reason, the people were quiet and the drinks didn't seem to flow as freely as they did when he was there. He would breeze through the door like he was God himself blowing new life into the place with his very presence. I could see why Margaret had fallen so hard for this man, but I couldn't understand why she would allow him to molest her daughter and not do anything about it. At that point, I didn't have time to figure it out, I still had a plan to execute. In this very bar is where it would all come together.

After staking out the bar for almost a week, I found out that he had a brother who lived in the neighborhood with his family and that the brother sold insurance for the same company as Do-Man. Well, well, well. How convenient for me. I called the insurance company and told them that I wanted to take out a small policy. They told me they would send someone to my home within the next couple of days. I told them that I wanted Lee Otis Boxx, because I heard that he was real good. The woman on the phone set the appointment for the following Tuesday at 4:30 p.m. This was going to be easier than I thought. With the brother coming to my house, I could really find out about Do-Man and his family. She knew she didn't have a lot of time so she would have to work quickly.

I had just finished baking one of my famous Bundt cakes and was pouring the chocolate icing over the cake when Lee Otis rang the buzzer to the apartment. He walked in and had to acknowledge the sweet smell of homemade cake. No one with a half-way working nose could be on guard with that comforting aroma gently making its way throughout the apartment. I greeted him at the door with my baking apron on, which was covered in flour, and my silver hair was just a little messy from all of the baking I had been doing. My grandmotherly appearance would certainly put him at ease and make him feel that he could trust me and tell me everything I wanted to know about him. I stood at the door wiping my hands on my apron and said, "You must be Mr. Boxx from Unified."

"Yes Ma'am. Are you Mrs. Simpson?"

"I sure am. Come on in and have a seat," Opening the door wide to let him in.

"Wow, it sure does smell good in here, Mrs. Simpson. What are you baking?" he said as he made his way into the apartment.

"Oh, honey, that's just one of my Bundt cakes I made for my little granddaughter. She just love 'em. I have to darn near beat her wit a stick to keep her from eatin' the whole thang. Let me git you a piece and you be the judge." I headed back to the kitchen before he could answer.

Lee Otis looked around the apartment and decided

that it was clean enough for him to have at least a piece of cake with his potential client, although he had no idea what the kitchen looked liked. Sensing his reservation about the kitchen, I yelled out to him, "Mr. Boxx, come on back here in the kitchen. Back here is where I handle all of my important business." He made his way down the hall and sat down at the large kitchen table in one of the mix-match chairs. I gave him his cake and poured him a cup of coffee in a white coffee cup with a chipped handle. He graciously accepted the offering of cake and coffee, and was beyond pleased when he tasted the first bite of the deliciously moist Bundt cake. His own Mama didn't make cake that good.

"Mrs. Simpson, I got to tell you, this has got to be the best Bundt cake I ever had. I'ma have to have my wife call you and get the recipe."

"Oh, baby, that ain't no problem at all. Have yo' wife to call me whenever she ready to start making the best cake in the whole world." I laughed and sat down in the mix-match chair directly across from Lee Otis. As he slowly ate his cake, not wanting to finish it because it was so good, I asked him, "Do you have any children Mr. Boxx?

"Taking a sip of his coffee, he said, "Yes, I have three beautiful girls, Cora, Mattie and Ella." A slight smile ran across his face when he said Ella's name. I picked up on that right away.

"Ella must be your heart?" I said with a slight smile of my own.

"Yeah, she's the one that has me wrapped around her little finger. She's the quiet one of the three, and the baby. Now as much as I hate to admit it, I do tend to favor her just a tad bit more than the other girls."

I cut him another piece of cake and freshened up his coffee. "Yeah, I know what you mean when you feel that you have to protect one more that the others. That's just how I feels about my little grandbaby in there. She's quiet, too, and don't hardly speak up for herself. And her Mama don't seem like she capable of protecting her like she should. So that's where I come in. I'll do anything to protect that baby. You know what I mean, Mr. Boxx?" He shook his head up and down not wanting to swallow the sweet tasting cake, trying to savor each bite for as long as he could. He finally swallowed and said, "I sure do, Mrs. Simpson."

"Please, Mr. Boxx, call me Simp. All of my friends do."

"Okay, Simp, I'll do just that."

Some how he found the will power to refuse his third piece of cake. "If I eat another piece of this scrumptious cake, I won't be able to eat any of my wife's dinner. And that wouldn't be a good thing if you know what I mean." Easing back in my chair, I gave him a smile that showed the gold tooth in the side of my mouth. The plan was about to fall right into place. We talked a little longer about family, religion and the plight of the Negro. By the time Mr. Boxx got around to talking insurance, two hours had passed and he knew that he would have to rush through the presentation. He suggested that we meet in two days at 4:30 p.m. again, and next time he would be prepared to go straight into the presentation and sign me up with the perfect policy.

I agreed and walked him to the door and tried to get him to take another piece of cake for the road. He reluctantly declined and promised to have his wife call me for the recipe. After he left, I almost felt guilty for what was about to happen. After all, he was really a nice man. But his brother was not, and he had to pay for what he did to my grandbaby. I didn't care how nice his family was, although, I couldn't help wondering how such a bad seed could come from what appeared to be good stock. I told myself that one bad apple could spoil the bunch if it wasn't gotten rid of, and that's just what I intended to do: get rid of that spoiled, rotted apple before he ruined any other precious apples in the neighborhood.

The next part of my plan was to talk to some of the trashy women that Do-Man ran around with. Maybe I would tell them he had a venereal disease. Maybe not. Those tramps may think they gave it to him. I had to figure out some way to ruin his reputation with his whores. Oh, yes, I was going to destroy him piece by piece, if it was the last thing I did. Satisfaction came from knowing his own kin folk would help to bring him down.

CHAPTER 18

GRANDMA BABE

See, that's why I really didn't want my chilluns traipsing up to Chicago, no how. I had a feeling that bad news was waiting up there for Lee Otis and dem. I knew that Do-Man was gon' be nothing but trouble as soon as he hit the city limits. That's just the way he was. Shucks, he left here with a switch blade in between his legs. So, really, all Do-Man did was take his riotous living from one city to another. Heck, if you ask me, he could've just went on across the bridge to St. Louis and saved hisself a lot of time and money, driving all the way up there to Chicago.

I also knew that Ella didn't want to go. I should have demanded that they leave that gal back here wit me. I don't know why I didn't listen to my right mind when it was telling me to just keep that baby right here wit me. See, that's why it's so important to listen to yo' good mind when it's tryin' to say somethin'. But we usually too busy tryin' to do just what we want to do that half the time we be don' missed the message, and end up having to pay for the mistake later on down the line.

Well, when Lee Otis and Sadie came to me and said

they was thanking 'bout going up to Chicago to make a fresh start of thangs, I was all for it. But then I got to praying on that thang, and it just wasn't setting right in my spirit. I couldn't sleep for at least a week after they told me. Just couldn't get it out of my mind. Then, when they had the family meeting and everybody was so excited about them going to Chicago, and Do-Man was gon' get Lee Otis a job, I figured I was just overreacting. Looking back, I should've stood up and spoke my piece. Now, I know it wasn't nothin' but the devil holding my tongue. Ella would come into my bedroom every night and crawl in my bed while I was listening to my radio soap operas, and say, "Grandma Babe, have you ever been to Chicago?"

"Yes, baby, I've been to Chicago 'bout two or three times." I'd tell her while trying not to miss too much of my program.

"Do you think I'll like it up there?"

"Well, baby, that's hard for an old woman like me to say. It's been years since I been that way. And to tell you the truth, I can really only speak fo' myself. See, I'm just a plain 'ole country woman that likes simple country thangs. So, Chicago just wasn't the place for me. But you might find that you likes it alright." I told her while trying to hide my disappointment in all of them leaving.

"Grandma Babe," she said as she snuggled up to me, "I want to be a plain 'ole country woman just like you when I grow up. So I think that I should stay here with you so you can teach me how to be a plain 'ole country woman." I had to laugh at the way she just summed up my whole life in four words.

That child meant every word she said to me that

night. Here we were living in a time when most folks was tryin' to run from the very thang that's sustained them all they natural life, and this girl wants to stay put and really become a part of her history. I told her that I would teach her as much as I could with the time we had left. That seemed to pacify her for at least that night, 'cause once I said I would teach her to be a plain 'ole country woman, she curled up next to me and went right to sleep. I laid there in my bed that night thinking about my grandbaby's request. Teach her how to be a country woman. Didn't know it was something you woke and said you wanted to be. It was more like you woke up one morning and realized that that's what you were. Hell, when I was a child I thought I was gon' be a teacher. Couldn't wait to git to school so I could look at the way my teacher would be dressed and listen to the way she said her words and how she had such great command of the classroom. I wanted to be just like her. But at the end of the fourth grade my father fell ill and was in a sick bed for near 'bout a year. Well, I had to quit school and start helping my Mama and my older brothers and sisters in the field. My guess is, even if Daddy hadn't fell ill, my school time was near up anyway. Since none of the other chilluns in the family went to school much past the fifth grade.

When it came time to go back to school, Mama told me that I was gon' stay there and help them git the pigs ready for slaughter. I mistakenly thought that by showing the disappointment on my face that my Mama would have pity on me and change her mind. I found out how wrong I was after my face stopped stinging from the hand slap that she gave, for, as she put it, "being an ungrateful, whining baby." My little fantasy about being a teacher ended right then and there. I was on my way to being a plain 'ole country woman, pulling my weight just like the rest of them.

Ella was always different from the rest of my grandkids. She was always underfoot. Even as a little, bitty baby, Ella had a strong connection to me. The first time I held baby Ella in my arms, she just nestled her little head in my chest like she had found her home. Been laying her head on my chest ever since.

I tell you, every time I thanks about what happened up der in Chicago, my heart just aches and aches all over again. At first I wanted to blame her Mama, Sadie, but then the Lawd had to deal wit me on that one. The Lawd told me just as plain as day that it wasn't no more Sadie's fault than it was Ella's. I tell you, I had to fall down on my knees and beg the Lawd to forgive me all over again. It was like Satan, himself, was riding my back and screaming in my ears that this was all my doing. Lawd, have mercy! I prayed to God and told him, "Lawd, you know I ain't never meant no hurt harm or danger to come to none of mine. Why in the world something like dis have to come up on our doorstep?" Then I remembered, I was the one, all those years ago, shaking my behind at some juke joint.

I knew something wasn't right with Do-Man the day he was born. But what mother wants to admit that she sees the devil in her child? It was almost frightening to look at his sweet little face and see the devil staring back at me through my baby's cold, grey eyes. At times I wanted to kill my own child. But what mother with an ounce of love in her heart could kill her own child?

So I kept trying to ignore what was looking me dead in my face, tugging at my heart and whispering in my ear. I even tried to convince myself that I was losing my mind. But I knew. I knew all along. Why didn't I do something? 'Cause I kept hoping that things would get better. They just got worse.

I ain't never told nobody this but, I came real close to killing Do-Man, more than once. There was the time he was sleeping in his little bed and I decided that for the good of the family and Do-Man, I was going to remove him from this earth. I took a pillow and gently put it over his tiny face and held it in place until he started squirming and my mother sense kicked in. I couldn't kill my baby, no matter how he was conceived. Not listening to that little voice deep in my soul simply prolonged his fate. He wasn't simply born to die, he was born to be murdered. Since I had willingly helped to create this child, I carried the responsibility of cleaning up the mess I made. Whenever I really think about how terrible of a thing this is, tears just well up in my eyes. I don' cried so many nights about this, that it's a wonder I got any tears left. My pain is coming at me from all angles. It's only by the grace of God that I'm still standing. Sometimes I wonder if him keeping me alive all these years was my punishment for being disobedient, keeping me around so I can see just how far reaching my sin really is. At times, I read the story of David in the Bible and see how the Lawd put a curse on David's house because of the way he sinned with Bathsheba. It sends chills down my spine every time I thanks about it. See, David ended up sinning 'cause he was in the wrong place at the wrong time - supposed to be off fighting with his army, but instead, he at home in Jerusalem. Just like me, I was supposed to be waiting for my husband to come home so we could get back together, but instead, I go running off to some juke joint wit some people that ain't meant me a bit of good.

Just like God struck David and Bathsheba's first son wit a deadly illness, I believe wit all my heart that God was telling me to kill Do-Man 'cause he was also born out of the worst kind of sin. After God killed their first son he ended up blessing them with another son, Solomon. Maybe if I had been obedient, the Lawd would have blessed me and Cleveland wit another child together, and maybe none of dis wickedness would have overtook my family.

CHAPTER 19

ELLA

Me telling my story all began with that crazy dream I had a couple of months ago. I had been in therapy for about three months and my therapist, Dr. Free, kept asking me to talk to the little girl inside of me. I thought it was absurd and couldn't bring myself to do it. My therapist said that I just wasn't ready to hear what the little girl had to say, but in order to get to the root cause of my problems I would have to address the issue. All I wanted to do was move on with my life and leave the past right where it was. Dr. Free kept telling me that the past was hindering my present and my future, and in order to move on I would have to face whatever childhood demons were haunting me.

I'll never forget the day Dr. Free suggested hypnosis. She could tell that I was skeptical. Actually, I was down right scared. Who knew what would come up and out while I was under hypnosis? I told Dr. Free that I wasn't ready and needed some time to think about it. I left her office a bit disoriented and decided to go home and get in bed. I must have gone to sleep as soon as my head hit the pillow. I remember sleeping really hard. My dream seemed very real to me. At first

I was afraid but something made me stay asleep and keep dreaming.

I remember seeing a little girl standing at the end of a long hallway, beckoning for me to come toward her. I stood frozen. The distance between us got shorter and shorter. When I was close enough to make out her face, I realized it was me when I was about nine years old. She had my famous pony tail that sat right in the middle of my head, a chubby round face, and my favorite summer outfit: cut-off blue jean shorts, a white tee-shirt, my blue bobby socks and my white tennis shoes. She looked like she had been outside playing. I couldn't speak to her, only look. My heart was racing. Why was she coming towards me? "Why don't you talk to me?" she said. Fear held my tongue. If I closed my eyes and opened them again maybe she would be gone. No such luck. Still there, only this time her image was crystal clear, no denying who she was, but what did she want?

In my dream, I stood and stared at myself. We stared at each other. She spoke first, "Do you think I'm good enough for you?" What did she mean? She didn't understand my confusion. I looked at her in her dirty play clothes, the very same ones I played so hard in that Grandma Babe would tell me I smelled like a puppy when I would finally go inside. "Do you think I'm good enough for you?" she repeated. I shook my head yes as if I were still that little girl standing before me.

"Then how come you don't talk to me?" she innocently asked.

I stood there hunching my shoulders, too ashamed to say it was fear that kept me from talking to her. She moved a little closer. I wanted her to stay where she was. I tried to back up but my feet were glued to that spot. She looked sad, like she wanted to get closer so I could touch her, hug her. I couldn't. I wanted her to leave, go back to wherever she came from. I closed and opened my eyes in the dream, only to find her standing right in front of me bigger than life. Frightened, I screamed, "Please don't hurt me!" She looked at me with the saddest eyes and said, "I just want you to love me." Tears began to roll down her face. "Do you love me?" She whispered. Yes, should have been my answer, but I knew the truth. I was ashamed of what she represented - my past. I didn't know if I loved the adult me. I finally managed to say, "Please go away." She held out her hand for me to grab. I wouldn't take it. I began to cry, stomp my feet and shake my hands real hard just like I did when I was a little girl when I couldn't get my way. "No!" I screamed. "I don't want your hand. Go away and leave me alone!" I shouted through my tears. She, too, began to cry. Her tears were not the tears of a spoiled brat as were mine. Hers were those of a sad child, abandoned by all who claimed to have loved her, and now the face of her very own soul turned it's back as well. She finally withdrew her hand, turned and walked away until she faded from view. I fell to my knees and wept. Was I so disgusted in myself that I couldn't allow the nine year old part of me to have a voice in my present life? Some things are just better left alone - she was one of them.

I woke up from that dream in a cold sweat and a pounding headache. It all seemed so real. Should I tell my therapist? She would definitely want to know. But then she would start talking all that hypnosis mumble jumble again. I wasn't in the mood. I made it clear to the little girl in me that she wasn't welcome in my dreams or anywhere else in my life. I got out of the bed and made my way to the bathroom. When I looked in the mirror I saw the little girl's reflection. Was I seeing a ghost? This had to stop. I ran out of the bathroom and called my therapist right away. Her answering service picked up.

"Good Morning, Dr. Free's office, how may I help you?" The too cheerful voice on the other end sang.

"Yes, I need to see Dr. Free right away." I said.

"Okay ma'am, this is her answering service. Someone will be in the office around 10 o'clock this morning. You can call back at that time to make an appointment," she sang once again.

I started to argue but then realized it wasn't worth it. I would just call back in a couple of hours. I was afraid to go back in the bathroom, but had no choice. I washed my face, brushed my teeth, even got in and out of the shower without looking at the mirror. I couldn't face her last night and I couldn't even look at myself this morning. I brushed my hair back into a pony tail and hoped for the best.

I waited until the clock struck ten on the head and called Dr. Free's office hoping to get her assistant, not that damn answering service. The phone rang two times and a not so cheerful voice greeted me on the other end. "Hello, Dr. Free's office, how can I help you?" is what the gloomy voice said.

"Ah, yes. My name is Ella Boxx and I'm calling to see if I can get an emergency appointment with Dr. Free this morning." I was trying my best to stay positive. Gloomy didn't bother asking me to hold. The hold music told me I was waiting as it sang what it assumed was my favorite tune. I waited for what seemed an eternity only for her to return and say, "I'm sorry, Ms. Boxx, but the Doctor is completely booked today. I can possibly squeeze you in next Thursday at 10 a.m. Will that work for you?"

"No, that won't work for me. I need to see Dr. Free this morning, not next week. Listen, you don't understand, I've been having nightmares since last night. I woke up this morning and was still having the same nightmare," I frantically said. Gloomy placed me on hold again. I could feel the irritation rising up from my stomach. If she came back to that phone and said I couldn't see the doctor I was going to have a fit. To my surprise, Gloomy came back to the phone with some good news. "Okay, Ms. Boxx. I just spoke to Dr. Free and she said for you to come in at 12 noon. So relieved, I almost looked at myself in the mirror.

By noon, I was almost a basket case. I was afraid of what Dr. Free was going to make me do, but I needed to talk. An empty waiting room greeted me. Patients would enter in one door and leave through another, protecting everyone's privacy. The soft ringing of the bell and a blinking green light said it was your turn to see the doctor. As soon as my behind touched the couch, the bell began to ring, signaling my turn to see the good doctor. "Hello Ella, come in and have a seat." She said with a guarded voice.

"Thanks for squeezing me in," I said as I made my way over to the oversized couch that sat directly in front of the huge plate glass window. Her office sat 25 feet in the air, overlooking the Atlantic Ocean. The view from the couch was amazingly tranquil. Some days it felt as if the ocean would come and take my issues, my problems, every one of my worries, out to sea and give them the proper burial they deserved. I would leave her office feeling free and lighter than the wind that gently swept across the ocean. This was not one of those days. Her look made me uncomfortable. Finally, I asked, "Is something wrong, Dr. Free?" She grabbed her note pad and said, "The message said that you were having nightmares that carried over to the morning. Is that right?"

"Yes, and it terrified me to no end."

"So, tell me about this nightmare," she said easing back in her chair.

"Well, a few weeks ago, you asked me if I could talk to the little girl inside of me, what I would say. I told you I wasn't sure because I was uncomfortable talking to her."

"Yes, I remember."

"Well, last night the nine year old me appeared in my dream. "

"What did she say?"

"She asked me if I thought she was good enough and did I feel that she was worthy of love."

"And what did you say?"

"I couldn't answer."

"Why do you think that was?"

"I don't know."

"Have you thought about why you don't want to talk to her?"

"A part of me is afraid."

"Afraid of what?"

"Afraid of what she may say to me."

"Do you think she will blame you for the sexual molestation?"

"I know she'll blame me for what happened because I blame myself," I said as I tried to choke back the tears.

"I think it might be time to for you to face your fears concerning your past. That's the only way you'll be able to move forward."

I sighed. I knew that she was right and the time was now. I leaned back on the couch and said, "I think I'm ready to do the hypnosis. What do I have to do?"

"The first thing you need to do is relax. I want you to lie down on the couch, close your eyes and begin to take in some deep breaths, and let them out very slowly. This will help to slow down your heart rate."

Her soothing tone was already beginning to relax me. I followed her instructions. I laid down on the couch and tried to get as comfortable as I could while closing my eyes and breathing slowly. Then I heard her say, "Try to completely relax." I did as I was told and the next thing I knew it was as if I were asleep but not asleep. It was the strangest feeling. I heard Dr. Free say, "Ella, I want you to pull up the image of yourself when you were nine years old." She must have know that my heart rate had increased because I heard her say, "Stay calm, Ella, everything is going to be okay. Just continue to breathe and relax." I did just as I was told and began to take really deep breaths. "Okay, do you have an image of the young you?"

"Yes, I can see her."

"Alright, where is she?"

"She's standing outside of my grandmother's house in East St. Louis."

"What is she doing?"

"Nothing."

"What would you like to say to her?"

"I want to ask her if she hates me."

"Go ahead and ask her."

"Do you hate me?" I asked the nine year old me.

"No, I don't hate you, I love you." she said.

I began to cry. Dr. Free asked, "What did she say?"

Between the tears I told her she loved me. "What else do you want to say to her?"

I said, "Little Ella, I'm sorry about what happened to you. Someone should have been there to protect you from your uncle. I know that you were afraid every time he came into your room and…" I had more to say but I began to breathe erratic and Dr. Free told me to relax and that she would bring me out of the hypnosis.

I laid there on the couch sobbing like a baby. Dr. Free was pleased with the session. I felt drained, vulnerable, exposed. Sitting up on the couch I couldn't look the doctor in her face. Where was this shame coming from?

Dr. Free said, "Ella, please don't feel ashamed by what just happened. Believe it or not, you have made a huge step today. And you have only yourself to thank. Remember, you're the one who called me for this emergency session. You should be very proud of yourself." She leaned forward and gently took my hand down from my face and said, "Listen, Ella, I want you to go home and write a letter to the nine year old Ella explaining what happened to her. I think that once you begin to write it all down it will begin to lose more and more of its power over you."

I had finally stopped crying and was concentrating on what she was saying. She looked me in my eyes and said, "Do you think you can start on that this week, and have something for me by next Thursday?"

I shook my head up and down while trying to gather my things so I could leave. As I stood up to make a mad dash to the exit door, she reached out and grabbed my arm and said, "This really was a good session. Don't worry, we're going to get to the bottom of your fears soon enough. Just give it some time."

I looked at her and said, "If they don't get to me first."

CHAPTER 20

DO-MAN

What is the fascination with me and these little girls? Y'all all know I did what they accusing me of. It's just that I never meant to get caught. I loved Annette, the little girl from East St. Louis, like she was one of my nieces. Even I couldn't believe how her mother would leave her with me like she did. I don't know if I meant for anything to happen with her or not. It's just that she was such a pretty little thing. Always hugging up on my neck, wanting me to give her a horsy-back ride or fly her around in the air like she was an airplane. I got so comfortable wit her 'til next thing I knew, I was getting aroused whenever I would think about playing with the little girl. That's when I knew that she would be my next victim.

Truth be told, I really don't think that this one was my fault. You can blame the girl's Mama for what happened. She was so busy trying to keep a man, run the streets and do whatever else she called herself doing, that she left her own child open for a predator like me to swoop right in and devour her whenever I felt the urge. Unfortunately for her, I began to feel the urge quite often. I even think little Annette liked it. Don't call me sick. I ain't sick. I say I think she liked it because when it first started she really didn't say anything. I don't know if she was just scared or what. But she didn't say anything. She didn't tell her mother or nothing. So of course in my mind, that was my signal to keep going. So I did.

Sometimes I would take her for long rides in my car and we would end up at that same river bank my step daddy used to take me to when I was a little boy. I found myself saying some of the same things to her that he said to me, except there would be times I could swear that she didn't mind doing whatever I asked her to do. Because she was so young I had to break her in slowly. So I would tell her to do simple things like touch or rub me when I was hard, and eventually I would have her to kiss it. She had to be around seven or eight years old at the time.

The only reason we got busted is because she started breaking out around her mouth. Come to find out, this other broad that I was messing around with had some kind of VD and passed it on to me. I had no clue that something was wrong with me until one day I was taking a piss and it burned like hell. The first thing I thought was that my old lady had given me something. But I figured I better not be too quick to accuse her of stepping out when I knew all along that I was the one in the wrong. So I went to that fine broad I was messing around with, Barbara Jean, and asked her what the hell was going on. Sure enough she admitted to giving me the clap. Ain't that a bitch? The broad came straight out and told me that she done gave me some venereal disease. I tried to choke the hell out of that bitch, but she must have been waiting on me to come after her, 'cause before I could get both of my hands around that skinny heffa's neck, she came up with a butcher knife big enough to scare a gorilla. I decided she wasn't worth me losing my life over, so I slowly took my hand from around her neck and eased my way on out of her place. I made my way down to Ms. Hattie Mae's house. Ms. Hattie Mae was like the neighborhood witch doctor. No matter what was ailing you, Ms. Hattie Mae had a cure for it.

I took my two dollars and my burning dick on down to Ms. Hattie and before I could even get in the door good, she looked me dead in my eye and said, "See you been round there to 'ole Barbara Jean's place."

"Ma'am?" I said as she stepped aside to let me in her home.

"You heard me, boy. You been round there to that nasty woman's house. You mens is gon' learn yet to stay way from that woman. She ain't right and she sho' ain't clean!" she said looking me up and down. I followed her to the kitchen in the back of the house where she kept all of her medicine.

I wasn't sure if I should follow her or not, so I just stood there and waited for her to tell me what to do. "Well, don't just stand there looking stupid, boy. Come on back here so I can give you something for that thang of yours." She never turned around or stopped walking as she gave me my instructions. I did what the old bat told me to do. I walked back there to the kitchen and watched her pull down two bottles of some brown liquid stuff. I had no idea what it was. I just needed the tonic to work - and quick.

Before she mixed the stuff in the bottles she turned to look at me and said, "Is you got some money wit you? 'Cause I wants you to know that this here potion ain't free."

"Yes, Ma'am. I got two bits right here in my pocket." I said, patting my front right pocket. She didn't move. That was my cue to put my money next to the big old book she kept on her table at all times. At first glance I thought it was the bible, until I saw a skull and cross bones on the front. That's when I decided I better put my money on the table, get my concoction and get the hell out of there. She told me to drink two tablespoons of the brown liquid three times a day for two days, and at the end of day two I should feel just like my old self. Then she told me, "Make sho' you stay 'way from that nasty Barbara Jean." With that I went home and began to take my medicine.

I don't know what she put in that potion but after just one tablespoon I began to feel like my old self. I was real tempted to stop taking the medicine, but something told me I better take it just like she said. So I did.

Well, a few days after I went to see Ms. Hattie, little Annette's mouth began to break out. At first her Mama thought is was something she ate. Maybe she was allergic to something. But she knew that wasn't it because the girl hadn't been eating anything out of the norm. Then, one day one of little Annette's uncles happened to be by the house talking to the little girl and noticed the bumps around her mouth. He started asking her questions about where the bumps came from. She couldn't give him the right answers. He put two and two together. He knew exactly what those bumps were because he had been to see Barbara Jean before and his girlfriend ended up with those same bumps on and around her lips.

I just so happened to be out at my favorite bar when all of the discoveries were made, otherwise he probably would have killed me on the spot. Guess Mama was right - I really was destined to be murdered, just not that night. Somehow by the time those three dudes found me at the bar, my old lady had convinced them not to kill me. Up until the day I was killed, I never could figure out why that woman spared my life. Guess I'll never know. Anyway, when they cornered me outside the bar, the one brother who had that knife up to my groin actually punctured my right ball. I thought that I felt something stick me but I wasn't sure. Not to mention, I was scared those dudes were going to kill me. I didn't realize that I had been stabbed until I got in my car and felt something wet sliding down my leg. "Ah shit, I done wet my fuckin' pants." I stopped the car, jumped out and almost fainted when I saw all the blood falling from underneath my pant leg. I tried not to panic, but it was hard when I didn't know if I was hemorrhaging or not. So I figured my last stop in East St. Louis needed to be Ms. Hattie's.

I don't know if she was expecting me or what, but when I dragged myself up the six steps to her oversized porch, the front door was wide open. "Come on in here, boy," she said, watching me limp across her threshold, blood trailing behind me. "This here be the last time Ms. Hattie gon' ever treat you." I slowly made my way into the house and she instructed me to go into the makeshift operating room, get undressed and put on the little gown hanging behind the door. I did as I was told and eased my way onto the table. Ms. Hattie came in right after I was on the table. She washed her hands at the dirty sink in the corner of the room, pulled out the necessary instruments to perform the delicate operation. The alcohol on my nuts burned like hell. Then she put something on them that felt really cool, like somebody was blowing ice on my balls. After a few seconds of the cool balls, I had no feeling in that area at all. Once she was satisfied that I wouldn't feel anything, she picked up this long ass needle and the next thing I knew I felt her heavy hands slapping my face telling me it was time for me to wake up and that I could pay her once I was dressed. How much should I pay Ms. Hattie for her home surgery? More than two bits that for sure.

The pain I felt was a small price to pay considering what I had just gone through that night. I put my clothes on and reached in my back pocket for all the money I had in all the world - exactly $50.00, most of which I had just won shooting crap. I gave Ms. Hattie half of that and used the other $25.00 to git on up to Chicago that same night. Surprisingly, Ms. Hattie understood and wished me well. I thanked her for all that she had done for me over the years and I told her that I would never forget her.

I left East St. Louis that night and never returned, at least not living and breathing. By the time I got to Chicago, I had decided that I was gon' try and change my wicked ways. I was gon' do right by the people around me. Heck, I was even gon' see if my oldest brother would move up here with his family. Yeah, my life was about to change - for the better is what I was hoping.

Well, no sooner than I got up there to Chicago I found me a job with the Unified Insurance Company. Basically, I just bullshitted my way in. They knew that

I didn't have the qualifications for the job, but because I was such a smooth talker, nice dresser and I looked good, they were willing to take a chance on this old country boy. I did real good when I first started. I was bringing in so much money it was crazy! All I had to do was learn the basics about those insurance policies and then I was good to go. Of course, the majority of my clients were females; and somehow these women would find money every week to pay their little polices. I never had a problem collecting my money. They would be practically hanging out of their windows and doors with the envelopes to pay me my money. At one time, I thought about being a pimp. Hell, I figured, I'd just be trading in one hustle for another.

Anyway, things were going just fine until I realized just how willing these women were to have a total stranger around their kids. I felt like a kid in a candy store. These women would ask me if I would take their sons out to play catch, help them with their homework, take them to the store... anything to spend time with their kids. I really did try to contain myself, but it was just too much for even me to handle. That's when I ran into Simp's daughter and granddaughter. I don't know what made me take a chance with that little girl. I guess one day I actually took time to look at the girl and I saw how pretty she was. Something in her little face just sparked something inside of me and I knew she would be my next victim. And just like all the other single mothers that I dealt with, her mother was no different. She made it too easy to have access to her daughter. All I had to do was show up and the little girl was mine for the taking. Had I known that Simp was her grandmother, I probably would have backed off. But knowing me I wouldn't have. Hell, I molested my own niece.

I have to admit, there was something different about this little girl. She was very quiet. It was almost like she was scared to talk or something. When I would take her to the store she was barely able to hold her head up while we rode in the car. Even when I would try and bribe her with candy, she would just keep her head down and not say anything. The most I could get out of her would be a mumble here and there. I almost felt sorry for her. That feeling quickly passed. I began to look at her non-talking as a good thing. I stupidly thought that I didn't have to prep her like I did all of my other kids. I just took it for granted that she would keep quiet. How was I supposed to know that the one person she would open up to was her Grandma Simp? Well, once that cat was out the bag, my life became a living hell. You wouldn't believe some of the crazy shit that lady tried to do to me.

She called my job so many times that I thought they were going to fire me the next time the phone rang. Then because they didn't get rid of me after the phone calls, this crazy broad just started showing up outside of the Unified Building with a damn picket sign that said, CLEOPHIS BOXX IS A CHILD RAPER! CLEOPHIS BOXX IS A CHILD RAPER! CLEOPHIS BOXX IS A CHILD RAPER!

Now how in the world she gon' go 'round saying something like that about me in front of my job? I told them to call the police on that crazy broad. Needless to say, my boss finally called me in his office to ask me what was going on. I told him I had no idea of what this woman was talking about. He must have held me in his office for more than an hour trying to get to the bottom of the situation. I sat there and looked that white man in his face and told him over and over that I had no idea what that woman was talking about. By the time I got finished doing a two step around, over and under all of his questions he called the Chicago Police and had them remove the vagrant woman in front of his place of business who among other things, was disturbing the peace.

The cops got there in record time. When they tried to remove Simp, she put up such a fight that they ended up cracking her over the head with one of their Billy clubs. I almost felt sorry for the old broad. But hell, she had no business trying to 'cause trouble for me on my job. I heard that she actually spent two nights in jail for making those cops go upside her head.

Shortly after that incident, my boss called me into his office and told me that there had been several discrepancies with my payments. Of course, I played the fool and acted like I didn't know what the hell he was talking about. But the truth of the matter was I had been pocketing the premium money from the time I started with the company. Yeah, I would turn in some of the money, but I think I kept more than I ever turned in. It's a good thing that none of my clients died while I was their insurance man, 'cause half of their policies lapsed a few months after I signed them up. It's a wonder I didn't get fired sooner than I did. Hell, I know I would have still been rolling had it not been for that trouble making Simp. She just couldn't mind her own business. Yeah, yeah, I know y'all saying that it was her business. But if you look at it from my point of view, that was a matter that Simp's daughter should have been handling . . . from the looks of things, it didn't bother her one bit. If it did, she sho' didn't say nothing to me about anything. That's a perfect example of how desperate those women were to have a man in their lives. They would do anything and allow anybody to be over their kids. It's just a damn shame if you ask me. I know, didn't nobody ask me.

CHAPTER 21

SIMP

That stupid boy don't know the half of what I did to git rid of his sorry behind. Not only did I go down there to his job and cut a fool, but I drug his family and so called friends into my little plan. How dare that low life bastard say I need to mind my own business? My grandbaby is my business. But you know what? Ain't no sense in getting all upset about what a dead man got to say 'cause it really don't amount to much no how. But since he started telling y'all what I did to him, let me finish.

After I got his brother to sell me that stupid life insurance policy, I decided that I would use his brother to do my dirty work. I knew it would work after I found out that his brother had a daughter a little older than my grandbaby. Well, if my instincts were right, and I knew they were, then Do-Man was more than likely doing the same thang to his own niece. All I had to do was prove it. So I started snooping around the little girl's school to see what I could find out. It wasn't that difficult because she went to the same school as my grandbaby. So when I would pick my baby up I would just watch that other little girl and see how she interacted with the other kids. And sure enough, she didn't have one friend on that entire school yard. The bell would ring and the kids would come flying out the doors, glad to be free from the time they got out of school until the time they reached home. All of the kids would make a mad dash for the school yard, just a rippin' and runnin', jumping all over the place acting like kids do when they been pent up for too long. That's what all the normal kids did, but not Do-Man's niece, oh no. She came walking out that school house slow as a turtle. If I didn't know better, I would've thought the teacher had to push the po' chile out the door and make her go home. She slowly walked down the stairs with her head held down. I don't recall seeing that po' baby hold her head up one time. And those fast tail sisters of hers were nowhere to be found.

She started walking in the direction of her house when all of a sudden I saw Do-Man's Cadillac pull up to the curb. There he was looking just as ignorant as usual, blowing the horn like some crazy man. The po' little girl was 'bout scared out of her mind. I could tell that she didn't want to get in the car. He was being so persistent, she probably felt she ain't had no choice but to get in. That's when I knew without a shadow of a doubt he was doing to her what he did to my grandbaby. She went on and got in the car with her uncle. I could feel the fear on that child's face. You just don't know how my heart went out for that baby. But I couldn't do nothing to help her at the very moment. But rest assure, I was working my plan to the letter. Oh that bastard was gon' pay for all the dirt he was doing, and all the pain he was causing. And the great thing about my plan was the price he was going to pay for what he did was so high that he wouldn't ever have to worry about paying for anything else again.

Everyday for two weeks, I watched that chile' go through the same routine after school. I would say a little prayer for her each time I saw her get into his car. I would also tell her that it wouldn't be much longer. My plan was starting to fall right into place. One night I went down to *The Corner Bar*, grabbed a table in the back, and watched all of the activity that went on. I saw who all the players were in Do-Man's world. I learned that old drunk Calvin Jones was the biggest shit talker of the group and, the biggest gossip. That man gossiped more that any woman I ever met. And it didn't matter if he was drunk or sober. He was always running his mouth, letting other people's business fly out. So there it was, he would be the one to get the ball rolling in my little plan. All I had to do was plant a little bug in 'ole Calvin's ear and he would do the rest. Oh yeah, by the time I got finished with Do-Man his chile' raping days would be over for good!

I decided that I would go back to *The Corner Bar* the next Sunday, which was blues night. The regulars would be there in full force since half of them got paid on Fridays, and the other half would have their welfare checks. The money and the drinks would be flowing freely all day and night. By 4 p.m. the bar was almost filled to capacity and the party was in full swing. I looked around to see if Calvin Jones was there, sure enough, he was propped up on his favorite bar stool. I swear, that man gon' die sittin' right there on that same 'ole bar stool with a drink in one hand while trying to grab some young girl's ass with the other, all the while holding that cigarette between his upper and bottom teeth, taking a pull every now and again.

Well, I made my way on over to where he was and asked him if I could buy him a drink. I know, that was a stupid question. Of course I could by a drunk a drink. He had worried the hell out of the young lady who was sitting next to him 'til she finally just got up and walked away, leaving an empty seat just for me to talk to my old buddy Calvin. We sat there and made small talk while we drank our first drink. I let Calvin pick up rounds two and three. After round three Calvin started with his gossiping. I thought to myself, just the fertile ground I needed to plant my seed. Calvin was on his third, "Have you heard?" when I interrupted him and said, "Calvin, have you heard about that man who's been going around molesting little girls in the neighborhood?" He almost fell off his barstool. He couldn't believe what he was hearing. So he asked me to repeat it. I gladly said it again. This time he leaned into me and said, "Who in the hell got the nerve to come in our neighborhood and do something nasty like that?" He took another sip of his Old-Granddad and then looked at me as if to say, "I know damn well you gon' tell me who been messing around with our kids like that." I gave him a sly smile and leaned in closer and said, "Now, don't tell nobody, but I heard that it was Do-Man." I said in a hushed voice. Calvin Jones didn't quite hear me at first because he took another sip of his bourbon and said, "Whatcha say, baby? I didn't quite hear you." I looked around to make sure no one else was listening and then I leaned in even closer to drunk Calvin and said, "I heard that Do-Man was molesting little girls in the neighborhood. I even heard that he was molesting his own niece."

Calvin couldn't believe his ears, but before he could respond Cassy, the barmaid, walked up to him and said, "Alright Calvin, it 4:15 and you said you needed to be out of here by 4 o'clock for your 4:30 appointment at home." He looked up at her and said, "Yeah, yeah you right." Then he looked over at me and said, "Are you sure Do-Man done raped his own niece?" I took another sip of my own drink and said, "Calvin, in all the years you been knowing me have you ever known me to be a gossip?" Drunk Calvin actually looked like he was pondering what I had just said to him. Before he could answer I said, "I wouldn't lie about something as serious as this. I just think something needs to be done. We can't have no predator like that running loose in our neighborhood. Something needs to be done." Calvin was just about to say something when the bartender strutted her tail back over and said, "Calvin, you told me to remind you that you and yo' wife got an appointment and you said you didn't want to be late. You better start making yo' way home fo' you miss it completely."

Calvin looked down at his half empty glass and decided that what was left in the glass was more important than what I was trying to say. He steadied himself as he stood up from his bar stool, threw his head back and downed the rest of his Old-Granddad. Then he looked at me and said, "Simp, I sho' would like to stay here with you and figure out what we needs to do about Do-Man, but I got's to git home and see about my wife." Then he leaned in real close to me and said, "You know, she be worried about me when I don't git home on time. But I tell you what," he slurred, "We can meet right here tomorrow afternoon to finish discussing this situation. What do you think?" I looked at that old fool and knew without a shadow of a doubt that I wasn't meeting him anywhere, not to mention, I really didn't think he would remember our conversation once the new sun marched across the sky.

As Calvin stumbled his way out of the bar, I sat there thinking this might have been a big 'ole waste of time. But little did I know, fate was dealing me a six-no trump and I was gon' run a Boston on Do-Man. All I had to do was sit back and let the cards fall where they may. I had no idea that Calvin's appointment was with Do-Man's brother. That really wasn't a part of my plan, but hey, whatever works.

Do-Man made his way to the bar around thirty minutes after Calvin Jones stumbled out of the joint. By that time I had found myself a quiet little table in the corner where no one would bother noticing me. I had a clear line of vision to see every move that chile' molester made while he was sitting there at the bar drinking his whiskey and talking to all of those loose women he liked to hang around with. I sat there for almost an hour just watching that dirty dog laugh it up, drinking and talking shit to all of his low life friends. Just when I said to myself that I had had enough, in walks Do-Man's brother. From where I was sitting, I saw him from the time he came in until he was taken out the door. That poor man walked in that bar looking like he had just talked to the dead. And what they had to say wasn't so nice. He stepped inside the bar and just stood there slowly looking around the place. I think I was the only one to notice that he was carrying a gun like it was a briefcase, in his left hand just dangling by his side.

His search stopped once he spotted Do-Man sitting at the bar laughing and talking. Mr. Boxx slowly made his way over to his brother and without saying a word, he raised the gun from his side and pointed it right at Do-Man's head. Before Do-Man could stop his grinning Mr. Boxx began to unload that gun on his own brother. There didn't seem to be a first shot or a last shot, just a series of shots fired and a bar full of people screaming and running. I do remember hearing someone say, "Damn, dat nigga got a gun!" and everyone trying to get out of the way.

From my bird's eye view, I saw the look of shock on Do-Man's face when he felt the heat from that first bullet rip right through his chest. Instead of running like the other party-goers, my anger and hatred for the man made me stay planted right where I was. I had to see him go down for myself. I wanted to know without a shadow of a doubt that that animal wouldn't be molesting any more little girls, or boys for that matter.

By the time the police got there I'm sure Do-Man was already doing his first dance with the devil. 'Ole Satan, himself, probably left the pits of hell to come to earth and escort his most favorite son back home. I have to admit, I did feel a little sorry for Lee Otis, but hell, it was for the greater good of the neighborhood and little girls all over, especially my grandbaby. I was just glad that my grandbaby didn't ever have to worry about seeing that man again.

I figured that 'ole Calvin's 4 p.m. appointment must have been with Do-Man's brother. He had mentioned that he and his wife were talking about getting insurance policies. This thang couldn't have worked out better if I had prayed directly to Jesus for divine intervention. Well, the cops came and escorted the poor brother out of the bar in handcuffs. Once everyone regained their composure, they all started to gather around outside and watch that unlucky man be put in the back seat of a police car and driven to a dingy jail cell where his life would never be the same. But I couldn't worry about that. I had to do what I had to do to protect my own. I'm sure that as time went by, he would be more than willing to thank me for what I did. I hoped he would, anyway.

A little while later, I heard that his wife and kids took the news really bad. It was a triple whammy for the family. I was actually surprised that they stayed in Chicago instead of moving back to East St. Louis where they came from. Maybe the mother looked at it like that would be running from your problems. I gotta give it to her though, she hung in there and didn't allow what these neighborhood gossips had to say run her out of her house.

One day I saw her picking up Ella from school and Ella still seemed just as down and depressed as ever. I wanted to tell Mrs. Boxx about this church program that I had started taking my grandbaby to twice a week...if you really want to call it a program. My grandbaby would talk to the pastor of the church twice a week. I think those talks really helped her. After about a year of going to see the good Reverend, she actually started coming out of her shell. She wasn't no social butterfly or nothing like that, but she started smiling more and more and she would even talk to me without me having to start the conversation.

Yeah, I wanted to tell Mrs. Boxx but she just didn't seem like the type of woman that would take kindly to a total stranger coming up to her and suggesting that she take her daughter to talk to some unknown pastor about being molested by her uncle. You know, back then black people weren't in to going to talk to somebody about their problems. They would rather keep it all bottled up inside or drown their grief in a bottle of booze. That's probably what's wrong with so many of us today. We're walking around with all this toxic garbage trapped inside of us, and just don't know how to get rid of it. Instead of taking it to the garbage can and leaving it there for the trash man to come and collect, we dump it all out in the streets and dirty up our families and neighborhoods with our mess. Then we sit back and say we just don't understand what's wrong with our communities.

I wasn't gon' let that mess continue in my family. So after everything went down, I started praying to God that He show me what to do. The very next day while I was working in the kitchen of these white folks that I used to cook and clean for, I overheard the lady of the house say that her 20 year old son must be crazy to want to help with all of that civil rights stuff that was going on. And because of his strange, behavior, she and her husband were going to send him to a psychologist. Before that day, I could barely say the word psychologist. So everyday she would be on the phone with her friends and family trying to figure out the best place to send this boy to get his head examined. So I figured, if this perfectly normal white boy needed to talk to somebody, then certainly my bruised up grandbaby needed some help.

Well, while I was sitting at church that next Sunday, listening to the preacher talk about taking your burdens to the Lord and leaving them there, I figured he was the man my baby needed to talk to. When I seen how good it was working out for my grandbaby, I figured this 'talking to somebody' thang was the best thing going, so I wanted to tell everybody that I thought needed some help about it. Then I figured that I had already done Sadie Boxx the best type of service she could imagine anyway. It was because of me that that demon was no longer around her baby. Eventually she would get her chance to thank me. You can rest assure that I'd see to that. But in the mean time, that little Ella just seemed to look sadder and sadder with each passing day. All I could do was pray for that girl and hope that everything would be okay for her. But my number one priority was my grandbaby. So that's what I began to focus on.

I even tried to get my stupid daughter to go and talk to the preacher but she told me she didn't need to talk to nobody about nothing. Said she wasn't gon' go and tell some preacher all of her business. I just shook my head 'cause I knew the truth. My own daughter was the one that needed the most help. But she was just like all the other black people I knew - too afraid to deal with the truth. She was so messed up that she didn't even try and get her own daughter back. Not that I would have given her back, but any normal mother wouldn't stand for somebody coming in and taking her chile' away, I don't care who it was. But that just goes to show how deep the pain is that she's feeling.

Maybe I been around white folks too long, but I believe just like they do that if something is wrong, then find a way to fix it so it don't keep coming back to bother you. Guess that's what I did 'bout that 'ole

Do-Man. I fixed some unborn child's problem without them ever having to worry about it. My work is done, at least for now.

CHAPTER 22

LEE OTIS

I don't know if it was my pride, my shame, or pure guilt that made me tell my wife not to ever bring the girls up here to see me. I stood strong on that for about the first month. Then the loneliness kicked in and I was yearning to see my family. I felt like the girls would look at me differently if they saw me in that damn prison uniform. I thought they would lose all respect for me, especially Ella. Somehow I had to explain myself and hopefully they would understand and forgive me for what I did, especially Ella.

When I first went in, I would call home every chance I got. When Sadie told me that the girls were starting to act out because I wasn't there, I knew it was time to start talking directly to them. So I sat down and wrote each one of them a letter. My first letter was to Ella.

Dear Ella,

I pray that you are alright. I can't begin to tell you how much your Daddy misses you. And I certainly can't wait to see your pretty little smiling face again. Boy, how I miss your smiling face. I miss coming home from work and you running to the door to greet me to tell me all about your day before even your mother had a chance to say hello to me. I seemed to have been your everything. The one you looked to for guidance and protection. And yet, I seem to be the very one who let you down.

Ella, I hope that one day you will be able to forgive me for tearing this family apart the way that I have. I want you to know that I only did what I felt I had to do to protect you and your sisters from being harmed anymore. What your uncle did to you was terrible and no one should have to go through that, and that's why he had to pay for what he did. Ella, I would do it again if I had to. I just pray that God will forgive me for my actions. I also pray that you don't blame yourself for any of this. What your uncle did to you was wrong and he had to be punished. He should have been punished a long time ago but that's neither here nor there.

Anyway Ella, I want you to know that I truly love you and would do anything in this world to make you happy and to protect you at all costs. Please try not to worry about me, just know that I'll be okay as long as I know that we'll all be together again as one big family.

Continue to be good and do your very best in school. I'll see you soon.

Love you a whole bunch,
Daddy

That was just the first of many letters I wrote to Ella. I hoped she got them all and was able to tell what was really going on in my head and my heart. It was hard trying to talk to her about the whole ordeal with her still being a kid and all. I don't think Sadie really tried to discuss anything with her. And I know her sisters didn't talk to her about anything. They barely said two words to her when everything was fine at home. The poor girl didn't have any friends, so I was basically all she had. But I was stuck in a jail cell like some caged animal. Ain't that a bitch!

Well, I finally told Sadie to bring the girls to see me. I couldn't believe my eyes when I walked out there to the visiting room and saw how much my family had changed in just a few short weeks. It looked like Cora and Mattie had turned into all legs and little Ella looked like a beautiful flower whose pedals were dropping off one by one, and soon she would be nothing more than a lonely stem waiting to be blown away with the wind. It took everything inside of me not to break down when I saw my baby. When she finally looked up at me, I could see a ray of light trying to makes its way from her dark and hollow eyes. It was eating me up on the inside to think that I had contributed to this pain in any way. I kept hearing Sadie's words run through my mind, "Stop beating yourself up. It's not your fault that your brother molested Ella, and as far as what happened to him well, you did what you had to do." But as I stood there staring at my baby, none of that seemed to matter. All I saw was a little girl whose life was ruined and I wasn't there to protect her. And when I'm being really honest with myself, I even blame her mother for what happened to her. Her mother should have noticed some changes in the girl as well. But she didn't. She was too busy trying to work outside the home and neglected to care for my children.

I haven't told Sadie any of this yet. I'm just waiting for the right moment to speak my piece. But in the mean time I need her to take good care of my kids and herself.

When the four of them came into the room, the first thing I did was kiss my wife, then I hugged Cora and Mattie. I stepped back and took a long look at Ella. She was standing there with her head down unsure of what to do. So I cleared my throat and said, "Hey, Miss Molly, you just gon' stand there and leave me here with my arms stretched out waiting for you to come jump in or what?" She shyly brought her head up so her chin was no longer touching her chest and gave the best smile she could muster up. Finally, she began to move towards me. I couldn't believe how withdrawn she was. "Come on, Miss Molly, give daddy a hug," I encouraged. She slowly made her way to me only to give me a half-hearted hug. I looked at Sadie hoping she could silently tell me what was going on, but all she could do was drop her eyes to the floor.

I tried to hug Ella back to life but when I let her go, she still looked like a lifeless little lamb that had nowhere to go and couldn't remember from whence she came. I actually had pity for my own daughter. But what the hell could I do from behind bars? I told the girls that I needed to talk to their Mama for a minute and they needed to go sit on the other side of the room for a while. Once they were out of ear shot, I turned to Sadie and said, "Listen, I need you to take the girls back to East St. Louis and I need you to do it quick." She looked me square in my eye and said, "Lee Otis, I'm not taking those girls back to that little country town. They like it just fine up here. Plus, I don't think it's right for us to just up and leave like we running from something. We ain't did nothing wrong so why should we be running away like some dog with his tail between his legs? Naw, we ain't going nowhere. 'Sides that, how we suppose to come see you if we all the way down in East St. Louis somewhere? Naw, we staying right here."

I did my best to stay cool, so I cleared my throat and said, "Yeah, Sadie I hear what you saying but we got to thank about Ella right now…"

"We got two more kids 'sides Ella. Now Ella gon' have to git over this thang 'bout Do-Man and git on with her life." I couldn't believe what I was hearing. "Sadie, you of all people should understand what Ella is going through, not only as her mother but as somebody who went through the same kind of trauma…"

"Ella didn't go through half of what I went through back there in those woods. So don't you even try to compare the two! Furthermore, I thought you and I wasn't gon' ever discuss what happened to me no more." I could see the fire jumping out her of green eyes. That meant that the discussion was now over, or so I thought.

"Listen, I'm sitting her in a damn jail cell because I killed my brother! Now that should tell you that I will do anything to protect what's mine." I saw the fire dim a little. "Now we need to figure out what's best for the family, but more importantly, what's best for Ella. 'Cause I don't give a damn about Ella not knowing the half of what you went through. The fact that she knows any piece of it is too much as far as I'm concerned. So by the end of the summer I want you and the girls to be prepared to move back to East St. Louis. Is that understood?" I tried to calm down but it was hard. Sadie started biting her bottom lip. That meant one of two things, either she was trying to keep from crying or she was so enraged that she wanted to hit me. I didn't give a damn either way. The bottom line was, she was going to have to take the girls back to East St. Louis. Sometimes the whole family has to take a hit for the well-being of one person, and sometimes one person has to take a hit for the whole family. It was now time for the family to take that hit. Convincing Sadie to make that sacrifice was going to be difficult, at best. Somehow I would get her to come around and see things for what they really were.

She looked at me with those cat green eyes of hers and was about to protest but decided this was not the time to argue with me. She was right. I wasn't backing down from that decision. No way in hell was I going to make my baby continue to suffer in that apartment after everything that happened. Sadie simply got her purse and coat and prepared to leave. She stood up and was not even going to say goodbye. I reached out and grabbed her hand and said, "Don't go away angry. I'm just trying to do what's best for Ella and everybody in the family." Then I kissed her hand and held it for a moment before I let it go. I could see her eyes begin to soften as I held her hand. She told me she would think about it and then turned to leave. Cora and Mattie came back to the table to give me hugs and tell me goodbye. I noticed that Ella hung back in the area that the girls were sitting in. After I said my goodbyes to the two older ones, I walked over to where Ella sat staring off into space. I sat down in the empty chair next to her and tried to put my arm around her. The way she almost jumped out of her seat, you would have thought she saw a ghost. I knew in that very instant that my baby had to get the hell out of Chicago so she could begin to put this whole thing behind her. I tried to touch her hand but she jerked it away. I told her that I wasn't going to hurt her, I just wanted to hold her hand for a moment before we said goodbye. She looked up at me with those hollow eyes and I almost cried. How in the world was my baby ever going to get over this ordeal? Or was I asking too much of God when I prayed every night asking Him to take away the pain and shame that she must be feeling day after day. From the looks of things, God had yet to answer. I decided to say a quick prayer right then and there. "Lord, I know You busy but we need You right here and right now. I'm asking that you send your angels down here to help little Ella git through this pain. 'Cause she sho' could use Your help." After I finished, I grabbed her hand and said, "I love you, Ella." Again, those hollow eyes. She never said a word. My heart exploded from the pain. God was gon' have to do something quick.

I watched my family walk out of the visiting area and out of my life, again. The first chance I got, I called down to East St. Louis and told Mama that she had to convince Sadie to move back home with the girls. She told me that she was already working on it but Sadie wasn't buying it. "For the life of me I don't know why that girl is so stubborn," Mama said with a sigh. I had to agree. I couldn't figure out why she would want to stay in Chicago. Then Mama said, "I thank she too ashamed to come back here. Too scared 'bout what people gon' thank. But I tried to tell her, none of that don't mean nothing. These folks 'round here can talk all they wants, but they ain't doing nothing to take care of her family, so they opinion don't matter."

My shoulders slumped. Something inside of me

told me that I was fighting a losing battle with Sadie. The only way I could help Ella was to git out of this jail.

CHAPTER 23

SADIE

I don't know why Lee Otis was talking about me and the girls going back to East St. Louis. Wasn't nothing back there for me or the girls. Ella was gon' be alright. All she needed was some time to adjust. Hell, I made it okay. Didn't nobody say 'let's pick up and move' when those animals raped me. Life went on as usual. And that's just what we was gon' do in this case. Period.

First, that damn Butch come up here trying to get me to move back. Then Babe started calling with all that non-sense. I can just hear it now if I were to take my children back to East St. Louis: everybody would be talking about how I couldn't even take care of my family and we couldn't make it in Chicago. Furthermore, why would I want to leave Lee Otis up here all by himself? Well, I wasn't going nowhere.

When we got home from visiting Lee Otis, I told Ella to come to my room so we could talk. We sat down on my bed and I got straight to the point. "Listen, Ella, you gon' have to get your attitude together. 'Cause see, everyone thinks we need to move back to East St. Louis. And I'ma tell you right now, we ain't going back there. Now I know that what happened to you was pretty horrible but it ain't nothing compared to what some other girls your age and even younger have to go through everyday. So I want you to get it together and stop acting like the world ended 'cause something bad happened to you. Do you hear me?" She looked up at me with those sad-looking eyes and just shook her head up and down in agreement with me. I sent her back to her room because I couldn't stand looking into those eyes. They were the eyes of a 90 year old woman who had seen too many disturbing things in her long life. Those eyes were now in my nine year old child's head. I made her leave right away. It was almost frightening to look at her now. Cora and Mattie didn't know what to say or how to behave around her. I don't know why, but I thought that they would have been more compassionate towards their little sister and everything that she had been through. But then I had to remember, they were never all that nice to her in the first place. And now, since the incident, they had even less to say to her, or she had less to say to them.

Not long after we got home from seeing Lee Otis, the phone rang. Sure enough it was his Mama, Miss Babe. I wish I'da had some way of knowing who was on the other end before I answered, 'cause I sho' would have let that phone just ring and ring and ring. Anyway, I knew she was up to something 'cause of the way she was talking, all soft and whatnot. Anybody who know Miss Babe, knows she don't talk soft to nobody for no reason. That's when I knew I had something she really wanted.

"Sadie?" she asked nicely.

"Yes." I replied.

"Girl, it's good to hear your voice." She said, still trying to sound nice.

"It's good to hear from you, too." I lied.

"Yeah, yeah, so how are the girls?" she said, trying to make small talk.

"Oh, they alright, can't wait for school to git out. Other than that they doing fine." I figured she couldn't keep this small talk up much longer so I braced myself for what was coming next.

"You know I would loves to have the girls come stay down here wit me for the summer. It wouldn't be no problem at all. They could stay like they did while you and Lee Otis was getting settled in Chicago last year. I thank it would be real good for the girls to spend the summer down here. To tell you the truth, it might not be such a bad idea for you to come spend a little time at home, see some of yo' kin folk. You know we all need to go home every now and then."

I put a phony smile on my face so I wouldn't sound as angry as I really was. Then I told her, "You know what Miss Babe? I think I'm gon' keep the girls up here with me this summer."

"Oh, well, I just thought that with everything that has happened, you might want to send them someplace where they could take they minds off of all the bad things that went on up there," she said, still trying to sound calm but I could hear her trying to swallow the frustration that was determined to make its way into the conversation.

"Naw, I think they'll be okay right here in Chicago for the summer."

"Well, what about just sending Ella down here. I know it would do her a world of good to come spend some time with 'ole Grandma Babe."

I was tired of talking about this so I told her, "Miss Babe, I'm gon' think about it and git back to you." I said goodbye and hung up the phone before she could say another word. Hopefully, for her sake she wouldn't call back right away, 'cause I was no longer smiling that phony smile.

I decided to look in on Ella just to see how she was doing. I knocked on her bedroom door and opened it before she could answer. She was sitting in front of her window just staring out onto the street. I have to admit, I did feel a twinge in my heart when I saw her sitting there. But I kept telling myself that these were the times I had to be strong. A part of me wanted to reach out and hug her and tell her that everything would be okay. But a greater part of me was angry at her for tearing the family apart. If she had been more outgoing like her sisters, she never would have been here alone with Do-Man, giving him a chance to do whatever he did to her. But I had to remind myself, what's done is done. Ain't nothing we can do to change any of that now. All we can do is make the best out of this bad situation.

I walked over to where Ella was sitting and said, "Your Grandma Babe just called. She wanted to know how you were doing." She didn't bother to turn and look at me. "I told her you were doing just fine. You are doing fine aren't you?" No response. I repeated the question. She barely shook her head up and down in an attempt to say yes. Then I finally asked what everyone wanted know. "Do you want to go to East St. Louis for the summer?" To my surprise she didn't say a word. She didn't even bother to look at me. Maybe we were doing okay. Me, Cora and Mattie certainly didn't need to go to East St. Louis, and based on Ella's lack of response, I guess she didn't need to nor want to go either. So that was that. The next person to call me with that going back home mess was going to hear it from me - and good. Now all I had to do was make sure that Cora and Mattie kept an eye on Ella while I was at work. That was just to make sure that she didn't go wondering off no where. All they had to do was make sure that she came straight home from school and got in the house safely. They hated having to look after their sister but that was just too bad. I couldn't have her going off someplace getting lost and looking crazy and then have my nosy neighbors, or worse yet, the Child Welfare people come snooping around here trying to git all up in my business. Naw, I didn't need none of that type of attention. So that's why whenever I could get off work early, I would go and pick Ella up from school myself.

By the time school let out for summer break, Ella still wasn't talking that much to any of us. She would come straight home from school, go to her room, come out for dinner and then go right back to her room. She didn't do any homework and when I went to the school to pick up her grades her teachers told me that she would just daydream all day. They had all heard about what happened to her and that's why they didn't put any pressure on her but they really thought she should get some help.

Yeah, getting professional help sounds real good but when you barely have money to pay your rent how in the hell are you going to pay for one of your children to get some "professional" help. I thought that's what the school counselors were for. If they were that concerned about Ella then they should have taken the time to talk to her instead of talking about what a shame it was that she was molested by her own uncle. It didn't matter no how 'cause I was seriously thinking about shipping Ella back down to East St. Louis, anyway. I just wasn't sure how that was going to look.

The thing that really got me to thinking about it was when Cora and Mattie came in my room one day after school and told me how embarrassed they were of Ella. The kids at school had started teasing her because they thought she was so weird. They practically begged me to send her to East St. Louis. I had no idea that this whole thing was affecting them like that. Maybe I could send Ella back home for the summer and just see how it worked out for her. As it stood now, she didn't talk to any of us in the apartment. She wouldn't even share what her Daddy would say to her in those letters he wrote to her once a week. I figured the least I could do was let her have her letters. Those letters were the only time she would show any sign of real life in that broken face of hers.

My decision to send Ella back home came when the lady across the alley came and rang my door bell one Saturday morning around 7 o'clock, and told me that Ella was in the alley kicking a dead cat up and down the alley. I knew then that Ella had really snapped and that it was time to do something. I sent her sisters out there to get her from the alley and while they were gone, I got on the phone and called Miss Babe and told her that I was willing to send Ella down there for the summer.

To my surprise, Miss Babe wasn't as excited as I thought she would be. She was upset that I waited so long before coming around to everyone else's way of thinking. Then she said, "Me and Butch will drive up there day after tomorrow to git her. We should be there round noon. I 'magine we'll stay for a couple of hours then turn on around and head back home. We'll talk to you then." She hung up the phone without saying goodbye or anything. I almost called her back to tell her not to come. But my good mind told me that this really would be good for everyone. So I waited for the girls to come back in from the alley. I took Ella to her room and sat her down on her bed. "You want to tell me why you were kicking a dead cat down the alley?" She shrugged her shoulders and mumbled, "I don't know."

"Did you kill that cat, Ella?" I said, not really wanting to know if she did. She didn't answer, she just held her head down staring at her hands. I figured it was a lost cause to keep asking her about that damn cat. She wasn't gon' tell me nothing I didn't already know.

"Listen here, Ella. I guess you acting out 'cause you still upset about what happened to you." She didn't say anything. " Well, I just got off the phone with your Grandma Babe and we both agree that it would be best if you go back home for the summer, and hopefully that will help you to come up out of this funk you been in for the past few months. And if by the end of the summer you are feeling better, then you can come on back to Chicago with me and your sisters and start school again. Would you like that?" She looked up at me and said, "When is Grandma Babe coming to get me?"

I should have known. That's the only thing that would get that girl to talk. Well, everybody would be getting what they wanted. The family back home would have their precious Ella back with them, Lee Otis wouldn't have to worry about his baby girl, my other two girls would be able to have a normal childhood and not be concerned about people looking at them funny because of their weird sister, and I would finally have a little peace of mind.

CHAPTER 24

GRANDMA BABE

Yeah, Sadie's tail finally called me talking 'bout she thanks it's time for Ella to come on down here with us. Well hell, we been trying to tell that crazy woman that for the longest. But some folks got to find out that fat meat is greasy fo' they selves. But because we was talking about my grandbaby I wasn't gon' argue with her. I just told her that me and Butch would be there on Saturday afternoon to git Ella. If Sadie had any kind of good sense, she would pack up her and them other two gals of hers and all of 'em would be on they way home. But like I said, I'm just glad she gon' let Ella come back.

What Sadie don't know is that the lady who came and knocked on her door got people down here; and when she saw Ella out there in that alley she called her cousin Mable, who goes to church wit me, and Mable called me. All I could do was fall down on my knees and pray that the Lawd would step in and do something quick. And sho' nuff, within 30 minutes of Mable calling me, Sadie was on the phone saying she was sending Ella here for the summer. What Sadie didn't know was that I had no plans of sending that gal back up there to that God forsaken city. No way, Jose! My grandbaby was going to stay right here wit me where I could keep an eye on her and nurture her back to health.

Butch couldn't believe his ears when I told him he needed to take me to Chicago. I told him we would be coming home with Ella 'cause it was Sadie's idea to send her. We pulled up to the apartment right before noon and when Butch let me out of the car I could see Ella looking out of her bedroom window. I stood there for a minute just looking up there at my baby. Butch had to come around to my side of the car and grab my arm before I was able to move. It was if I could hear that child's pain floatin' down from that window. It took everything inside of me not to break down and cry right there on that city sidewalk. "Come on Mama, it's gon' be okay," I heard Butch say to me as he helped me up the stairs to the apartment.

Sadie greeted us at the door with that 'ole phony smile she kept plastered on her face. It made me sick just to look at her. But I knew I had to be nice. We went on in and sat down in the living room. She offered us some coffee. Butch readily said yes; I declined. All I wanted to do was pack Ella up and get gon' from that demon possessed place. The evil spirits were so thick up in there it's a wonder you could breathe. Ain't no telling what all went on in that apartment, let alone the whole building.

Cora and Mattie came out and gave us hugs. They sat down in the living room and talked to us while Butch waited for his coffee and I waited to see Ella walk in the room. After we had been there for about twenty minutes, Ella finally came out of her room. I almost didn't recognize her when she walked over to hug me. Her eyes had absolutely no life whatsoever. I wanted to take a stick to that crazy ass Sadie and beat her within an inch of her life. How in the world could she just walk around day in and day out watching this girl die a slow and painful death? What kind of mother was she? She should have been the one in that bar with the gun that night. But who am I to judge? All I know is, I was glad to be gittin' Ella out of there.

Ella slowly walked over to me and put her arms around my neck and held on for dear life. I sat her down on my lap and began to rock her back and forth like I did when she was a baby. The flood gates had finally opened up and the dam was about to break. That baby hadn't been able to express herself since all of this stuff went on. I found myself singing her favorite little song, "Jesus Loves Me." That song always calmed her down whenever she was scared or upset about something.

After I rocked her for a while, Butch got up and said, "Well, Sadie, do you have Ella's bags packed? I thank we need to be gitting back on the road so we can git home fo' it's too, too late." Sadie went on back to Ella's room to git her bags. It took her a long time to come back. I just figured that she had a few more things to pack and that's what took so long. She finally came out with all of Ella's bags and placed them on the floor by the front door. Judging by the number of bags Sadie brought out, I wondered if she planned on the child ever coming back. I didn't say anything. I figured it was best to just let it all play out the way it was suppose to play out.

Ella finally calmed down enough for us to git up

and make our way to the door. I don't know why, but I told Sadie not to worry, we would take real good care of Ella and that we would call once we made it home. Butch and I hugged everybody and said our goodbyes and made our way back to the car. Sadie tried to hold Ella back and give her some damn last minute instructions on how to behave. I told Sadie don't even worry about none of that. "I'm sure Ella will be just fine." Then I gently pulled Ella away from her mother and moved her on down the stairs so we could git out of that building and back to our car.

Once we had everything loaded up and pulled off, I felt myself breathe. I didn't realize it, but the whole time we were up there I was practically holding my breath. It almost felt like we had taken someone's precious stone without them knowing how valuable it really was, and we had to get as far away from them as fast as we could before someone realized the mistake that had been made. Yep, Sadie had just let her most precious jewel walk right out the front door. And before she missed it, I wanted to be as close to home as possible.

After about an hour on the road, Ella said, "Grandma, I'm hungry." She almost sounded like the old happy-go-lucky Ella that I sent up there to Chicago last year. I turned around to look at her and I saw those same lifeless eyes which let me know we had a long ways to go before my sweet little Ella would be back. I said a quick prayer to myself right then and there. "Lawd, please restore my grandbaby to the healthy, beautiful little girl that You created her to be. I knows You can do it, 'cause You can do anythang but fail. In the name of Jesus, thank you."

I said to Ella, "Now you know Grandma Babe done packed up some good sandwiches just for you. And if Butch can drive like he got some good sense then we might let him have a sandwich or two. What you thank?" She tried to smile but it looked like it hurt. I reached in the bag and handed her a ham sandwich with mustard on it just like she liked. Then I gave her a bag of potato chips and told her to look in that cooler on the back seat for some sodi water. All I could say was, well at least the girl had an appetite.

We finally made it on in to East St. Louis around 8 p.m. Sally was at the house waiting for us to get back. As soon as she heard the car pull up she came outside to meet us. I told her all I needed her to do was to help Ella git ready fo' bed. Butch unloaded me and Ella's stuff and made his way to his house down the road. I had never been so happy to be home in all my days. I didn't even make Ella take a bath before she got in bed. I let Sally put her right to bed, and then I tried to stay up and talk to Sally for a spell, but I was so tired that I started nodding between words. So, Sally let herself out and I went on to bed.

The next morning I let Ella sleep a little late. I woke her up at 7:30 and told her to git ready for breakfast. I made sure that I fixed all of her favorites: biscuits, hash browns, sausage links and pancakes. I topped it off with a big 'ole glass of milk. When Ella came to the table, I thought I saw a tiny sparkle dance across the dead eyes. She sat down at the table and waited for me to bless the food and then proceeded to eat like she hadn't eaten in days. Her wanting to eat was a sign that she was ready to git back to living.

So I sat down at the table and we ate breakfast

together. She didn't have a lot to say. I did most of the talking. "How you feel about being here for the summer?" She shrugged her shoulders. Now, I guess since she been living in Chicago, she forgot that I don't go for no shoulder shrugging. I asked her again, but next time I threw in; "And gal, don't you shrug yo' shoulders when I ask you a question." She looked at me and said, "I think it's going to be okay." I looked at her and said, "I know it's going to be alright. You back down here with yo' Grandma Babe. What more could you ask fo'?" She actually smiled.

"Listen, Ella, I'm going to do everything in my power to make sure that you are protected from any and all fools at all times. I don't want you to ever worry about horrible things happenin' to you again. And if someone around here says anything to you that makes you feel uncomfortable or tries to do anything to you that you know is not right, all you have to do is let me know. And just like yo' Daddy did, I will kill the son-of-a-bitch that thinks he can git away with treating my grandbaby like that." Fear made a showing in her eyes this time. I quickly reassured her, "Don't worry baby, Grandma ain't going to jail or nowhere else I don't want to go. See, your Grandma knows the law around here. Ain't nobody stupid enough to mess with me or mine in this town." She gave me a little smile.

Then I told her about the chores that she would have to do starting tomorrow morning. I didn't want her to think that just 'cause we went and got her that I was going to coddle her and she wouldn't have to pull her weight. She needed some good hard work and some strong love to help her git through. And that's just what Ella was going to receive during her stay with me.

Ella stayed real close to me that first week she was home. Even when I had her out there in the yard she was either looking around to see where I was, or she was running back in the house every chance she got. Although she was starting to come around a lil' bit, she still didn't talk for the most part. I had pretty much prepared myself for a long hard road with my grandbaby. That was just fine with me 'cause I ain't had nowhere to go but church, the grocery store and out to what was left of my fields. And she ain't had nowhere to go either, 'cept wherever I went.

So, basically, we spent the whole summer underneath each other. Truth be told, I needed Ella just as much as she needed me. See, in the midst of everything that was going on people did tend to forget that I was in mourning for two of my boys. One I knew I'd never see again in this life or the next one, and I was just praying that I lived long enough to see the other walking around a free man again. But I knew the Lawd was gon' give me strength to make it through. He always did and He always would. One day out of the blue, Ella just walked in the kitchen, sat down at the table and said, "Am I ever gon' see my mother and father again?" It caught me so off guard that I almost dropped to my seat that I had just stood up from. I eased myself back down in my chair and said, "Well, yeah Ella, I reckon you gon' see yo' Mama and your sisters real soon if you wants to. But now yo' Daddy, well, now you know that's a different story. I really don't know how long he gon' be in jail. The Judge give him 20 years." I tried to talk to her as calmly as I could 'cause I didn't want to upset her in anyway. She sat there quietly listening to me talk when I finally said, "Ella, you thank you 'bout ready to go back to Chicago?" That child looked at me like she had seen a ghost. She quickly said, "No, no, Grandma Babe. I was just wondering if any of them was gon' come down here to see me anytime soon, that's all." She got up from the table and began to wash the few little dishes in the sink. I told her, "You know you can call yo' Mama and sisters anytime you feels like it, right?" She shook her head up and down. I knew then that she had said all she wanted to say for the time being. When the urge hit her again she would let me know it was time to talk again.

That summer seemed to fly by. And with each passing day little Ella seemed to get stronger and stronger, although, she never did get back to the care free little girl that I watched go off to Chicago a year earlier. But at least she was talking. I knew school would be starting soon so I figured I should at least call her Mama and find out what she was planning for Ella. I had a feeling that she was gon' let her stay down there wit' me, seeing as how she rarely called to check on the child. I thank she may have come down to actually see her one time, and that was to bring her some things that she needed. Me and Butch went up there to get Ella at the beginning of June and Sadie didn't come down there until the beginning of August. Her and the girls stayed for the weekend and turned right around and went back home. Sadie didn't even stay with us. She went and found some long lost cousin of hers and stayed over there for the weekend. I could tell that Ella was disappointed but I told her that there really wasn't no room at my house for all those folks, no how. She knew that was a lie, but she never said anything to me about it.

Right before school was to start I got a call from Sadie saying that she thought it might be best if Ella went on ahead and stayed down here for the first part of the school year. I tried to play it cool and act like I was disappointed that she wouldn't be coming to get Ella, but it was hard. I told her that it wouldn't be no problem for Ella to stay on down here. Then I told her she should think about letting Ella stay for the whole school year. Right after those words left my mouth I began to regret saying them. I knew Sadie would look at that as me trying to manipulate her or take control of the situation. See, with her, everything had to be on her terms in order for you to get what you wanted. So I changed it up a little and said, "Well, what I mean Sadie, is I know you still trying to get adjusted to Lee Otis being gon' and everything, I just want you to know that if you wants Ella to stay here for a couple more months or for the whole school year it don't make me no difference. You just let me know what you want me to do and consider it done."

CHAPTER 25

ELLA

Eight years later my mother still hadn't come to get me from East St. Louis. As a matter of fact, I can only remember her coming down there to see me a hand full of times. Grandma Babe became my mother, father, doctor, spiritual advisor…my everything. She was my world. If it weren't for Grandma Babe, I would be completely messed up instead of just partially screwed up in the head.

Even though my grandmother was there for me, I still had a lot of unresolved issues that needed to be dealt with. By the time I graduated from high school, I had about three friends. I didn't even go to the senior prom; hell, I had never been on a date. Most of the kids thought I was odd so they stayed away from me. Being a straight A student afforded me the chance to go to just about any college I wanted. Most of the kids who came out with me ended up getting married and entering the work force. I wasn't ready to face the real world, so I opted to go on to college. Grandma Babe tried to get me to go to Southern Illinois University in Carbondale, Illinois since it was close to home. But I knew that I needed to get a little further away from home than SIU.

Just like I had to get away from Chicago because of Do-Man, there were demons that I was running from in East St. Louis as well. It was as if Uncle Do-Man had opened the door of perversion on me. Every one of my male high school teachers tried to come on to me at one time or another.

I was so shy and scary that I walked through the hallways with my head down everyday. I wore the most matronly clothes I could find. Grandma would always get after me about dressing so homely, as she would put it. I dressed that way for many reasons. One, that's how I felt. Even though the thing with Uncle Do-Man had happened years earlier, I still felt ashamed and unsure of myself. I certainly didn't want some other grown man to find me attractive. Another reason I dressed the way I did, is because I didn't want any of the boys to notice me and ask me out. That would have been a disaster. I guess the other reason I dressed the way I did is because I didn't want the girls to notice me either. I didn't have one friend in the entire school. And that's just the way I liked it. They all thought I was strange. The teachers knew that something was wrong with me because I was such a perfectionist. My work had to be just right and I had to get nothing less than 100's on all of my assignments or I would be hanging around the teacher's desk after class asking why I didn't get a perfect score. And if they actually told me that I had done something wrong, I would be so devastated that most of them would take pity on me and give me the extra point just to keep me from being distraught.

I didn't know the teachers knew anything was wrong

with me until in my junior year when my guidance counselor, Mr. Crane, called me down to his office. First he complimented me on being a straight A student and being on the honor roll every marking period. Then he told me that he was a bit concerned about my obsessive behavior over my grades and that he wanted to run some test on me to get a better understanding of what made me "tick". He asked if he had my permission to do such a test and I told him yes. In my mind I was thinking that I should have Grandma give him permission but I was too afraid to say anything because I didn't want to upset him in any way.

He began asking me a series of questions that at some point took a turn down a road I wasn't so comfortable with. "What kind of dreams do you have?" he asked, staring me in the face. "Do any of them involve having sex with boys or grown men?" My heart began to pound and I could feel the sweat starting to form under my arms. "Have you ever had sex with anyone, male or female?" My heart was racing even faster and I just prayed he couldn't see the sweat that was now forming on my forehead and upper lip. It took everything within me to stop my leg from doing its own jumping dance underneath the desk. I couldn't do anything about those damn tears. Mr. Crane looked at me and said, "It's okay, Ella, you can tell me the truth. I won't tell anyone, and I won't hurt you. This will be just between us."

Then I started to hyperventilate and was on the verge of passing out. That's when he finally said, "Okay Ella, I think we've covered enough for today. You can get your things and leave. But remember, we need to keep this between us." I fumbled around trying to gather my things and finally stood up to leave when he said, "I have to be honest with you. The only reason you responded the way you did is because there must be some truth to the questions I asked of you." I just ran out of the room, down the hall and out the crash doors to the fresh air that was waiting to greet me as I stepped outside. I ran to the bushes on the side of the building and began to vomit up years of pain and shame. Then I began the three and a half mile walk home.

The trip home felt more like a walk through a mine field rather than a walk down country roads. I was hearing all kinds of voices and seeing images that made me sick. At one point, I dropped my books and fell to the ground holding my head in my hands just trying to make it all go away. The tighter I held my head, the louder the noise in my head got. The next thing I knew, I was face down in the dirt calling on the name of Jesus. My grandmother would say that the hants, that is, those demons, were having a field day with my mind. I told Jesus that day if He would just take this madness away from me, I would be a good girl and do whatever He wanted me to do. I was so caught up in my pleas to Jesus that I didn't even notice Uncle Butch pull up along side of me in the middle of the road. Next thing I knew, Uncle Butch was picking me up from the ground and putting me in his pick up truck. He didn't say one word. He drove me straight to grandma's house and carried me in the door.

Grandma stood in the middle of the floor when she saw Uncle Butch bring me in. He looked at her and said, "Mama, you better come take her and put her to bed." My grandmother rushed over to me and said to Uncle Butch, "What in the world happened to this child?"

"I don't know. I just happened to be driving down the road when I saw her face down on the ground calling out to Jesus."

"Calling out to Jesus?!" Grandma shouted.

"Yeah, she was calling on Jesus."

"Lawd have mercy. What in the world was this child calling out to Jesus fo' in the middle of the road?"

"Mama, I don't know what's going on. I didn't ask no questions. I just scooped her up from the ground and brought her straight here," said Uncle Butch as he decided to help Grandma walk me to my bed room. They laid me down on the bed, and Grandma began taking off my clothes. I remember shivering and her saying, "Chile, what's done happened to you? Did someone do something to you?" I don't know what I said to Grandma, but my next memory was of her escorting me to school the next day demanding to see the principal along with Mr. Crane. By the time the two men came out to see us a small crowd had gathered in the front of the office with people wanting to see what was going on with the eerie girl and her grandmother.

Principal Buckley came out and told everyone to go back to class. He then escorted Grandma and me into his office. Once seated, he said, "How are you doing Ms. Boxx?"

I could tell that Grandma was trying to contain herself, but it looked like she was going to lose the fight with herself. The force that had been building up inside of her since last night came rushing forth like a tornado. The words that flew out of her mouth seemed to push Mr. Buckley back in his seat. He made the mistake of trying to interrupt her and the words became more powerful. Grandma Babe looked at Mr.

Buckley with fire in her eyes. His light brown skin turned red. Grandma shouted, "What kind of camp is you running up here?!" She continued before he could answer. "I wants to know what the hell y'all got going on up here. My baby was found in the middle of the road crying out to Jesus! What in the hell did y'all do to her to make her damn near lose her mind?!"

"Mrs. Boxx, let's calm down so we can get to the bottom of this." He said trying to take control of the situation.

"No, I will not calm down! Somebody up her at dis school done something to set my baby off and I want to know who and what!" Grandma said sitting on the edge of her seat. Mr. Buckley turned and looked at me and said, "Ella, can you tell us what happened?"

I tried to speak but the words disappeared from my mouth before I could even put them in a sentence. I attempted to lift my head but gravity had other plans. So I sat speechless watching an ant make its way across the concrete floor. Once again my Grandmother came to my rescue. She said, "I'll tell you what happened. Some quack you call a guidance counselor had the nerve to ask her if she been having sex dreams and if so, who do she wanna have sex with?! Now what I want to know is, who is this person, and why in the hell is he asking my baby some nonsense like that?!" Mr. Buckley turned to look at me and asked, "Is that true, Ella?" Head still down, I barely shook it up and down to indicate it was true. He then said, "Who asked you those questions, Ella?" I could hear the concern in his voice. Oddly enough, I began to feel comforted by his voice. I slowly lifted my head and tried to look him in the eye the way Grandma always told me to do when talking to someone. I mumbled out Mr. Crane's name. I almost felt like I had betrayed Mr. Crane in some kind of way.

Mr. Buckley could hardly believe his ears, but before he could respond, Grandma Babe huffed out, "Okay, the gal done told you who the pervert was, now what you gon' do about it?" He turned his head back to me and said, "Are you sure Mr. Crane asked you those questions?" I shook my head up and down again. Then he said, "What were you talking about to make him ask you those types of questions?" Before I could answer, Grandma jumped in again. "Listen here. It don't matter what they was talking 'bout. The girl don' told you what happened. Now you needs to git Mr. Crane on down here so he can explain thangs for himself." Mr. Buckley realized that he was fighting a losing battle with Grandma, so he called his secretary and told her to have Mr. Crane sent to his office immediately. He then turned to Grandma and said, "Mrs. Boxx, may I get you something while we wait?" Grandma looked at him like he had two heads. He put both of his hands up as if to say, please forgive me for asking such a dumb question.

Mr. Crane walked through the door whistling and stopped right in the middle of blowing the air between his lips when he saw me and Grandma Babe sitting across from Mr. Buckley. I immediately became nervous. I was afraid that my ability to even shake my head up and down would somehow vanish. Mr. Buckley stood up and told Mr. Crane to come in and have a seat. After he was situated, Principal Buckley said, "Well, Mr. Crane, the reason I called you to my office is because Mrs. Boxx here has lodged some serious complaints against you. And I wanted you to have a chance to defend yourself." Before the principal could say another word Mr. Crane jumped up and said, "I don't know what this little girl is up here lying about, but I ain't did nothing to her. The only thing I ever did was talk to her because she seemed lonely and depressed. That's all I ever did. I swear fo' God, I ain't did nothing to that girl!"

That was all Grandma Babe needed to hear. She lit into Mr. Crane so bad that I was beginning to feel sorry for him myself. By the time she finished reading them both the riot act, the secretary buzzed in and asked the principal if he wanted her to call the police. Grandma Babe yelled out, "Go head on and call the police 'cause I'm sure they would like to know what kind of perverts is working in the schools these days!" Mr. Buckley immediately told his secretary not to call anyone and that everything was under control. Then he hopped to his feet and said, "Listen, everyone. Let's all calm down and handle this like rational people. Now, Mr. Crane, did you ask Ella those questions? All I want is a yes or no." The room was still and quiet as we waited for his answer. You could see the pleading in his eyes as he looked at Mr. Buckley. Mr. Buckley repeated himself and then said, "Just yes or no." Mr. Crane looked him dead in the eye and said, "No." I thought Grandma was going to have a stroke. She jumped up out of her seat and was just seconds away from treating his neck just like those chickens she would kill in her yard. Had Mr. Buckley not come from behind the desk to stop her, Mr. Crane would have been flying around in the air with Grandma's hands wrapped around his neck waiting for it to snap.

"You are a low-down, dirty liar!" Grandma shouted. Then she said, "I want this man removed from this school right now. He shouldn't even be allowed to look at chillun', let alone be in a school full of 'em!"

The principal said, "Well before any action is taken, an investigation must take place. As it stands, now, it's his word against hers."

"My grandbaby ain't got no reason to lie on this fool. If she said he asked her those filthy questions then he did, and ain't no telling what else he had in mind. Now I wants' to know what you gon' do 'bout it, Mr. Buckley?"

"I do understand what you're saying, Mrs. Boxx, but we must conduct an investigation before we can do anything. Now I'm going to have to ask you to leave."

"I'm not going anywhere until I know that this man is no longer around any children. And if you don't remove him, I will call the authorities on you and this school!"

Mr. Buckley looked at Mr. Crane and said, "I will have to place you on suspension until we can sort this out." Grandma was half-way pleased with the temporary solution but looked Mr. Buckley square in the eye and said, "Please don't think for a minute that I won't be watching this situation very closely, 'cause I will. If I have to, I'll come to this school everyday to make sure that he ain't nowhere around here, and to also make sure that you doing what you just told me you was gon' do. I hope I'm making myself very clear, Mr. Buckley." And with that she gathered her things and headed for the door. I knew that was my cue to get up and make my exodus as well. Nerves had me tripping over my chair as I tried to get out of that office without making eye contact with Mr. Crane. I can't recall at what point I forgot to breathe while sitting in that office, but the humongous gulp of air I took in almost stung my lungs as I stood in the hallway.

Grandma Babe was already half-way down the corridor before I could even get out of the office. I heard her calling my name and I ran to catch up with her. She told me that I was going home with her and that I would return to school the next day once that fool was on suspension. As we walked back to Grandma's house, I couldn't help but think, why didn't my mother stand up for me the way that Grandma had this morning? My mother never said a word about what happened to me. It was as if it didn't happen. Although now I realize that the circumstances were different, Daddy killed Uncle Do-Man before anyone could say anything to him, but it seems to me that she should have been outraged that something like that happened to her own child. When she first found out, she appeared a bit shocked but not outraged. She seemed to have the attitude that it was already done, and now we had to find a way to get over it and move on with our lives. She never even asked me how I felt about the whole ordeal.

Not Grandma. She wasn't going to let anyone harm me in any way. She would kill a thousand men to protect me. For the first time in a long time, I actually felt worthy to be a part of the human race. Somebody actually stood up and fought for me. I felt the tears welling up in my eyes. Before the salty fluid could make its way down my cheeks I found a piece of tissue and dabbed my eyes. Had Grandma seen me crying, she would have had a fit, turned around, gone back to that school and killed Mr. Crane.

We made it home and Grandma didn't say anything else about that morning's events to me; but as soon as Aunt Sally came by for her daily visit, Grandma went right into what happened, what all she said and wasn't going to put up with from that school or the principal. She told Sally she was going to give them exactly one week to gather whatever information they needed to get rid of Mr. Crane before she went back up there and showed out again. Sally agreed with Grandma and asked how I was doing. Then Grandma did something she had never done in all my years of knowing her. She actually called me into the kitchen and told me to have a seat because she and Sally wanted to talk to me. I couldn't believe it. She didn't allow anyone to sit at the table when she and Sally were talking. That was their time and their time alone. And everyone in the family knew it. I walked into the kitchen and Grandma said, "Here, gal, sit down right here next to me." I did as I was told and didn't know what to do after that. Should I pull my chair up to the table? Would I be staying long enough to move my chair up? Was I going to be allowed to talk? Did they even want to hear what I had to say? Why was I even there?

Grandma said, "Ella, tell Sally what you told me 'bout that freak they calls a counselor up there at that school." After I told Sally what happened she said, "Is his name James Crane?"

"I think so."

"Mama, you know his grandmother. If that's the same James I'm thinking of, his grandmother used to play the piano at the church up there on the hill. You know, Mt. Moriah Baptist Church. You know the one I'm talking 'bout, Mama. The church where they said the pastor had been molesting those little boys. Eventually, the congregation kicked the man out 'cause it was just too many complaints. Well, the lady who played the piano, Ms. Ettie James, had a grandson that spent a lot of time with the pastor. Word is, the pastor had his way with that little boy and the poor child was never the same." Grandma sat there trying to figure out who Sally was talking about. "Mama, you got to remember that." Sally said. "I think he went to school with Butch. Might have been a couple of years older than Butch. But I think they went to school together."

"You know what, Sally? I do vaguely remember something 'bout Ettie's grand boy not being wrapped too tight cuz of some pastor at that church. That's how come I ain't never let none of y'all join down there. I always knew something was wrong with that so-called preacher. He just looked like something wasn't right 'bout him. So you say that this here Mr. Crane is the same little boy?"

"I sho' do think so. If it ain't him, then it must be his brother. But I don't remember him even having a brother. Yeah, Mama, it's got to be the same one."

They both looked at me as if they had forgotten that I was an invited guest at their table. Then Grandma said, "Ella, has that man ever tried to touch you in any way?" I felt my throat tightening up and my ears starting to ring. Here we go again. Why didn't these people just leave me alone? What had I ever done to anyone to deserve this? My voice finally decided it was ready to be heard, "No," I said just above a whisper. Grandma looked at Sally as if she didn't believe me.

Sally looked at me and said, "Ella, you know you can tell us anything. We are right here to protect you. So if he did anything you just let us know. Okay?"

I nodded my head up and down but thought to myself, if everyone is here to protect me then why do these things keep happening to me? Why don't you protect me before these men touch me and say all kinds of strange things to me? I remember thinking, what is it about me that says it's okay to be treated that way? I made sure that I dressed as plainly as possible, I was polite and minded my manners, I did whatever I was told, I made straight A's in school and yet I was still the one being harassed by everyone. Why me?

Grandma said, "Well, tomorrow I'm goin' back up to that school with you and I'm gon' tell that principal what you said, Sally, and I'm gon' do everything in my power to make sure that damn freak don't end up back in that school." Then she looked at me and said, "Ain't no need in you being scared, Ella. Sally was right. We is here to protect you. And not just me and Sally, the whole family is here for you, but you gots to let us know if something ain't right. Okay?"

I shook my head in the affirmative. I didn't like being the honored guest at their table. I was ready to leave. Finally, I whispered, "May I please be excused?" Grandma didn't make a fuss she simply said, "Yeah, gal. Gon' in there and start on your homework." I quietly left the table and went to my room. I sat down on my bed and began to cry. Thoughts of running away came to mind, then, I thought about just ending it all. That way I wouldn't have to deal with all the demons from the past and the demons that were waiting for me in my future would have to find someone else to haunt. That really did seem like the most logical thing to do. Just end it all and my family wouldn't have to worry about protecting me from anything or anyone, anymore. They could all live their lives and take care of their own children. Besides, why should they be so concerned about me when my own mother didn't care enough to protect me? Hell, I hadn't even seen my mother in over a year. And I couldn't remember the last time she called. It was as if she and my sisters had created a brand new life without me and my father. I just felt like I didn't belong anywhere.

Grandma Babe took me to school the next day and told the principal what Sally said about Mr. Crane. Mr. Buckley said that he was going to start his investigation that very morning and that Grandma didn't have to worry about anything. Mr. Crane was officially suspended, pending an investigation, and Mr. Buckley said that he would personally keep an eye on me to make sure that I was doing okay. And he would report anything unusual to her right away. I could tell that Grandma really didn't want him to personally keep an eye on me, in light of the current situation, but I guess she figured he knew she would just as soon kill him, as look at him, if she thought for one minute that he was inappropriate with her granddaughter. She left and Mr. Buckley told me to have a seat in his office. I just kept thinking, God please don't let this man try anything with me 'cause I don't know how much more I can take.

He came in and sat behind his desk and said, "Ella, before I send you to class I want you to know that you can come directly to me if you have any problems with anything. Is that clear?" His voice was so soothing, and the look in his eyes said that he really did care about what happened to me. I almost forgot to answer. He said, "Did you hear me?" I snapped out of my daydream and said, "Yes sir." He smiled and told me to go to class and to make sure I stopped by his office before I left for the day. Then he stood up and walked to the door, opened it up and waited for me to exit. I couldn't believe it. A man other than my father showing genuine interest in me. I wanted to turn around and hug him and then just spend the rest of the day in his office. But I just kept on walking.

As I made my way down the hall, I noticed that the other kids were trying not to stare at me. I slowly ran my hand down the back of my dress just to make sure that it was okay. I looked down at my shoes and I hadn't stepped in anything. I smoothed over my hair, which was pulled back in its usual pony tail. Why were they trying not to stare and whisper? I finally made it to my first period history class, only to find the entire class gathered around the teacher's desk. When I walked into the classroom the teacher looked up in surprise and said, "Ella, I didn't think you would be in class today." I didn't respond. I simply took my seat in the front of the class and put my books underneath my seat. She told the rest of the class to take their seats. That was the longest forty-five minutes of my life. I couldn't figure out for the life of me why everyone was leering at me. What had I done now? I didn't know how much more of this I would be able to take. I felt like the pressure was mounting on my head and chest. I don't even know if I waited for the bell to ring before I made a b-line to the hall way. As I tried to make my way to my next class, I heard my name being paged over the PA system. "Ella Boxx, report to the principal's office immediately. Ella Boxx, report to the principal's office immediately." I turned around and headed to Mr. Buckley's office.

When I got there, he told me that he wanted me to spend the rest of the day in his office because, somehow the situation with Mr. Crane had leaked out and he didn't want me to have to deal with all the stares and questions so soon. So he excused me from all of my classes for the rest of the day and made me his assistant. That was just fine with me. He had me filing, answering and making phone calls and he actually began to talk to me. He asked me about what happened to me when I was younger and I couldn't believe my ears when I heard myself actually tell him all of the details. I had never even told my father everything that happened. But for some reason I knew that he wouldn't judge me. I even found it comforting to talk to him.

The thing that made him different from everyone else is that he actually looked at me. He looked me in my eyes and wanted to hear my words, know my thoughts and, feel my pain; he looked at me and wanted to see me. He wanted to hear about the terrible things that happened to me and help me put them in some kind of perspective. That was something no one else had been able to do. I don't know if it was because I wanted him to do it, or because I knew he could and would if I just let him. He would because that's who he was.

I could have knocked that clock off the wall when it quietly shouted 3:15. Never in the history of my school career had time flown by that fast. I looked at the clock and cursed it with my thoughts. Then I wondered if the clock at home would have such fleeting time throughout the evening and into the morning. Probably not. I would go home and suffer through the night like I usually suffered through the school day.

I was right. Time drug it's feet that evening and I was kicking mad. The next day I arrived fifteen minutes early to school and headed straight to the principal's office. I was ready to report for duty. I knocked on Mr. Buckley's door and was told to come in. Once inside I was hit with terrible news. "Good morning, Ella." Mr. Buckley said barely noticing that I was there. "Good morning." I said back.

"Listen, I'm afraid I won't be able to use you today. I have a meeting outside of the school, so I'm sending you back to class, but you should be just fine. We'll see how it goes today and maybe you can help out in the office on tomorrow." My luck was just going from bad to worse. Didn't he know that I didn't want to be bothered with those stupid teachers and those even dumber kids. I wanted to spend my time with someone who was smart and funny and who would actually talk to me like I was a human being and not some freak of nature. Unfortunately, I had no choice but to do as I was told. Without saying a word, I turned around and walked out of the main office and to my first class. To my surprise, Mr. Buckley was right. Things were back to normal. No one even noticed me walking down the hall that morning. I guess some other poor soul had the pleasure of being ridiculed by the school that day. There were a few stares, but for the most part, things were back to normal. By the end of the week, I was back to being the girl no one knew or even saw. I was invisible Ella once again.

Mr. Buckley finally finished his investigation of Mr.

Crane and found out that not only had he asked those same types of questions to other students, but that he was also having an affair with a 16 year old junior. He was fired from the school and the girl's parents were going to have him arrested for statutory rape until they found out the girl was eight weeks pregnant. They tried to make her have an abortion but she put up such a fuss and threatened to tell all of the family secrets that her father paid a visit to Mr. Crane and see what they could work out. When it was all said and done, Mr. Crane left his wife and married that teenage girl. They ended up having five kids together.

CHAPTER 26

LEE OTIS

Man, you just don't know how happy I was when I got the news that Ella was back in East St. Louis. Sadie finally came to her senses. I don't know if it was me telling her I would leave her when I got out of jail, or promising her that money would be mailed to her every month to help out with rent, groceries, utilities and whatever else she needed if she just sent Ella back home. Whatever it was, she sent my baby back where she belonged. So I made sure that each and every month she and the girls were taken care of. I was going to do that, anyway, but she didn't know that. As far as Sadie was concerned, we were broke and that's just the way I wanted to keep it. But in reality, I had money stashed away that she had absolutely no knowledge of. I had been holding on to the money for a rainy day. Well, we were about to have 20 years worth of rainy days. I just hoped I had enough money to last until I got out of the joint.

Let's just say the money was retribution for Sadie being raped when she was a girl. See, when me and my brothers went to pay those crackers a visit for the last time, we went inside the old barn where they conducted their business, which was moonshine. When my brothers and I were done conducting our business with the two crackers that were left, we saw something sticking up out of the hay. So Butch went over to see what it was, and low and behold it was a huge black trunk. There were six trunks stacked up two-by-two. We found a crowbar and cracked those bad boys open and you guessed it, six trunks full of money! At that moment, I was glad that I had only asked two of my brothers to come with me, Butch and Robert. For what we were doing, I needed men who could be trusted not to go out get drunk and end up telling all of our business to anyone who'd listen. We each got two trunks and vowed never to say anything to anyone about our findings. We took the money and hid it. I didn't touch any of mine until we moved to Chicago. Then I only took a couple of hundred dollars just to make sure we got our place and I gave Sadie a few dollars to go out and buy some things for the apartment. I kept $500 cash in the house at all times, just in case of an emergency. Well, my real emergency was here. I thought about using the money for my legal defense but, I figured that once the jury heard the evidence and all of the circumstances surrounding my crime, they would surely find me innocent. Things don't always turn out like they should. Plus, I couldn't chance people asking me where all that money came from.

Sadie kept trying to figure out where this money was coming from. But I never would tell her. She just thought my family was sending her money out of the goodness of their hearts. I set it up with Butch to send her $100 a month. That way she could pay the rent with no problem. But I told him not to send it until I had been in jail for at least two months. I was hoping that after not being able to pay all of her bills for a couple of months, she would be willing to move back to East St. Louis. That woman is so stubborn she went out and got another job to make ends meet. That's when I called Butch and told him to start the payments right away. I think the other reason she sent Ella back home is because it was going to be one less mouth to feed. I really didn't care what her real reasons were. I was just glad she did the right thing.

Once Ella was back in East St. Louis, I started receiving letters from her at least twice a month. My heart would skip a beat every time I got mail and saw my baby's handwriting on the envelope. Most of her letters were telling me about what her grandmother had her doing around the house and how glad she was to be back in East St. Louis. It would break my heart to read that she still didn't have any friends. No friends around the house and not one in school. I wrote and asked Mama about it, and she would write me back and say that these things take time. It just seemed like it was taking too much time. Ella was a beautiful girl. There was no reason why she shouldn't have any friends. She was so much like her mother it was scary. I just prayed that she didn't have the same emotional wounds that her mother carried for all of these years.

Come to think of it, Sadie wanted to stop having children after the first two. I convinced her to get pregnant with Ella. I must admit, it was a difficult pregnancy. She was sick all the time, had terrible mood swings, and couldn't seem to keep on any weight. We thought we were going to lose her a couple of times.

That's when Mama stepped in and started giving her some of her 'mother's finest medicine,' as Mama used to call it. I don't know what was in those concoctions, but whatever it was, it did the trick. Sadie stopped throwing up whenever she looked at food and was actually able to eat a decent amount of food.

Sadie was so depressed after she gave birth to Ella, that she barely touched her. She didn't want to look at her. I couldn't even get her to give the baby her breast. Sadie laid in bed for four weeks. I thought she was going to die fo' sho'. Once again, Mama stepped in and snapped Sadie back into reality.

Mama came over every day and bathed Sadie, fed her, made her put on fresh clothes and made her comb her hair and brush her teeth. All while she was nursing her back to health, she would talk about the baby. At first Sadie didn't want to hear anything about her new baby, but Mama would simply ease in a mention or two every chance she got. Then one day, Mama had me to bring Ella in the room with Sadie so she could see her beautiful green-eyed girl for herself. The first time Sadie really looked at Ella, she began to weep. At first we thought she was overcome with joy, but when she screamed out, "Get that baby away from me!" we knew it was just the opposite.

Then one day, Sadie's cousin Nadine, came to visit. She took one look at Ella and said, "No wonder she don't want nothing to do with that baby. The child looks just like her mother." "Her mother? Chile, what you mean 'her mother'?" Mama said.

"I mean just what I said. That baby in there look just like Sadie's real Mama." Then she pulled out some snuff and began to pack her cheeks.

None of us had ever seen Sadie's real mother. We just assumed that Sadie had never seen her either because she never mentioned the woman. Sadie didn't touch little Ella for at least a month. Everyday, Mama would try and ease the baby in to Sadie, and everyday Sadie would simply turn her back to the baby and tell Mama to take her away. That's how I became so attached to Ella. Every time Mama would take the baby back to her little crib, I would go and pick her up and just rock her in my arms. Then I found myself carrying her around with me everywhere I went. As soon as I got home from work I went straight to her crib. I didn't even go and say hi to Sadie.

One day I was sitting on the front porch just holding Ella like I always did, when Sadie walked out and said, "I want to hold her." Shocked, I got up and tried to hand her the baby. There was no attempt to take the baby from me. I asked her, "Would you like to hold her?" She didn't answer. I waited with outstretched arms for her to take the baby, but she never did. She continued to look at little Ella. Finally, she turned around and went back in the house.

I couldn't figure out what had just happened. First, she said she wanted to hold the baby, then, she just stood there staring like some crazy woman. I sat back down and rocked Ella until she went to sleep. I must have rocked us both to sleep because the next thing I knew Mama was on my porch saying, "Boy, what you and that baby doing out here on the porch like two hobos?" I woke up to the sound of her laughter. She reached down to take the baby out of my hands and said, "You better give me that baby fo' she fall right out of yo' lap onto dis here porch."

When I told Mama about what happened earlier, she said, "Yeah, well I'm not surprised. I don't know if she'll ever want to have anything to do with this baby gal. But don't worry, son, you gots yo' whole family right here to help you wit whatever needs to be done. We all right here fo' you," she said as she took Ella out of my arms and began kissing her in between words. Then she looked me square in the eyes and said, "Son, you don' lost control of yo' house and you needs to git it back, and quick." She was right, and that's just what I had planned to do.

CHAPTER 27

SADIE

Lee Otis is right. I didn't want anything to do with Ella when she was first born. I didn't want to have another child after Cora was born. I was happy and content with the two beautiful girls we already had. Plus, I felt I could keep a better handle on things with just two girls, as opposed to three.

See, there's only a couple years difference between Mattie and Cora, and they did absolutely everything together. They were inseparable. So I had it fixed in my mind that they would somehow take care of and protect one another if for some reason I wasn't around to help them. I just felt in my gut that if I had another child, things would be completely different. The new child would be too far behind in age for the other girls to really appreciate. I tried to convince Lee Otis that it was best that we stick with two but he just had to have his way. I think he was really hoping for a boy. Serves him right. That's why he ended up living in a house full of women.

Well, sure enough he got his wish. Within three months of him pestering me about having another baby, I was pregnant. And I'm telling you, it was the worst pregnancy I ever had. I was so sick that I couldn't even look at food. I lost so much weight that the doctor was afraid I was going to lose the baby. As sick as I was, I didn't even care. I know that sounds cruel but you just don't know the pain and agony I went through carrying that child for nine and a half months. I'm telling you, I was sick as two broke-down dogs from the time his sperm found my egg, until the day I gave birth. It's a wonder me and the baby didn't die.

After all I went through just to get that girl to the outside world, I really didn't want to see her little face. None of the people around me really understood what I was going through. To them, I just seemed crazy and they couldn't figure out why I didn't want to have anything to do with my own baby. Well, I'll tell you. All during my pregnancy with Ella, I had dreams, or should I say nightmares, about a white woman coming to my house right after I gave birth to Ella and snatching the baby right out of my arms. I started screaming like a crazy woman and no one heard my cries. Then after the woman ran out of the house with the baby, I heard gunshots. I didn't know if she had killed the baby or someone had killed her or her and the baby. I was so hysterical that I just passed out. When I came to in my dream, the white woman was standing outside of my bedroom window holding a dead cat in one hand and my baby in the other. She had them both by the neck. At first I couldn't tell if the baby was dead or not. The only way I knew the cat was dead is because I saw blood sliding from its mouth and his lifeless body was limp in her hand. I tried to scream but there was no sound. No sound and no one around to help me.

I would finally wake up in a cold sweat. My sheets

would be wet and Lee Otis would always say, "This can't be good for the baby." I thought to myself, "To hell with this baby. What about me?"

I had only seen my mother once in my entire life. I remember thinking, how could someone so beautiful be so ugly at the same time? One day, my stepmother and I were in town to pick up some supplies when this woman came stumbling out of the town watering hole. It looked like someone had literally kicked her out. She came flying out onto the street and landed right in front of a man riding his horse. Fortunately, the horse was just walking and not running. He pulled up on the reigns to make the horse stop completely and waited for her to crawl from in front of him. I remember the man asking, "Are you okay, ma'am?" She looked up at him and slurred, "Git the fuck away from me, nigger, before I have the Sheriff arrest you for trying to rape a white woman." The man pulled the horse's reigns to the right, kicked the horse in the side and galloped away, leaving the white woman lying in the middle of the road.

I heard my stepmother mumble, "Don't make no sense, that woman out in the middle of the road like that. Ain't nothing but a piece of po' white trash. That's all she is - po' white trash!" The woman lying on the ground tried to get up two or three times, but failed with each effort. Finally, she decided to crawl to the side of the road, where she ended up about three feet away from us. My stepmother decided it was time for us to leave. She grabbed me by the hand and turned me in the other direction. That's when I heard the white lady say, "Where the hell do you think you're going with that gal? Bring her back here so I can take a look at her!" My stepmother's grip tightened and she tried to speed up her pace, but the woman on the ground hollered out, "If you don't bring that gal back here for me to see, I'm gon' call the Sherriff on yo' black ass!" My stepmother stopped dead in her tracks, slowly turned around and we both began to walk towards the woman. By that time, she had pulled herself up from the ground and was sitting on a chair that was in front of one of the stores. We stood in front of her and the woman reached out to touch my hand. I was scared. She had the same grey eyes as me. Looking into her eyes was like looking at a glass mirror. I saw things in her eyes that I didn't understand, things that frightened me; things that no child should ever see. I saw myself in her eyes. I looked down at the ground. The woman said, "Don't be afraid, darling. I'm not going to hurt you. I just want to get a good look at you."

"Do you know who I am?" I shook my head no. "I'm yo' Mama," she said with a sad smile. Then my stepmother said, "It's time fo' us to go." She grabbed me by the hand and turned to leave. The woman sitting in the chair said, "Don't you just walk away from me, I'm trying to talk to my daughter!" My stepmother quickened her stride and before I knew it we were down the road on our way back home.

After we had been walking for a while, I finally asked my stepmother, "Why did that lady say that she was my mother?" She looked down at me and said, "Hush up, gal. You always trying to be in grown folk business. Don't even concern yo'self wit the likes of her. She ain't nothing and nobody. And if you ever see her on the streets again you do best by running fo' yo' life. 'Cause I'm telling you, she dangerous and she slick like a low-down snake. You hears me, gal? You see her on the streets, you turn and run fo' yo' life. I means it."

I knew that was the end of that conversation. So I figured I would wait for my father to come home and eavesdrop on their conversation. Sure enough, before his butt could touch the top of his seat, she lit into him about running into my mother on the street. I remember her saying,

"I took Sadie to town today, like you told me to, and we ran right into that whore of a mother of hers. Laid out their in the middle of the road drunk. Had just got kicked out of some saloon. But to make matters worse, she made me brang Sadie over there to where she was so she could get a good look at her. I'm telling you, it took everything in me not to cuss that two bit wench out. The only reason I didn't is 'cause she threatened to call the Sheriff if I didn't do what she wanted. I really wanted to beat the hell out of her. But she wasn't worth going to jail over. So I kept my peace and let her look at Sadie. Then you know what she had the nerve to sit up there and say? She gon' tell the child that she was her Mama. I could have stomped her right there on that porch. The only reason I didn't is 'cause I don' already spent five years of my life doing hard time. I was tempted to do another five years."

When my stepmother finished talking, she put his plate in front of him so he could eat his dinner. He never said a word. I stood at my door, just waiting for him to say anything. He opened his mouth to shove her beef stew and cornbread in but nothing came out except a loud belch once he was done with his meal.

Once again, my father was not going to help me. I stood at my bedroom door wondering if the woman we saw in town was really my mother. A part of me was hoping that she was. Because underneath the dirt on her face and the pain I saw in her eyes, I could see that she was once a very beautiful woman. I had nothing else to hold onto, so I grabbed the beauty of the woman and clung to it tightly, believing that one day I would grow up to be a beautiful woman myself.

As the days went by, I heard my stepmother tell that same story over and over to anyone who would listen. That's how my older cousin Nadine came into the picture. She would come to our house almost every day. She was one of the few friends my stepmother had, which was surprising because Nadine was simply beautiful. She was half Black and half Indian, giving her an exotic look that the white men in town secretly loved and adored. This made her one of the favorites at the brothel that she and my real mother lived in. Nadine was the one who would tell my mother what was going on with me.

I don't recall ever seeing my mother again. I know for sure I never spoke to her after that day. But those grey eyes burned a permanent memory in my soul. So when I started having the nightmares years later, I knew it was her coming after me. But what in the world could she possibly want? And why had she killed my baby in the dreams?

Once I gave birth to Ella, I just couldn't bring myself to look at her, let alone hold her. I knew for sure that I would see my mother in her face. When cousin Nadine came by to visit and told Lee Otis that the baby looked just like my mother, I knew then and

WHY?

there that I would never have anything to do with that little girl. I was doing it for her own good. If I just stayed away from her everything would work out fine. I figured her father could raise her. His mother would certainly help and then I could get back to raising the children I actually wanted.

But Ms. Babe wouldn't leave well enough alone. She came to our house every single day. Whenever she would come in the room with the baby sticking her out for me to grab, I would turn my back to her and act like I was a deaf mute. She would stand there for a while, trying to coax me into at least looking at the baby, and after getting nowhere, she would finally turn and leave.

Then one day, she came in the room empty-handed and, for a split second, my heart skipped a beat. I thought something happened to the baby. I guess she could see the concern dance across my eyes and I saw a slight smile flirt with her lips. She sat down on my bed and said, "Listen Sadie, I'm not gon' keep trying to force you to love your own baby. I guess you just like everybody else - you got yo' own demons to contend wit. And unless you wants some help for whatever is bothering you in the head, ain't nothing nobody can do to help you. This is something you gon' have to work out fo' yo'self. Now today gon' be my last day coming over here helping out wit the baby and everythang unless you says you wants' me to keep coming. Otherwise, I'm gon' leave all this to Lee Otis. So you let me know what you wants me to do."

I turned my back to her and thought, finally, she wont be coming to my house everyday. She stood up, "Well, I'm gon' gone back out there and see what I can do for the baby and Lee Otis, and then I'm leaving. Just yell if you wants to talk befo' I leave." And with that she walked out of my room. I wasn't sure how I felt about her threatening not to come back. I knew Lee Otis couldn't handle the baby, hell, he had to work everyday. Somebody needed to be there during the day to tend to the little girl.

I walked out to the porch later on that evening and told him to let me hold the baby. When he tried to hand her to me, something gripped my arms and wouldn't let me touch her. So I just looked at her, and sure enough she looked just like my mother. It was frightening how much she looked liked my mother. Those same almond shaped eyes, except I didn't know what color her eyes were. They looked like a mixture of green, grey and brown, it just depended on which way the sunlight hit her eyes. It was almost too much to take. The only difference was that the baby's skin color was a deep yellow with red undertones. I had to admit, she was the prettiest of all my girls. She had the obvious pretty features, but if you looked deep into her eyes, you could see something beautiful trying to come out; but something evil was trying to keep it locked up. It scared me and I couldn't look at her anymore. I practically ran back in the house.

Poor Lee Otis just didn't know what to do. Once I was back in the bed, I yelled out to the porch for him to come in the room. I told him to tell his mother to keep coming to the house during the day, not for me, but for the baby. The only thing that I did do for Ella during her first days of life was give her a name. But even that wasn't the nicest thing I could have done for her. Yes, Ella was one of my dead aunts. But what Ella didn't know was that she was my least favorite aunt. And she died a brutal death. Her husband found her in her lover's bed and killed her and the lover. Yeah, Ella was set up to fail and I did a pretty good job of making sure that came to pass.

One day, Ms. Babe was at the house and she brought the baby into my room and put her in the little crib. Said she would be right back, and left out before I could protest. And like clock work, as soon as Ms. Babe walked out of the room, that baby started crying like there was no tomorrow. I waited for Babe to come back and check on the baby, but she acted like she was deaf. She never did come back into that room. I wanted to scream to the baby to be quiet. She just kept crying and crying and crying. The next thing I knew I was walking over to the crib to pick her up. Before I knew it, I was holding the little thing in my arms. I had to admit, I began to feel something, holding my fat little baby. But I was determined not to let my feelings show for her. All I wanted to do was get her quiet, and back to the crib she would go.

I had been holding her for at least an hour by the time Ms. Babe finally came back to check on her. When she saw me holding her she turned around to leave, but I immediately called her back so she could take the baby from me. "Uh, Ms. Babe, you can come take the baby now." She walked right out that door like she didn't hear a word I said. That one simple act is what forced me to start taking care of my baby. I tell you, that was one of the hardest days of my life.

You would think that after time, it would have gotten easier, but the more she grew the more she looked like my mother and the harder it was for me to look at her. I never admitted it to anyone but, I hated my mother. I hated who and what she was. I hated her for not being a mother to me, and I hated her for letting my stepmother raise me. Before I knew it, I was transferring those same feelings onto Ella. That's why after everything that happened with Do-Man and Ella, I eventually let her go on back to East St. Louis. I figured Ms. Babe started raising her, she might as well finish. So, it wasn't as difficult to send her down there as people might think.

I knew that once Ella went back to East St. Louis she would never come back to Chicago to live under my roof. It was best for all of us.

CHAPTER 28

UNCLE BUTCH

Yeah, we all knew Ella wasn't going back to Chicago. I don't know why Sadie put up such a fuss in the first place. She ain't bit mo' wanted that gal than the man in the moon. I saw it fo' myself when I went up there the first time, right after Lee Otis went to jail. I had never seen a mother so cold when it came to the welfare of her own child. But that's just how Sadie was when it came to Ella. Never really had a kind word to say to or about her. I always did thank it was a shame the way she treated that gal. But that was my brother's wife and kid. So I just tried to mind my own business. Now had anyone bothered to ask me fo' my opinion I sho' woulda' gave it.

I'll tell you this, too. I hated sending that woman money every month. The only reason I sent it on time every month is because my brother told me to, and Sadie was taking care of my other two nieces. My brother going to jail was really the best thing that ever happened to Sadie in my opinion. Because of him being locked up, she was able to get rid of the child she never wanted and she got money every month like clock-work to make sure she and her children were comfortable.

And despite everything that happened, my brother still loved her. Sometimes I would shake my head in amazement at the love he had for that woman.

As you can see us brothers would do anything for each other, even murder. See, Lee Otis don't really like to talk about what happened to those crackers that raped Sadie all those years ago. Well, like he said, he found out about the whole thing after they was married. I guess that's why he felt obligated to get revenge on those crackers. When he first brought it to me, I told him we should just leave it alone. That was something that happened years ago. Besides that, why would he want to stir up that kind of trouble in our little town anyway? 'Cause if word ever got out that some niggers killed some crackers, you might as well kiss East St. Louis, and all surrounding areas, goodbye! Then I told him, "Man, she look like she doing fine now, anyway. Just leave it alone."

Then he told me, "Butch, me and Sadie just saw the bastards that raped her. They were right outside the ice cream shop acting a fool like they do. I'm telling you, it damn near scared poor Sadie to death. Now you know I can't have my wife afraid to go into town because some ignorant crackers may taunt her every time they see her. Butch, we got to do something."

I didn't like the sound of that 'we got to do something.' But I asked the question anyway, "What did you have in mind?"

That's when the wheels started turning in his head. He came up with this plan to get rid of those crackers one by one. He figured because they were white trash, and a nuisance to everyone in town, that no one would really miss them.

He knew that there were five of them, and that they hung out at an abandoned barn in the middle of a corn field. Apparently, that was the same place Sadie was raped. We went and staked out the place for about a week so we could get their routine down. Every evening around 5 o'clock, two brothers, Jason Lee and Wild Cat, would pull right in the barn. The others would stagger in about an hour later. They would go in the barn and usually stay there for a couple of hours and then they would leave. All five of them would be drunk as skunks when they left.

Lee Otis decided we would pick 'em off one by one as they left. We went after the weakest one first. That was Bobby Johnson. He was a scary punk who did whatever those guys told him to do. When he pulled up to his shack of a house and stepped out of the raggedy Chevy, we knew he was ours for the taking. He was so drunk, I don't even know how he was able to see straight. It didn't matter. Whatever he was able to see on the way home was gon' be the last thing he ever laid his filthy eyes on again.

Just as he was about to reach for the leaning screen door, I put a potato sack over his head and Lee Otis hit him in the head with a brick. We drug him deep in the woods behind his house where we had a big piece of tarp spread out on the ground. We laid him down and began to chop him up in to small pieces. Once we were done, we rolled up the pieces in the tarp and put it in the back seat of my car. Then we drove over to Mama's place and threw the pieces in the pig pen. The next day we sent our younger brother in to town to see if he could find out anything, see if anyone was talking about that missing cracker. We listened out for over three months, and nothing. The only people who actually missed the poor bastard was his four running buddies.

They made the Sheriff go out to the man's place to investigate. The Sheriff came to the conclusion that the man decided he didn't want to be in East St. Louis anymore and he just took off. The other four crackers weren't buying it. They tried to stir up the people but most of the people were glad that he was gone, and prayed that he wouldn't come back.

We continued to stake out the barn and we heard them saying they would kill a nigga to get revenge for their friend and brother. It didn't matter which nigger, they just had to kill one to make an example out of one; to let the other niggers know that they were not to be messed with. We knew right then we would have to make our next move real soon. Our next move would have to be the following night.

We decided we would take out two this time. Maybe that would scare the last two into not retaliating on Negroes in town.

Well, once Ella finally moved back to East St. Louis, the whole family pitched in to make sure she was comfortable. We all offered to let her stay at one of our houses 'cause we all had kids, but Mama insisted that Ella stay with her. It was almost as if Mama felt partially responsible for what happened. I kept trying to tell her that it wasn't her fault. She can't control the demonic actions of other folks. All she can do is try to live right herself. That's what I would always tell her but I could tell she was taking on the guilt of this entire thang.

Ella really didn't talk that much when she moved back to East St. Louis. She stayed locked up in the house most of the time. I could understand that. But then it got to the point where she never wanted to come out, and Mama had to literally force her out of the house, even to go to church. It was like she had found her safe haven and wasn't going to leave for anything.

My daughter, Katie, would go over to the Mama's house and try and talk to Ella, but Ella really didn't have much to say. Eventually, Katie stopped trying. She said Ella was weird. I told Mama she might want to let her talk to someone, maybe the pastor or something. Mama said she would handle it her way. I backed off and let Mama do what she felt was best.

CHAPTER 29

ELLA

After Grandma heard what had been going on with Mr. Crane, she wanted to take me out of school all together. As far as she was concerned, I had gone to school long enough, anyway. I would be of more use to her helping out around the house. Plus, I was reaching the age where I needed to be thinking about getting married and having kids. It was a shock to hear my grandmother talk that way, because ever since I could remember, she always talked about how important education was. Education was the ticket to get you anywhere you wanted to go. She would always quote the Bible scripture, "In all thy getting, get understanding." And then she would say, "See, I understands that the white man can and will give you material thangs while you here on this earth. And whenever he feel like it, he can take it away. But the one thang he can give and not take back is an education. 'Cause see, once you learns something, it's yours to do with as you please. You can share it with other folks or you can keeps it fo' yo'self. But whatever you choose to do, it yours."

So when she started telling me that I needed to

think about a husband and having kids, I was a bit frightened. Fortunately, Aunt Sally began to talk to her and made her come back to her senses. I did overhear her telling Sally that the reason she was so concerned about me thinking about a husband is because she really didn't think that I would ever get married after all the things that had happened to me. I even heard her praying to God one night, begging Him to heal my mind so that I could live life like a normal person. Funny, I used to beg God for the same thing. Maybe He would listen to Grandma.

Well, Aunt Sally and Uncle Butch finally convinced her that I needed to at least finish high school and that I wasn't so messed up in the head that no man would want me. After all, my father did marry my mother. So, I continued with school.

Unbeknownst to Principal Buckley, he was my best friend. I couldn't wait to see him during my study hall and after school. He would always ask how things were going with my classes, my teachers and the other students. It was the concern in his voice that would penetrate straight to my heart. He would do the simplest things that would get me excited, like resting his hand on my shoulder to say "good job," or looking me in my eyes while talking to me, and somehow seeing the real me - the scared, messed up in the head, just longing for love from a man, me.

He never said he saw all of those things, but I could tell he knew they were there.

CHAPTER 30

SADIE

Me and the girls went to East St. Louis for Ella's graduation. I must admit, when I saw her walk across that stage and get her diploma I got a little teary-eyed. She had made it. Now I wondered what she would do with the rest of her life. I secretly prayed that she wouldn't end up like me. Sadly, in many ways, she already had. But she still had time to correct that. Unfortunately, I couldn't give her any advice on anything. Not that she would have listened to me anyway. Ella and I barely said two words to one another. I knew it was my fault, but again, I prayed that the girl would be okay.

Whenever I would call to talk to her, she was so busy that she usually wouldn't even come to the phone. I know she was angry with me for never really going to visit her. I just didn't know what to say. Believe it or not, I did feel bad about everything that happened. I just didn't know how to say it. Plus, I had my own set of issues to deal with. Hell, I had a husband in jail, and he was going to be in jail at least another four years. Here I was a single mother trying to make ends meet the best way I could. Some of my friends told me that I needed to get myself a man to help me with my bills and the girls. I tell you, I thought about it long and hard many a night. But the thought of having some strange man laying up over my girls was just disgusting to me.

Don't get me wrong, I did have my share of gentleman callers, but I wouldn't allow any of them to spend the night. Because of that, they really didn't want to help me like I know they could have. But that's okay, 'cause Lee Otis made sure that his family sent me some money every month. I just needed more.

I was surprised to hear that Ella had gotten several scholarships. I didn't even know she had planned to go to college. I was so proud when they called her name and said she had received a full scholarship to South Carolina University, and that she was the valedictorian of her class. You know it cut like a knife to know that I didn't have anything to do with her academic success. But I really was happy for her.

After the ceremony, I noticed that the principal was hovering over Ella like a proud father. I thought that was kind of strange. But no one else seemed to think twice about it. Ella seemed to enjoy the attention he was giving her. What in the hell was that all about? Was something going on between them, or was he trying to get something started? I remembered thinking he looked rather young to be a high school principal - maybe early 30's. Still, too old for Ella.

When we went back to Babe's house after the graduation, I asked Sally what was going on with the principal and Ella. She said, "Oh child, ain't nothing going on 'tween them two. He just took her under his wing and kinda watched over her while she was in school. You know how delicate Ms. Ella is. Seem like she always need somebody to watch over her."

I looked at Sally and said, "Or maybe that's just the way y'all been treating her all this time, so she really believe that she need somebody to always watch over her." Sally just looked at me with that judgmental look I had grown accustomed to seeing from that side of the family.

She gave me a half-smile and walked away. I didn't care. I knew what I saw and wasn't going to hold my tongue just because they felt I didn't have the right to say anything concerning Ella. I was still her mother and if I wanted to exercise that right, I could anytime I wanted.

To be honest, I don't know why I was so concerned about that man and Ella. Truth be told, it would probably be the best thing for her if she did hook up with a man like that. He was older, stable and able to protect her. Three things that she needed.

There were so many people at Babe's house for the graduation luncheon, that you almost couldn't walk through the house without bumping into somebody. As I was making my way to the kitchen, I bumped right into the principal. Well, well, well, I thought to myself.

"Do you always take such personal interest in your students?" I said to him as he tried to squeeze his way past me.

"Excuse me?" he said.

"Do you always go to the graduation parties of your students? Or is Ella just special?" I said with a smile.

"Well, yes, I try to be as involved with my students as I possibly can. I'm sorry, I didn't catch your name."

"Please forgive my manners. I'm Sadie Boxx,

Ella's mother."

I extended my hand to shake his. I could only imagine the pee that wanted to make its way down his leg, but because he was at a party he would do his best to hold it back. Good luck.

He stuck his hand out to shake mine and said, "It's nice to finally meet you, Mrs. Boxx. You have a very special daughter. Like I said at the ceremony, it was truly an honor to work with her for the past four years. I'm really going to miss her."

I couldn't believe my ears. I heard everything he didn't say. This man was in love with Ella. It was just oozing out with every word. Lord, have mercy! Just how far had he taken this thing? And did anyone else know? I politely excused myself and went to find Ella. I realized that some things just don't change. Here it was, a house full of people, all there for Ella, and I find her sitting off in a corner all by herself. She was a spectator at her own party. The whole party thing must have been Babe's idea.

I went over to Ella and said, "So, are you enjoying the party?" She looked up at me and said, "Yeah, its okay."

"I would say this is more than just an 'okay' party. You got the best food in East St. Louis here, it looks like half the town is here, including your principal and you're the guest of honor. What more could you ask for?" Her face lit up when I mentioned the principal. Then she said, "Yeah, I guess when you put it like that, it is a pretty nice party."

"So why are you sitting over here in the corner watching, instead of talking to all of your guests?" She shrugged her shoulders. "Are you nervous?" She shook her head no. I was about to tell her to go and mingle, but the principal walked over to us and said, "Ella, I just had the pleasure of meeting your lovely mother. I see where you get your beauty." He said smiling at her. She looked up at him and dryly said, "Thank you."

He didn't know what to do after that response, so he excused himself and headed towards the back door. I looked down at Ella and said, "Right now is not the time, but you and I really need to talk before I head back to Chicago." She never looked up. I said, "Did you hear me?" She just shook her head up and down. I stood there for a second or two debating if I should say anything else. I decided to leave it alone for now. I made my way to the kitchen to get some punch.

Ms. Babe had the oven door open taking out another full pan of pulled pork. I remembered that was Ella's favorite. I walked over to Ms. Babe and said, "Can I help with anything?" She gave me the 'only reason you here is 'cause you Ella's Mama look.' She wanted to tell me to get the hell out of her kitchen. Even she was too polite to say such a thing, so she just said, "Oh no baby, me and Sally got it. Go head and enjoy yo'self."

I took her advice and left her kitchen. When I got back to the living room, I noticed that Ella had traded her corner seat for a folding chair outside next to the principal. I watched them talking through the window. At first it looked like they were having a serious conversation then all of a sudden he broke out in laughter. Even Ella laughed a little. What in the world could they be talking about? I wanted to go out there and find out but something told me to just keep watching. After the laughter died down, he put his hand on top of hers and I could tell that he was talking softly to her. She had this look on her face that said, 'I don't care what happens in this world tomorrow, just don't stop talking to me today.' I knew that look because that was the same look I had when I first started courting Lee Otis. That man had a way of taking all my cares away and making me feel like I was the best thing that ever graced this earth. Except, Lee Otis was only three years older than me, not fourteen. I'm sure part of the reason Ella was looking so sad is because she was missing her Daddy.

The party finally started to wind down around 8 o'clock that night. I told Cora and Mattie that they could spend the night with Butch's girls and I would stay at Babe's house with Ella. Once everyone was gone and all the food put away, I told Ella to come with me to the porch so we could talk. She looked at Babe for permission. Babe nodded her head towards the porch. We got out there and I suggested that we both sit on the porch swing. She did just as I asked.

I began to gently swing back and forth. Looking straight ahead because my heart was in my mouth, I said to Ella, "You may not realize this but, I'm very proud of you and everything that you've been able to accomplish. Your grandmother really did an excellent job in raising you." I saw her begin to squirm in the seat like she did whenever she was uncomfortable about something. I cleared my throat and decided to keep talking.

"I really do wish I could have done more, as far as raising you. But back then, I just wasn't equipped to deal with everything that was going on. Do-Man doing what he did, your Daddy killing him and going to jail... all of the pain that you were going through. I just didn't know what to do or how to handle it all. I know this may sound like a bunch of excuses, but it's the truth. Thank God for your grandmother stepping in, otherwise, I might have had a nervous break down and things really would have taken a turn for the worse." I was actually starting to feel okay. I was getting it all out and she was actually listening to me. Or so I thought. Out of nowhere, Ella turned to me and said, "Then why was I the only one to move back down here to East St. Louis? Why didn't we all move back down here and continue to be a family? Isn't that what Daddy said he wanted?"

I couldn't believe my ears. Ella was actually speaking up. I wasn't sure how to respond. I guess I always knew that she would ask that very question one day. I just kept hoping that it would be later. Later finally became right now. We stopped swinging. I stood up and walked to the banister on the porch. I turned around and looked at my daughter who was looking more and more like my mother with each passing minute and said, "It's time for me to tell you the whole truth." I took a deep breath and began to tell Ella all about how my real mother abandoned me when I was just a baby, how I was raped when I was a girl, and how no one came to my rescue until years later when I met her father. I even told her that I didn't want to have anymore kids after Mattie was born. It all came flying out of my mouth like a rushing wind. There were some things that I didn't want to tell her but they fell out of my mouth with everything else. By the time I finished talking, I felt like someone had turned me upside down and emptied everything out. I felt lighter but I could tell Ella felt even more heavy.

I didn't know if I had done the right thing, but I knew it had to be done. I figured at that point, maybe Ella and I could begin to work on some kind of a relationship. She didn't share the same feelings. What I initially thought was sadness in her eyes, showed itself to be contempt, borderline hatred. She looked at me and said, "How dare you come here after all of this time and tell me that you never wanted me in the first place? Was that supposed to make me feel better about our situation? Am I supposed to forgive you because your life was a mess, and that makes it okay for mine to be one, too? I wish that you and my sisters had just continued to stay away. I haven't seen any of you in almost four years and you come down here for my graduation like you really have something to be proud of. You did nothing in molding me into the person I am today. As far as I'm concerned, Grandma Babe is my mother and I don't have any sisters! All of you can go back to Chicago and leave me alone for the rest of my life." She got up from the swing and walked back in the house and went straight to her room.

I wanted to call her back out to the porch, but deep down I knew she was right. Who was I to come in there after all of this time and say anything to her about anything? I should have just sent a card saying congratulations and good luck with the rest of your life. But she was my daughter and I wanted to share in this special day with her.

When I went back in the house I could tell that Babe and Sally had heard our conversation, at least Ella's side anyway. Neither of them said anything to me, nor I to them. I just went and sat down on the couch. I could have used a good stiff drink. Babe came into the living room with a glass of brown liquor and sat it down in front of me. "What's that?" I asked.

"Something to take the edge off." she replied.

She wasn't going to get an argument out of me. I gladly took the glass and began to drink. Then I had to remind myself that I was only trying to take the edge off, not get plastered. I put the glass down on the cocktail table and sat back on the couch. The edge was beginning to feel a little softer already. I looked at her and said, "Thanks. You must have been reading my mind."

She said, "Naw, I wasn't reading yo' mind, I just heard all the thangs yo' daughter just said to you." She paused. I was surprised that she was being so nice. She continued, "Now we all know that we've had our differences, and some of the decisions you've made over the years, well, I won't even pretend that I understand. But they was yo' decisions and I went along with them." I hoped she wasn't going to give me a lecture. That would have been too much. "But as a mother, I do feel yo' pain. It don't never feel good when you ain't on one accord with one of yo' childrens. And don't nobody really understand what you going through except you and the good Lawd. Now, I'm not gon' sit up here and tell you how you should have handled that situation 'cause what's done is done. I just wants you to know that we ain't never tried to turn her against you in any way. What ever feelings she has, they all hers. But I will tell you this. I don't thank it's ever too late to try and mend a broken fence. If that's what you really wants. See, Ella is a real, sweet girl, and if you just show her that you genuinely care, she'll eventually come around. But now that's up to you. I'm just offering some cheap advice." With that she got up and went back in the kitchen to put the rest of the food away.

I heard what Babe was saying, but I really didn't know if I was up to putting forth that effort to try and salvage a relationship that Ella and I never had in the first place. After all, I was practically a stranger to her. I went to bed that night and decided I would just leave Ella alone to live her life the way she saw fit.

Maybe after enough time had passed, she would find it in her heart to forgive me and at least sit down and have a conversation with me. That might be too much to ask.

I don't know why I thought it, but I wondered if she would invite me to the wedding when she and the principal got married. All I could do was hope and pray.

CHAPTER 31

LEE OTIS

April 17, 1973 rolled around like a frozen jar of molasses. That was the day I walked out of Statesville Prison a free man. I was beginning to doubt if I'd ever see freedom as a mere mortal again. I had gone before the parole board three times, and each time I was denied. I figured this time would be no different. So I didn't bother to get my hopes up. I didn't even prepare my parole board speech. I simply went in and sat down before the all white board, answered their questions and was about to tell them that there was no need to continue with the charade, when one of the women on the board asked, "Mr. Boxx, do you have any remorse for what you did?"

I looked that white lady dead in the eyes and said, "Its questions like that that let me know you really haven't read the particulars concerning my case, because if you had, you would have to come to the conclusion that I must have been insane during the time of the murder, seeing as how I killed my brother for molesting my daughter. So let me ask you, ma'am -Would you have any remorse for killing your brother for raping your daughter?"

The white lady was now the red lady. Nerves made her rub the back of her neck with one hand and tap her #2 pencil on the desk with the other. I sat there a moment waiting for her, or anyone else, to respond. They didn't. I stood and told the guard I was ready to leave. The following week, I received a letter from the parole board telling me I was going to be released on Tuesday, April 17, 1973.

I think I was still in shock when I walked outside and the bright sun hit my face and the cool breeze brushed past my cheek. The breaths I took were hard and deep. Just knowing that the air I swallowed didn't pass through barbed wire and over a stone wall, made it that much sweeter to inhale. My outstretched arms welcomed freedom to my chest to rest its weary head. On that day, I walked out of that concrete building, looked around and there was Sadie running towards me. She jumped into my arms and I held her like my life depended on it. In that split second, I knew I would never leave her side again. Despite all of the issues she had, and Lord knows she had a lot, I loved her with everything I had. And I knew she loved me just the same.

Now, as glad as I was to see Sadie, I was secretly hoping that Ella would have come up here to see me get out. Maybe she was waiting back at the apartment. Sadie looked in my eyes and could tell that I was thinking about Ella. She simply said, "She's not coming."

I tried to pretend everything was fine and said, "Oh, I didn't think she would travel all this way just to watch me walk out of prison."

Sadie tried to make light of the situation and said, "Well, all isn't lost. Your Mama and the whole gang will be up here in two days, and we gon' have a feast to beat all feasts."

"Two days? Why they waiting so long to come?" I said, annoyed that they weren't waiting for me when I got out.

"Because I asked them to wait a couple of days so you could get re-adjusted to your surroundings and your wife, if you know what I mean." She said with a wink.

"That's why I love you, girl, 'cause you always thinking. What's taking you so long to get in that fancy car and drive me home where I can get to know my wife all over again." We both laughed and hopped in the metallic gold 1969 Electra 225.

We got back to the apartment and nothing was the same. She had changed the furniture, painted the walls a different color, beads were hanging from the ceiling in some of the doorways, and strange-looking posters were on the living room walls. I almost didn't know what to think. I tried to pretend that it was cool, but the look on my face said it all. Finally I said, "All of this shit is coming down tomorrow. It looks like a bunch of hippies live here." I didn't mean to hurt her feelings but this was just too much for my first day home.

Sadie didn't say anything. I'm sure she knew I wouldn't like it, but that's how she had been living for the past couple of years, so I couldn't be too hard on her. All I knew was I couldn't stand it. I needed to have more familiar surroundings. The outside world had already passed me by. Everything was different when I got out. The music had changed, the cars were different and hairstyles were just crazy. Who would have ever thought that grown men and women would proudly walk around with nappy hair so big that it bounced up and down when they walked down the street? Some of these people looked scary. I was just glad that Sadie hadn't gone that far. Negroes were now called Black, and Black and White people were walking side by side, protesting the war, calling for people to, "Make love not war."

Although, I have to admit, when I saw Sadie standing outside the prison with that little short dress on and those boots that came up past her knees, I was turned on. She looked sexy as hell. I couldn't wait to get her home. Although, she could have warned me about the apartment before I went up there and stepped into the groovy love den. But it was cool because at least for the next 48 hours, that's exactly what it was going to be, a love den.

After I looked around the entire apartment and tried to let things sink in, she walked up behind me and put her arms around my waist and buried her head in my back. I was so glad that she was behind me because I didn't want her to see the tears rolling down my face. I had been longing for my wife to touch me just like that for the past ten years. I needed her to just hold me and hold me and never let go. At that moment, I just kept saying to myself how thankful I was that she didn't leave me while I was in prison. I didn't care what all we went through, I was never leaving her again.

I held her arms around my waist for what seemed an eternity. Then she led me to the bedroom, and to my surprise, everything was exactly the way I remembered. For that she was going to get the super-duper special love making treatment. We fell on the bed and she eased her way on top of me and began to unbutton my shirt. Wow, I didn't remember her being so aggressive. I kept thinking, I didn't want her to take those boots off. Just make love to me in those boots and I'm yours for life. She pulled off her dress and I wanted to cry all over. I couldn't believe how beautiful she still was after all this time. I told her not to move. I needed to look at her beautiful body before I made love to her. She smiled and sat on top of me rubbing my chest. 'Thank you, God, for giving me this angel,' I said to myself.

I began to gently feel her breast. How soft, yet firm, they were. I couldn't wait to put them in my mouth. I began to caress her sides and allowed my hands to slide down to the small of her back and then grabbed her plump behind, which was always my favorite. Thank God she didn't take after her real mother in that department. My hands were doing their own dance across her body. It was so soft and just a little plump. My excitement was growing. Had I made love to her right then and there, it may have looked like rape. So I continued to feel her body and mentally made love to her for a while.

I must have been taking too long because the next thing I knew, Sadie had taken off her boots and stockings and was taking off my pants. I said, "Can you do me one favor before we start?"

"Whatever you want baby."

"Can you put those boots back on?" She didn't say a word. She bent down, put the boots on, and climbed back on top of me. We made love for hours.

It started off nice and slow, but by the time it was over, we were both sweating like we had been in the cotton fields of Mississippi. Man, was it good.

When we finally came up for air, Sadie went in the kitchen and warmed up the supper she had cooked for me. Yeah, it was all my favorites. Baked neck bones, lima beans, candied yams, macaroni and cheese, hot water cornbread, and freshly squeezed lemonade. I'm just glad we made love first. All that heavy food would have put me right to sleep. This way I had the best of both worlds.

After we ate, slept and made love again, we finally began to talk. I was holding her in my arms stroking her hair when I said, "We have got to get this family back together." I felt her tense up.

"Do we have to talk about that right now?" she asked.

"No, baby, we don't have to talk about it right now, but I do want us to start thinking about it."

Then she said, "You do know your whole family will be here day after tomorrow?"

"Yeah, but I want to get our family back together. Cora and Mattie off living in California doing God knows what, and Ella living down in South Carolina where ain't nobody heard from her in I don't know how long. We just need to be a family again."

"Okay, baby. We'll deal with it later." She rolled over and put her plump butt up against my leg. That's all I needed. We would talk about family later.

The day before the family was to come to Chicago, I decided that Sadie and I would go down there and stay for a few days. Plus I had a few things to settle up with my brothers. And since Sadie had learned how to drive and we had a nice big, brand, new car, why not put it on the road and see how it drove? My driver's license had long expired so Sadie would have to do all of the driving. We hit the road at 4 o'clock in the morning, that way we could stop and take our time and still make it down there before nightfall.

We pulled up to Mama's house around noon. Everybody was there. All of my brothers and sisters, their kids and grandkids, the neighbors...even Mama's pastor, Rev. Sykes, was there. When we got out of the car I was hit with the smell of roasted pig coming from the back. Mama remembered that was one of my favorites. And the first person I saw was Butch as he came from the back of the house with his long white chef's apron on. We hugged for what seemed forever. Then, one by one, the whole family came out on the porch. I couldn't believe how much the family had grown since the last time I'd seen them. Mama was standing right there in the middle clutching her chest trying to hold back the tears. No one made a move. They were all waiting for Mama. I stood there looking at the woman that gave me birth, feeling like a little boy on the inside. She began to make her way down the stairs never taking her eyes off of me. I stood there frozen in my spot. She finally made her way to where I stood, and before she put her arms around me, she gently lifted her hands and began to feel my entire face. Then she slid them down to my neck and shoulders. She squeezed my arms, then grabbed my hands and held them in hers while she allowed the tears to flow from her sparkling eyes. The tears began to roll down my face. Then, all of a sudden like a force of nature, she threw her arms around me and I stooped down and put my arms around her and began to swing her around in the air. Laughter flew up to the sky from the rest of my family members standing on the porch. The flood gates opened because they all ran off the porch and began to hug me, kiss me and slap me on the back of my head.

Sadie got lost in the sea of relatives trying to get at me. We stood outside of Mama's house for almost 15 or 20 minutes with everyone laughing, saying hello and telling me how much they missed me. Mama finally broke up the crowd and told everyone to give me some breathing room and let's all go inside. Before I could make my way inside, Mama pulled me to the side and said, "Have you heard from Ella?"

I was trying real hard not to think about my baby girl at that particular moment, but Mama brought her up, "Naw, I ain't heard from her yet. I don't know if she knows I'm out or not." trying not to sound too hurt.

Mama looked at me and didn't say another word about it that night. But we all knew she knew I was out of jail. Then Mama said smiling, "Come on in here, boy, this is a happy day. Let's go and have ourselves a good time." She grabbed me by the hand and led me into the house.

The house smelled just like it did whenever we would have big barbecues for some special occasion or for no reason at all. There was so much food on the kitchen and dining room tables, I almost got dizzy just looking at it. Mama fixed me a big ole plate of everything there. I had my pulled pork, collard greens, black-eyed peas, corn bread, baked sweet potato, a piece of catfish that had just come out of the kettle, some chitterlings and a big old glass of fresh, squeezed lemonade. I was in heaven. Yes sir, I sat there and ate it all! I had to stop Mama from piling even more on my plate.

At some point, I found myself sitting alone on the couch. It gave me a chance to look around at the family and take it all in. I looked at how graceful my mother and brothers and sisters were all aging; how their kids were all there with them, most of them grown and married with kids of their own. Life had truly moved on without me.

I sat there thinking how this reunion was bittersweet. All of my nieces and nephews and great nieces and nephews were here, and my own children were nowhere around. I had to do something to get my own family back together. Before I could think about it for too long, people started coming back into the living room and sitting down wanting to talk. Then out of nowhere, one of Butch's granddaughters came up to me and said, "Uncle Lee Otis, why was you in jail?" The whole room fell silent and her mother was about to grab her and spank her. I said, "No, no. Don't spank her. She has a right to know why her uncle was in jail. She's a part of this family and we shouldn't keep secrets from our babies. That's part of the reason I went to jail, because of secrets." I took my little niece and put her on my lap and said, "What's your name?"

She looked up at with those big brown eyes and said, "LaToya."

"That's a pretty name, LaToya. How old are you?"

"I'm five years old."

"Oh that's a good age."

She smiled a toothless smile and let out an innocent

little giggle. It warmed my heart to hear that innocence in her giggle. I contemplated what I should say to this child who was still so free. I decided to tell her the truth. At least in a way that a five year old could understand.

"Well, Miss LaToya, you asked me an honest question so I must give you an honest answer."

The entire room held it's breath.

"LaToya, I killed a man for hurting my little girl. See when my daughter was about your age, someone did something to her that was very bad. And when I found out about it I lost my temper and shot him. I didn't mean to kill him but I was very angry at him for what he did to my daughter. And I think I would do it again if I had to. I would do whatever I could to protect all of the little girls and women in this family. If someone did something to you, I would protect you, too. You understand?"

To my surprise she said, "That's what Grandpa Butch tells me all the time. He said he would kill a nigger if he ever messed with me."

I couldn't believe my ears. The whole room fell out laughing. That's when Mama came in and said, "Alright, that's enough of all that killing talk. We gots better thangs to discuss on today. Git on off yo' uncle's lap and go somewhere and play," Mama said as she shooed my niece away with her dish towel.

LaToya hopped down and was gone just as fast as she had come. I looked at Mama and could tell she was having a hard time dealing with this. I walked over to her and said, "Mama, let's go out on the porch so we can talk."

"Boy, we in the middle of a party. I ain't got time

fo' no talking right now," She said trying to make her way back to the kitchen.

"Listen, Mama, I need to talk to you right now," I said with urgency.

"Can't it wait until tomorrow? After all, you gon' be here for the next two, three days, ain't you?"

I figured I'd back off and give here a chance to get ready for our talk. I told her, "First thing in the morning we need to talk."

"That's fine boy, now git on back in there to yo' party."

As I walked back into the living room, it hit me that I hadn't seen Sadie since we got there. Where in the world could she be? I walked around the entire house and there was no sign of her. So I decided to go out back, and sure enough, there she was talking to Butch and his wife. Then I saw her put a cigarette up to her mouth. What in the hell was going on? Sadie didn't smoke, or did she. Hell, I just didn't know anything anymore.

I walked over to the barbecue pit where they were all talking and said to Sadie, "When did you start smoking?" I thought she was going to be startled or try to give some flimsy excuse. She looked at me and said, "Man, I been smoking for years now." Then she turned around and went back to talking to Butch and his wife.

I stood there feeling like a complete outsider. What in the hell was going on? Maybe I would take Mama's words to heart- there was a party going on, so I might as well get back to it. I walked back to the living room and somebody turned on the record player. An Isley Brother's song came on, "Fight The Power." The whole house came running into the living room and started dancing. Mama grabbed me by the hand and pulled me into the middle of the room. We danced a while. By the time we left the floor my shirt was drenched with sweat. I thought I was going to pass out.

The party finally began to wind down around midnight. I think the last person left at one or one thirty. Sadie came on in from outside smelling like a chimney. That's when I told her, "Listen, baby, I know you say you been smoking for years, but you gon' have to quit that filthy habit. I can't have no woman of mine walking around smelling like no ashtray."

She turned around, looked at me and said, "Everybody is smoking now-a-days. And besides, it don't even smell that bad."

"I really don't care who all is smoking. I don't want you doing it. And that's that." To my surprise, Sadie didn't even bother to argue with me. Maybe she was just trying to keep the peace since I had just gotten back home and everything.

The next day she didn't have much to say to me. Guess she really was mad about last night. I didn't care. Anyway, Mama came into the room around 8 o'clock that morning. "Son, I got somebody on the phone who wants to talk to you."

Wiping the slob from the corner of my mouth I said, "Who is it?"

She stood in the doorway with her hands on her hips. "Listen, you need to hurry up and git to the phone. This here is long distance and ain't nobody got money to be wasting, waiting around on you to git to the phone." Then she walked away.

I jumped up and found my robe and headed to the

kitchen. Mama handed me the phone before I could sit down at the table. "Hello." There was dead silence on the other end. "Hello." Nothing. "Hello." I heard someone clearing their throat on the other end. I decided to wait for them to speak first. The voice on the other end finally said, "Daddy? Is that you Daddy?"

Now it was my turn to be silent. I couldn't believe my ears. I found some words to speak "Ella, baby, is that you?"

Her little voice was trembling. "Yes, Daddy, it's me."

Oh my God. Was it really Ella on the other end of that phone? "Where are you baby? I said, trying to choke back my tears.

"I'm in South Carolina."

I thought my heart was going to shatter into a million little pieces at the thought of seeing my baby girl again. "You plannin' on coming home soon?"

She paused. My heart stopped. "I don't know if I can get away, right now. But I'll try and come home once the semester ends next month."

I knew I couldn't pressure her into coming home right away. After all, she was in school. I guess I just thought that she would be so happy to see me that she would have dropped everything to be here. That's when the light bulb went off. "Baby girl, how about I fly out there to see you?"

She paused again, then "Just you?"

"Just me. I could come out next weekend and stay for a couple of days. How does that sound?"

Again with that damn pause. Was she afraid to see me? I don't know why. Hell, I'm the man that killed Do-Man for her. Mama must have seen the frustration rising up in my face. She gave me a look that said calm down and be patient. I took heed.

"Okay, Daddy. Next weekend will be fine. Call me and let me know your itinerary."

Before I could say anything else, she said good bye and hung up. I placed the phone back in its cradle. Mama came up behind me and put her hands on my shoulders and said, "Give her time, Lee, just give her a little time." I shook my head as if to say, I don't know what I'm going to do. She slipped a cup of coffee in front of me and sat down across from me. "So what did she say?"

"Basically, she said I could come and see her next weekend - by myself."

Mama gave me a little smile and said, "What's so wrong with that?"

"I just want us to be a family again, that's all."

"Well, you got to give her time. She been through a lot. And I know you thank she owe you something for what you did. But the truth is, she don't owe you nothing. Don't forget boy, it was yo' job to protect her. So you got to look at what happened as a part of you doing what you had to do fo' yo' family."

I looked at her and said, "You don't think I know that? I have thought about that everyday for the past ten years. I know it was my job to protect my entire family. I just don't understand why she don't want nothing to do with any of us. I tried to communicate with her while I was in prison, and everything was going fine for the first couple of years. Then, all of a sudden, she wouldn't write to me, she barely wanted to come to the phone when I would call...she just didn't want nothing to do with me..."

Before I could finish, Mama cut me off and said, "Boy, I don't know what you moping for. Didn't the girl just say you could come out there and see her next weekend? That sounds like a step in the right direction to me. Just take it slow for now, son. Everything will work out just like it's supposed to. Mark my words. Now let me git you some breakfast going while you go on out back and look at that shed door for me. Look like it want to come on off the hinge or something."

I took another sip of my coffee, left to throw on some clothes, and went out back to look at the shed door. Sadie and I stayed in East St. Louis for the next two days. We visited with some of our old friends and relatives who weren't able to attend the party. I finally got up the nerve to tell Sadie that I was going to visit Ella the following weekend. To my surprise, she didn't say anything. But I could see the uneasiness in her face when I told her. The only question she asked was, "How long will you be gone?"

"Just for the weekend," I casually said.

"Oh, that's good. I just hope you can resolve whatever it is that you're looking for."

"I'm not even sure what to expect when I get out there. All I know is, I need to see her face-to-face and look in her eyes when I talk to her."

Sadie looked a little sad, but she knew I had to do what I had to do. I have to admit, I did feel a little sorry for her. Poor Sadie, she refused to have a relationship with Ella, basically forcing her out of her life for good, and the two children she did everything for, completely turned their backs on her, leaving her all alone in Chicago when they got half- way grown. They ran off with some cult. Who in the hell would have believed some shit like that? When Sadie wrote and told me what happened I wanted to tear the bars down from my cell and go out and find the bastards that had talked my girls into joining some bullshit cult. Then I turned my anger on Sadie and questioned how in the hell could she let something like that happen? And how in the hell did they get caught up in some mess like that in the first place? I just couldn't understand it to save my life.

I finally got over it and decided I would have to deal with that once I got out. Sadie didn't tell me about what was going on until a month before I was to be released. But right now I had to focus on Ella. Like Mama said, at least she had agreed for me to come and see her. I was nervous about the whole visit. What would I say to her? How would she receive me? Would she hate me? I just didn't know. I don't think I got one good nights sleep that whole week leading up to the visit.

The day finally arrived for Sadie to take me to Midway Airport. I was so worked up about my trip, that I had Sadie get me to the airport at 8:30 a.m. for a 9:30 a.m. flight. We barely spoke during the ride. She asked me if I wanted her to come in and walk me to the plane, I told her not to worry, I'd be fine. She dropped me off right in front of the American Airlines terminal. I got out of the car and began the journey that I had looked forward to and dreaded for the past ten years.

CHAPTER 32

ELLA

My father's flight was scheduled to land at 11:45 a.m. I had decided to blow off all of my Friday classes in order to pick him up from the airport. And even though I didn't have too much to say to my family once I went away to college, I was excited about my dad coming to see me. I figured he wouldn't be getting out of jail for a long, long time. I remember coming home from the trial and hearing my sisters saying that Daddy would have to spend the rest of his life in jail. That stuck with me, and I never bothered to ask Grandma Babe when he would be getting out. I was probably afraid of the answer.

I got to the airport twenty minutes before his flight was to land. I checked to see if the flight was on schedule, and sure enough it was. Five minutes before the flight was to land my heart started racing. As if out of nowhere, the plane appeared on the runway. I saw them roll the stairs out to the plane and the passengers began to de-plane. I watched the people come out one by one, and kept thinking that inside of the plane was my past. A past that I had desperately tried to cover up and forget. Here I was about to see it face to face.

I began to hyperventilate. My first inclination was to turn and run. But my feet were glued to the ground. Damn, why did I tell Daddy he could come? Oh yeah, I was listening to grandma. If I bit my bottom lip any harder, I swear it was going to start bleeding. Did I forget to put on deodorant?

It seemed like everyone on the plane had gotten off and still there was no Daddy. He would have to be the last one to get off. Then it hit me, what if he looked completely different than what I remembered? Naw, Grandma would have told me that on the phone. What if he didn't recognize me? Before a million questions could invade my head, a tall brown-skinned man stepped out of the plane. Dressed to the nines and shoes gleaming from the high shine he no doubt did himself. If I didn't remember anything else about my father, I remembered how he took pride in his dress and having shined shoes at all times.

Daddy stood at the top of the stairs for a moment looking around like he was a movie star. I had almost forgotten how handsome my dad was. Even after ten years in prison, he still looked good. My knees began to buckle as he descended the stairs. He still hadn't noticed me. I tried to make my way closer to the stairs, but I still couldn't move. I would just have to wait for him to come near me. He made his way down the stairs and was looking around for his little girl. He walked right by me and I called out, "Daddy?" He stopped and turned around. He looked at me for a moment and then wrapped his long arms around my entire body.

That was the best hug I'd had in years. We stood there in each others arms for the longest time. Neither of us wanting to let go. Finally, I dropped my arms and took a step back. He released his hug but held me at arms length, and looked at me like he couldn't believe that his little girl had grown up. Then he said, "You turned out to be even more beautiful than I thought you would be." His voice began to crack, and tears welled up in my eyes. I had promised myself that I wouldn't cry when I saw him. Another promise broken.

He grabbed me by the arm and led me back into the airport. Once inside he said, "Which way out?"

"Well, did you check any bags?" I asked trying to regain my composure.

"Naw babe, you know your old man travels light. All I got is this one overnight bag."

'Babe.' It felt good to hear him call me babe. He said it like no one else could. It always made me feel like I really was his babe. No one else had that privilege but me, not even my mother. I was glad he didn't bring my mother. "Well, since we don't have to go to baggage claim, we can go right out the door up ahead."

We took a taxi cab back to my apartment which was just blocks away from the college campus. I stayed in a small, one bedroom apartment that had a let-out couch. I offered to take the couch, but Daddy wouldn't hear of it. He said he had slept on a cot that posed as a bed for the past ten years. A let-out couch was practically a bed fit for a king, as far as he was concerned.

Once we were settled in, I offered to cook us some lunch. Daddy said that would be good and even offered to help. As far back as I could remember, my father never lifted a finger in the kitchen. I couldn't believe my ears. I had to laugh at that gesture. I told him to have a seat and that I would handle it. I broke a glass and a plate all within five minutes of preparing lunch. Daddy walked over to the sink where I was standing and said, "Come on Ella, let's sit down and talk."

I knew that was the purpose of his visit but I wasn't ready to jump in and talk this soon. I was still trying to decide if I was glad he was there. He took me by the hand and led me to the small kitchen table and sat me down in one of the mismatched chairs. He sat down across from me and said, "I think right now is as good a time as any for you and me to talk." That was my Daddy - always straight forward and to the point. He didn't believe in wasting a lot of time, or words, on anything.

He took me by the hand and continued, "I can only imagine the thoughts you must have had about this weekend. And I say that because of the thoughts that I had myself. I didn't know how you was gon' receive me, so I prayed the whole way here that you would at least listen to what I had to say."

My hand started trembling. I thought I would be ready for this conversation by the time he got here, but at that very moment, I knew I wasn't. I slid my hand from his and was about to get up from the table when he said, "Ella, you can't run all yo' life. At some point you got to sit down and face this thing, otherwise it's gon' run you fo' the rest of yo' life. And you'll end up just like yo' Mama.

I knew he was right, but I wasn't ready to face him or the ugly past just yet. I stood up and said, "I understand what you're saying Daddy, but right now I'm just not ready."

"Well, when do you think you'll be ready, Ella? I'm only here for the weekend."

"Why don't we try this tomorrow, or even later on today? Right now I'm just not ready."

Daddy looked at me with those soft brown eyes of his and said, "Okay, Miss Molly. We'll do it your way. We'll talk later. How about I take you out to lunch? That way you can show me around town and your campus."

That was my dad, always able to turn a potential disaster into a problem solved. Most times, anyway. We got ready and left the apartment. I took him on a quick tour of the campus and then we found a nice little soul food joint to have lunch. After lunch, we walked around campus some more and eventually went back home. Fortunately, we ordered so much food for lunch that we each had a doggie bag and warmed up our leftovers for dinner.

I pulled out the T.V. trays and we ate dinner in front of the T.V. When we were just about done, I looked over at my dad and said, "Why did Do-Man do those awful things to me when I was a little girl?" I was surprised that my voice did not tremble when I spoke. My father put his fork down and said, "Babe, your uncle Do-Man was a sick bastard. I don't think anyone knows why he was the way he was. I tell you, Ella, I've asked myself that very question over and over for the past ten years."

I jumped in before he could say anything else. "Do you know that I blamed myself for you going to jail, and that's why I haven't had a lot of communication with you over the years. I was too ashamed of what I felt I made you do."

"Ella, I'm sorry you felt that way but, I would have killed a thousand men if it meant keeping you from

249

anymore danger. My only regret concerning Do-man is that I couldn't kill him more than once. See, that's why I wish you and your mother would have had a real relationship. She would have been able to explain to you that none of that mess was your fault. But because she's dealing with her own set of demons, there was no way she could have helped you through your situation. But we can discuss that later. Right now, I want to talk to you about what you were dealing with at the time and how you're doing now."

I wasn't sure I was ready to get all the way into the discussion, but I figured I'd give it a try.

"For the first few months that you were gone, I felt like my whole world had crashed in on me. Mama, Cora and Mattie seemed to blame me for you going to jail. They barely talked to me. When they did talk to me, it was more like yelling. So I found myself locked in my room most of the time. I would go to my window that faced the street you would always walk down on your way home from work, and pretend that you were going to turn that corner any minute, and you would have something underneath your arm with my name on it. That's how I made it through most evenings. Then Mama would yell through the door that it was either time to eat or time to get in the bed. I didn't know how much more of the loneliness I could take."

"One day while in school I was daydreaming, like I often did after what happened, and the teacher was calling my name, but I didn't hear her. So she came over to my desk and slammed a book down and said, 'Didn't you hear me call your name, young lady?' I snapped out of the daydream and heard this nappy-headed boy yell out, 'She dreamin' 'bout the day her uncle did it to her!' and he started laughing. That's when I lost it. I had no idea that my entire class knew what happened to me. But to make matters worse, they were going to openly tease me about it! Something inside of me died that day, and with it went my will to fight on any level. Instead of me lashing out at the boy, I just sat at my desk and cried"

"I was no longer embarrassed, I was simply defeated. The teacher took me out of the class and to the principal's office, where they called Mama on her job to come and get me. Do you know she made me sit at that school until 3:15 pm and told them that I was to walk home with my sisters? Needless to say, I walked home alone like I always did. By the time Mama got home, I was already in the bed. She came in to my room demanding to know what happened in school and why did I have them calling her on her job. She went on for about 20 minutes before she even noticed that I was sitting on the side of my bed and my feet were planted in a pool of urine. Shortly after that incident is when she decided to send me back to East St. Louis."

"I was actually glad when I saw Grandma and Uncle Butch at the apartment that Saturday morning. I didn't say anything. I just got my things and left. All Mama said was, 'bye.' I don't even remember her walking us down to the car. I do remember driving off in that car, not even bothering to look at the neighborhood that I was leaving behind. I never once turned around to look at the apartment that I hated from the day I saw it. I simply closed my eyes and prayed to God that I would never have to go back to that place again. At least He answered that prayer."

I decided to take a break and I got up to get some water. Daddy was just sitting there behind his T.V. tray, looking like his camp counselor had just told him a ghost story. I couldn't believe I had said so much. I could feel my heart beating a hundred miles a minute. Daddy patiently waited for me to return to the couch.

When I sat back down, he put my hand in between both of his big hands and said, "Baby girl, I'm so sorry that you had to go through any of that. You just don't know how I would pray to God every night that I could have been there with my family, especially with you. I knew you were going through a rough time when your mother brought you to visit me in jail that one time and you wouldn't talk to me. I knew then things weren't right. I begged your mother to not only send you back to East St. Louis, but I wanted her and your sisters as well."

I took my hand from my father and stood up from the couch and said, "I just don't understand how a woman could be so selfish when it comes to her own child. There's no way you can tell me that she didn't recognize the pain I was in. What really hurt is when she came to East St. Louis for my graduation party, how she actually tried to talk to me about what happened, and then wanted me to forgive her! How dare she come and ask me for forgiveness after all that time had passed? She barely picked up the phone or came to visit me while I was in East St. Louis? I should have been ashamed of the way I treated her, but I wasn't. I believed she deserved it, and much worse. The only reason I didn't curse her out is because I knew Grandma and Aunt Sally were listening in the kitchen. So I said what I had to say and I left. I guess you know I haven't spoken to her since. Grandma tried to convince me to call her a couple of times after I left for school, but I told her I had already said what I needed to say, and that the next time I spoke to my mother, she would be apologizing to me for not protecting me like she should."

I knew that he was surprised by what I was saying, but it was like a faucet had been turned on full blast and there was no stopping it. I was on a roll and I wouldn't quit until it was all out. As each word fell from my mouth, I felt a pound lighter. So I kept talking hoping that once I had finished, maybe I would have lost some weight in reality.

"The first few months at Grandma Babe's house were pretty difficult for me. You know I didn't have any friends and Grandma figured that if she worked me to death, I would be cured of whatever was ailing me. So I spent the entire summer working in her garden and tending to her smelly animals."

Daddy let out a little laugh because he knew exactly what I was talking about. I ended up telling him everything that happened to me up until that very moment. I even told him about Mr. Buckley or Charles as I now called him. I could tell that he was hurt to the core by some of the things he heard. But he came for the truth and that's exactly what he got. I just felt that I had no reason to hold it in anymore.

Finally, Daddy told me that he had heard enough and that maybe we should get some rest and start over in the morning. I agreed. I set up the couch for Daddy and then I went to bed.

CHAPTER 33

LEE OTIS

Yeah, I was pretty shocked at the things Ella told me. Sadie never let on that things were as bad as they really were. As Ella sat there and painted a picture of the horrible things that happened to her, I really began to regret shooting Do-Man and going to jail for all of that time. Had I known that my baby would have been this messed up as a result I never would have done it. Maybe I just would have choked his ass until he passed out and then proceeded to kick his crazy ass. But all of that is hindsight. On the other hand, had I not killed his sick behind, he would have continued to do those same nasty things to other little girls.

I was just glad that Ella found it within herself to open up to me and finally start talking. Maybe one day she and her mother would be able to talk. But that would take forgiveness on Ella's part. We would have to work on that.

The next morning, we got up and I told Ella that I wanted to take her to breakfast. She said she had a surprise for me but she was saving it until Sunday. We spent the day bopping around the college town while she showed me all the stuff I didn't see the day before.

It was good to just get out of the house and have a light day. We talked, laughed and ate junk food, something I hadn't done in years. It was good to see my little Ella actually laugh again. There were still a lot of things I wanted to say, but decided they could all wait. Nothing could have been more important than the feeling I was having right then and there.

I figured since we were having such a good time, that it would be a good time to ask Ella about her love life. "So, Miss Molly, is there anyone special in your life?" I actually saw her blush. I told her, "I'm sure you have somebody in your life. It's okay to talk about it." She just shook her head and smiled. She never answered, she just smiled and we continued to walk along the college campus.

CHAPTER 34

SADIE

Needless to say, I really didn't want Lee Otis to go visit Ella without me. But I had no choice but to understand. I took him to the airport and didn't say one word. I had to keep telling myself that it was only for three days. I guess I was hurt because Ella had refused to talk to me since the night of her graduation party. It's partially my fault. After that night, I never even called my daughter to see if we could possibly talk about it anymore. The morning after she all but cursed me out, I got my things together, my other two girls from Butch's house, and we headed back to Chicago. I didn't care what all went on between us, I was still her mother and she didn't have no right to talk to me like that.

Anyway, I picked Lee Otis up from the airport that Sunday evening. A part of me was anxious to find out what happened between the two of them and another part of me wanted to say that I didn't give a damn. I pulled up to the American Airlines terminal and he was standing right there waiting for me. His plane must have come in early. That was a switch. He hopped right in the car and leaned over and gave me a kiss. I said, "Welcome home."

"Thanks, it's good to be back."

Trying to keep the mood light I said, "If you keep running off and leaving me I'm gon' think you trying to stay away for good." I looked over at him to get his reaction. He kept looking straight ahead. He was trying to figure out how he was going to tell me whatever it was he had say.

"So, how was your trip?"

"It was pretty good. Much needed," he said still looking forward.

"How was Ella?" I said, forcing the words out of my mouth.

He didn't answer. Maybe he didn't hear me so I asked again.

"How was Ella?"

He finally turned his head to look at me, "You sure you want to know?"

"What's that supposed to mean?" I said as my voice rose a notch.

"According to Ella, you haven't spoken to her in almost a year. Now if that's true, why would you be so concerned about how she's doing?" he said calmly.

"Listen, Lee Otis, it ain't no secret that me and Ella ain't never got along. And after the way she treated me the last time I was in East St. Louis, I figured it was best to leave well enough alone."

"Yeah, she told me all about that. I see you ain't never bothered to tell me what really happened when you went down there. Sadie, I just can't believe that you hate our daughter so much that you would just let anything happen to her. You know, you ain't never really been a real mother to her. How you think she was gon' treat you after all them years of you never calling, writing or even going to visit her."

"Look here, Lee Otis Boxx. That girl ain't never liked me and you know it. You was the one she always went running to whenever things didn't go her way. And if it wasn't you she was running to, it was yo' Mama. So tell me, Mr. Know-It-All, when did I ever have a chance to be a real mother to the girl?"

His voice was becoming angry, "Sadie you didn't want that girl from the git go. So don't sit up here pretending that me and my Mama pushed you out of the way; you was never there to be pushed. All we did was step in and fill the void that you purposely created. And besides that, how long are you going to blame Ella for what happened to you as a girl? She can't help it if she look like yo' Mama. And it damn sho' ain't her fault that yo' Mama was a prostitute and left you with some people who didn't care nothing about you."

He was going too far and he knew it. But he was on a roll, so there was no stopping him. What I didn't understand was why he was so bitter and hostile towards me now? He knew the nature of me and Ella's relationship. God only knows what she said to him over the weekend. She always did have a way of getting him to be on her side. If he wanted to argue about this, then fine with me.

"Listen, Sadie, Ella told me some things this weekend that made me sick to my stomach. And a lot of it had to do with you and your basic neglect towards her." I couldn't believe he was talking to me like that. I told him it would be best if he not say anymore.

By the time I parked the car in front of the apartment building, we hadn't spoken for over 30 minutes. I was about to get out of the car when he leaned over and grabbed my arm and said, "Sadie, the girl was in so much pain I could hardly stand to look at her. She reminds me so much of you when we first started dating, it's scary. Believe it or not, she needs you and has always needed you. So, I think it's time you face your demons. Start working it out in your head. Then, maybe you can help somebody else, namely our daughter." He had a firm grip on my arm and a pleading look in his eyes. I don't know what that girl told him while he was down there, but whatever it was, it shook him up real bad. I didn't want to know.

We went in the apartment and ate the dinner I prepared in complete silence. I don't know what was on his mind, but all I could think about was how in the world did Ella need me so bad? I figured that since Lee Otis was out of jail, all of her worries would be over. After all, she did have a father that was alive and kicking and who was willing to do anything to help her. I know he gave her some money while he was down there. I don't even know where he got money to get down there from.

As far as I was concerned, Ella had it pretty good compared to me. At least she grew up in the same house as her real mama, daddy and sisters, unlike me growing up with that horrible stepmother. And no matter what Lee Otis, or anybody else says, at least I didn't give Ella away. I done said this a million times and I'll say it a million more times - I did the best I could with what I had, and that wasn't much.

CHAPTER 35

DO-MAN

I just need to clear up something before the gates open up and welcome me home. I feel the heat rising so they'll be coming to get me real soon. Some of you are wondering if I'm sorry for what I did to all those little girls, especially to Ella. What people fail to realize is that Ella and I were alike in many ways. We were both hurting and longing to be accepted. She was just so damn quiet that nobody really paid attention to her needs; I was so loud, funny and the life of the party that no one ever saw the real pain I was in on a daily basis. Just like Ella, I had no one and nowhere to turn for help. My brothers and sisters didn't have a clue as to what I was going through, my mother turned a blind eye, and my father created the whole damn situation in the first place.

I must have been about thirteen or fourteen when I first noticed little Anna, our next door neighbor. She couldn't have been no more than five or six at the time. Anna could have been a pretty little girl if someone had taken the time to clean her up or comb her hair. I don't think they even talked to the girl. She would come outside everyday in the same dirty blue dress, unruly hair and her poor little bare feet would be black as the dirt she played in. Every now and then, she would allow herself to get a glimpse of the world around her. She would lift her head and steal a peek with her huge brown eyes. I guess her surroundings were too much for her big eyes to handle because she would drop her head almost immediately.

One day I looked at little Anna playing in the dirt, as I had so many times before, and I no longer saw her as an innocent little girl. She was something to be devoured. I was terrified because it brought back all of those old memories of when my father would take me for rides in his old jalopy. Scared or not, it didn't stop me from wanting to touch that little girl. I couldn't tell my brothers because they would have told my mother. Hell, they might have beat the hell out of me, which is probably what I needed, a good ass whipping to straighten me out. I struggled with those feelings for weeks before they overtook me. It was as if I had no control over what was happening to me. One day I even went off into the woods just to talk to God. When I got out there, I was going to tell Him that He had to take those urges away from me, but instead of talking to God, I started plotting on how I was going to get that little girl out there just so I could touch her. I just wanted to touch her little brown face, run my hands across her thick wooly hair and down her back; and then I would pull her close to me and just hold her in my arms. I just wanted to touch her.

I knew I didn't have no business trying to talk to God. I had never talked to the Lord; Mama did all the talking when it came to Him. I didn't even know how to start a conversation with Him. So I just sat there in the woods trying to figure out what I was feeling and what I could do about it. My teenage mind told me that touching that little girl in any way was wrong. But I couldn't figure out why I had such strong urges to be close to her. The more I tried to fight those feelings, the more my determination said that the little girl would be mine.

Needless to say, she was my first victim. I have to admit, I was sick after the first time I touched her. But that urge had such a hold on me that I had no choice but to give in to its prodding. I was only sick after that first time. It was like I had learned how to drink and could finally hold my liquor; not liking the taste but loving the affects.

So, you asked if I was sorry for what I did to little Ella and the rest of those little girls. Let me put it to you like this: how can I be sorry for something I had no real control over in the first place? My destiny had already been decided, I was just living it out.

CHAPTER 36

ELLA

I told my dad that I would give him his surprise on Sunday before he left. We got up that Sunday morning to get ready for church. He was surprised, but glad to see that I was going to church on a regular basis, even away at school. What he didn't know, was that I had already tried the 'not going to church' thing, but Grandma called me one Sunday and read me the riot act. She told me that if she called down there again and I hadn't been to church, she would be on the next thing smoking. As she put it, "Hell hath no fury like Ms. Babe when she find out her children ain't in church!" I was too afraid of her to see if she was bluffing. I figured it would just be easier to go to church every Sunday and not lie, than to take that risk. She always knew when I was lying, anyway.

The doorbell rang promptly at 10 a.m. Daddy looked at me with a puzzled look on his face. I tried to ignore him, but the smile I was trying to hide kept forcing its way to my lips. "Are you expecting someone?"

I cleared my throat and said, "Yes, I am."

Daddy stood in the middle of the floor and said, "Well, aren't you going to get the door?"

My heart was pounding because I didn't know what Daddy's reaction to the surprise would be. It was now or never. I opened the door and there stood Charles Buckley. When he saw me he leaned in and gave me a peck on the cheek. I stepped aside to let him in.

You could have knocked my father over with your baby finger. I walked Charles over to where my father was barely standing and said, "Daddy, this is Charles Buckley. Charles, this is my father, Mr. Boxx."

Charles stuck out his hand. Daddy shook it. I was so glad that Charles didn't do that soul brother hand shake with Daddy. I don't think it would have gone over too well with him. I told Charles and Daddy to have a seat at my kitchen table while I went and got the coffee pot to pour them each a cup.

Daddy asked Charles how long he had known me, and Charles immediately looked at me. I jumped in and said, "We've known each other for…"

Daddy interrupted me and said, "I didn't ask you. I asked your friend how long the two of you have known each other." He looked back at Charles and waited for an answer.

Charles said, "Well, sir, I've been knowing your daughter since she was in high school."

Daddy took a sip of his coffee and said, "And what school were you in when she was in high school?"

Again, not sure what to say, he opted for the truth, "I was at that same school."

I could see my father's temples begin to flutter. I had to jump in.

"Daddy, let me explain." I began to say. He gave me that, 'was I talking to you?' look. Charles glanced at me as if to say, 'don't worry, I can handle this.'

"Mr. Boxx, let me assure you that nothing happened between Ella and myself while she was in high school." Daddy sat there sipping his coffee not saying a word.

Charles continued, "I was the principal at the time and Ella was having a difficult time with one of her teachers, and I sort of took her under my wing, allowing her to work in my office during her study break, and sometimes before and after school. It was through her excellent work ethic that I really got to know her as a person. There was a connection between us that couldn't be denied. But I waited for her to graduate from high school before I ever said anything to her. I even went to talk to Ms. Babe before I said anything to Ella. I wanted your entire family to know that I had nothing but the purest intentions when it came to Ella."

Daddy took another sip of his coffee and said, "How old are you Mr. Buckley?"

"I'm 39 years old, sir."

"You're 39 and she's 19. You don't think that's going to 'cause problems later on down the line?" Daddy said as he leaned forward in his chair.

"Well, sir, Ella and I have already talked about our age difference, and it doesn't matter to either one of us. We know that what we have is real. And that's all that matters."

"Real, you say? Real what? Real convenient for you, Mr. Buckley? And speaking of convenient, what are you doing down here anyway? Y'all livin' together?"

Charles was determined to stand his ground with Daddy: He leaned forward in his chair and said, "To answer your first question, its real love. I love Ella with everything I have. And to your second question, I say, no, it is not convenience for me. I was offered a professorship here to teach math. So that is why I'm down here."

Daddy took another sip and said, "So, why is Ella here?"

"Ella is here because she deserves to be here. This is one of the top rated schools for Blacks in the country. And they offered Ella a full scholarship to study at this university. With all due respect, Mr. Boxx, I understand that Ella has been through a lot, and is still going through a lot. But I assure you, I have nothing but the best of intentions when it comes to your daughter. And yes, I do plan to marry her just as soon as she graduates, if she'll have me."

I was standing by the sink listening to them talk about me as if I weren't there. I stood there biting my bottom lip wishing their conversation would end. I wanted to kick myself for listening to Charles in the first place. He's the one who insisted on meeting my father. He even talked me into inviting him down for the weekend. Had it been left to me, I might not have seen my father until someone in the family died.

Daddy finished his cup of coffee, leaned back in his chair and said to me, "Well Ella, looks like you got somebody who ain't gon' let you go no matter what I say. However, I will say this to you, young man. If I ever hear of you doing my baby girl wrong in the least way, I will hunt you down like a low-life dog and kill you. Never let it be said that Mr. Boxx wasn't clear about his intentions towards you if you mess over his daughter. I'm sure she told you, I done already killed one Negro over her, and will kill a hundred more if I have to. Am I clear, Mr. Buckley?"

For the first time in all the years I'd known Charles, I actually saw fear creep across his face. Oh, he tried to hide it, but it was too late. I had already seen it. Although I never worried about Charles doing anything to harm me, a part of me was glad that Daddy had put the fear of God in him. That way he would know that I really did have somebody out there, other than him, to protect me and he better treat me accordingly.

Charles responded to Daddy's last question with a simple, "Yes, sir." With that, Daddy got up from the table and said, "Are we going to church or not?"

"Yes, Daddy. Let me just grab my Bible and my bag."

"You got another Bible I can use. I didn't bring one 'cause I didn't know we was going to church."

I took the cups off of the table and placed them in the sink. Then I grabbed my jacket and we all headed towards the door. We made it to church just before the choir marched in on the new song they had learned, "Oh, Happy Day." That's just what this was, a happy day. I had two men with me who loved me with everything they had to give. And they were each willing to give it all to me. Oh, what a happy day.

CHAPTER 37

SADIE

About a week after Lee Otis got home from seeing Ella, the strangest thing happened. While trying to finish my Saturday morning cleaning and get out to the A&P before it got too crowded, the phone rang. Who in the world would be calling at 7 o'clock in the morning? "Hello?" No answer on the other end. The sound of crying stopped me from hanging up. "Hello?" I said again. The haunting voice on the other end said, "Mama, I want to come home." My heart raced to an unnatural rhythm; my fingers wanted to go numb and allow the phone to hit the floor. I struggled to keep a grip. It was Cora on the other end.

"Where are you?" I said trying to stop myself from shaking.

"California. I want to come home, but they won't let me."

"Who, baby? Who won't let you come home?" I pleaded.

"The people here at the commune," she said in a hushed voice.

"Why don't you just get your things and come on home?"

"It's not that easy. You just can't get up and leave. One girl tried to walk out the front door and they almost beat her to death."

I could hear the panic in my child's voice. "Call the police and have them escort you out of there."

"I'm afraid to do that. Most of the police around here don't have anything to do with us. They say we're all crazy because the women they tried to help in the past came right back. So they usually don't get involved unless the parents get involved and force the authorities to do something."

"Where is your sister? Is she trying to get out, too?" I was almost afraid to breathe.

"She doesn't want to leave. Mattie can't understand why anyone would ever want to go back to their old life. To tell you the truth, mom, I'm afraid to tell her that I really want to escape."

"Why are you afraid to tell your sister?"

"Ma, she's so far gone that I think she will actually tell on me just for talking about it. You just don't know how bad it really is out here. If they even suspect that you're thinking about leaving, there could be grave consequences."

"Well, where are you calling me from now?"

"They sent me to get some things from the store, so I snuck and called you from a pay phone outside the store."

"Can you give me the address to the commune?" I begged.

"I'll have to call you back. If I don't get back soon, they'll be looking for me," she said rushing off the phone.

"When will you call again?"

WHY?

"I don't know, maybe in a couple of days. I gotta go." She hurried off the phone.

I hadn't spoken to Cora, or Mattie, for over a year, and all of a sudden Cora calls me and says she wants to come home. I couldn't wait for Lee Otis to get home so I could tell him the news. He had gone out to get the morning paper. The door barely had a chance to close behind him before I ran up to him and started telling him about the phone call from Cora.

He looked like he was somewhat pleased about the news but not nearly as excited as I was. I didn't understand. Ever since he had been home, all he talked about was the five of us being a family again. Here one of our daughters was actually reaching out to us, saying she wanted to come home, and he was acting like it was no big deal. I bet if it were Ella calling saying she wanted to come home, even for a visit, he would have booked her flight and went and waited at the airport until the day her plane flew in.

So I asked him, "What's wrong with you? Aren't you happy she wants to come home?"

He looked at me and said, "Of course I'm happy our daughter wants to come home. I just can't help thinking about all those kids that get mixed up in those cults and the pain that they put their families through when they claim they want to get out. You know, it's not just a matter of them saying they want out. Those people don't just give them up. The leaders of those cults are into mind control. Basically, their followers end up being like slaves to the leaders. They do, go, eat, sleep, dress and say whatever the leader tells them. Trying to get somebody out of those things is pure hell."

I looked at him like he was crazy. Then I said, "How in the world do you know so much about those things, anyway?"

"Because," he said, "there was a white cat in prison, named Joe, who had a daughter that got caught up in all that mess. The man used to tell me that at first the girl was just hanging around all these hippy-dippy folks, then she started smoking pot and talking all that free love bull-shit; and the next thing he and his wife knew, the girl was calling them from some compound in Arizona, talking about she wouldn't be coming home and that they probably wouldn't ever hear from her again. She had a new family that understood her. Well, when Joe and his wife heard all of that, they got a private investigator to find the daughter. After about a month or two of searching, the investigator finally found the girl. The cult had moved from Arizona to the mountains in Colorado. Joe, his wife and the private investigator, all went up there to try and kidnap the girl. They were able to get the girl back to the hotel, but by the next day she had run off again. They tried it again a couple of days later, but the people in the cult were waiting for them. One of the men in the cult confronted Joe and Joe pulled out a gun and shot him dead. And that's how the cat ended up in prison. He says that the only reason he was convicted is because the boy he shot was the son of some big time U.S. Senator. So when you ask me if I'm happy about Cora wanting to come home, yeah, I'm happy, but I'm just thinking about what all it's going to take to make that happen. Sadie, I don't know if I have the strength for it at this point."

What in the hell did he mean, 'he didn't know if he

had the strength?' He better find the strength to deal with it! That's our daughter we're talking about. The next thing I knew, what I was thinking was coming out of my mouth. "You mean to tell me that you were willing to kill your own brother over one of your children, but you ain't willing to kill some strangers over another daughter? Please help me understand that logic."

He looked at me and said, "Sadie, I just did ten straight years of hard time. Do you really think I'm trying to go back because our crazy ass daughter decides that now she's had enough of living like someone who's lost her mind? That was a choice she made. Didn't nobody force her to do that shit. And let me tell you this. As long as yo' name is Sadie Boxx, don't you ever compare what happened to Ella to what those other two nuts decided to do. You hear me?"

Lee Otis was so angry that he looked like he wanted to hit me. I walked away without saying a word. I went on back to the kitchen and finished cooking dinner. I heard him in the living room watching television. How could he sit there and watch some stupid program and our child was trying to get home? If he thought he was getting away with this, he was sadly mistaken. If I had to fly to wherever she was by myself, our daughter was coming home. I don't give a damn what happened to some white man's daughter.

Didn't he realize that our daughter wanted to come home and that's what made the difference? Oh, he was gon' do something about this and he was gon' do something fast. He just didn't know who he was foolin' with. Hell, he ain't the only one in this family willing to kill somebody over his daughter. I would kill a nigger

D. A. Rhodes

or anybody else who stood in my way when it came to
Cora and Mattie. That included his black ass, too.

Two days went by and I hadn't heard anything from
Cora. Lee Otis didn't even mention the conversation.
Guess he thought I was gon' forget. Not hardly. We
had just sat down to dinner when the phone rang. I
jumped up to answer, praying that it was Cora.

"Hello?" I said, barely getting the phone to my ear
before speaking.

"Hey, sugar, dis Mama Babe. How you doin'?" she
said in her annoying normal country drawl.

"Oh, I'm fine, Ms. Babe. Hold on a minute." I
immediately gave the phone to Lee Otis and sat back
down to eat my pork chops, mashed potatoes and
green beans. He took the phone and walked into the
dining room. The phone cord was so long, you could
practically walk around the whole apartment with that
thing. They must have stayed on the phone for at least
twenty minutes. Now what in the world could they be
talking about for so long, especially in the middle of
our dinner? He finally came back in the kitchen and
hung up the phone.

He knew I was waiting for him to tell me what
that was all about. So what does he do? He sits down
and starts eating his food like nothing happened. I
don't know why he was acting so crazy. Forget it, I
broke down and said, "So what's going on with your
Mama?"

"Nothing much," he said as he put a big helping of
mashed potatoes in his mouth.

"Something must be going on, she kept you on the
phone for at least twenty minutes," I said, trying not
to sound annoyed.

"Everything is fine at home. She was just calling to see how we were doing. That's all," he said in between bites.

"It took you twenty minutes to tell her we were doing okay?"

He stopped chewing and said, "I just told you what she wanted. Don't keep asking me the same thing over and over." He went back to his pork chops.

I was so angry that I got up from the table, threw the food from my plate into the garbage, and tossed my plate in the sink, ignoring how it shattered as it hit the bottom of the sink. I stormed out of the kitchen. Lee Otis sat right there and finished his dinner. Then he got up from the table, left his plate right there, grabbed his jacket and headed for the front door. I was too mad to even try and stop him. I wouldn't give him the satisfaction. He slammed the door behind him and was gone.

Lee Otis stayed out until 3 the next morning. You best believe I was sitting straight up in the bed when he brought his tail home. He thought he was going to get in the bed without any explanation for his whereabouts.

"Excuse me, but where in the hell have you been?" I said.

"Look, woman, don't start with me right now. I done had a rough night, and I don't feel like hearing all that jibber-jabber from you tonight. Now if you don't mind, I'm about to get some sleep." He turned over and closed his eyes. I thought he must've been drunk talking to me like that, but he didn't smell like liquor. Maybe he was smoking some of those reefers that the young people were doing. Naw, something else was going on and I was determined to get to the bottom of it.

CHAPTER 38

LEE OTIS

I swear, that wife of mine should work for the FBI. She gets it fixed in her head that something is going on, and won't stop until she has all of the facts, or at least all the facts in her mind. Would you believe that she actually called my Mama to try and find out what we were talking about on the phone? Now, she should have known better than to call my Mama with some stuff like that.

Mama said she had a feeling that Sadie was going to call her and play detective. She just didn't know Mama was the head detective of them all. See, I would have told Sadie what was going on, but she don't know how to keep her mouth shut. Plus, she gets all excited and flies off the deep end about everything. So, we decided that it would be best not to include Sadie in the beginning stages.

After Sadie told me that Cora was trying to leave the commune, I got on the phone with Butch and explained everything to him and asked him if he thought this was something we could handle on our own, or should we call in the authorities? It was his idea to let Mama in on what we were doing. I agreed.

I didn't tell Sadie that Cora had actually called the day after she spoke with her. Cora told me everything that she told her mother. I got all of the information from her and told her to hold tight and that her Daddy was coming to get her. But before I committed to doing anything, I asked her several times if she was sure that she wanted to leave. She swore that she was. Then I told her, "Listen, baby girl, I'm not trying to go back to jail for nobody. Now when we come out there to get you, you gotta be ready to leave. There won't be any time for changing your mind. Do you understand me, baby girl?"

"Daddy, I promise you that I'm sure. I've never been more sure of anything in my life. *Please* come and get me. I don't know how much more I can take." She began crying on the phone. That was it for me. Something had to be done, and soon.

Butch and I made plans to go out to California the following week. Cora told me that Mattie vowed to never leave the compound. At that point, I told her we weren't going to force anybody to do nothing they didn't want to do. Maybe Mattie would leave at a later time. That's when she told me that the leader of the cult was talking about moving everyone to Israel.

This thang was really getting out of hand. Why in the hell were they moving to Israel? Right now, we had to concentrate on Cora. I told her not to breathe a word of our plans to her sister. She swore she wouldn't. Something told me that she would try and convince Mattie to leave. But again, I couldn't worry about that right now. My focus had to be on making sure that me and Butch's plan would work.

I called Butch a week before we were to head out west. There was something in his voice that said he wasn't all for the plan like he was when we first discussed the matter. I didn't want to ask him if he had changed his mind because of the answer I knew I would get. But I couldn't force him to do something he really didn't believe in. So, I bit the bullet and said, "Hey man, you still cool with our plan, ain't you?"

He assured me that he was still with it. His only problem was Mama. She actually wanted to be a part of the plan. No matter what he said, she still insisted on being a part of what was going on. I didn't have time to be dealing with Mama on this issue. So I decided to call her and tell her to back off, and that she would have absolutely nothing to do with this.

CHAPTER 39

SADIE

The mail was unusually late the Saturday I got the beautiful blue envelope out of the mailbox. I couldn't wait to get upstairs and open the pretty piece of mail addressed to Mr. and Mrs. Lee Otis Boxx. I tossed the other mail on the kitchen table and gently opened the baby blue envelope with no return address.

I damn near knocked over my coffee cup when I read the invitation.

Ms. Ella Mae Boxx
And
Mr. Charles Buckley
Request the honor of your presence
As they pledge their undying love
With
The exchanging of vows on
December 24, 1973
At 2 p.m.
At the True Pilgrim Of The Rock Church
1765 W. Pilgrim Ave.
Charleston, South Carolina
Reception to immediately follow

I couldn't believe it. Ella was actually getting married. From the moment I saw her with that Mr. Buckley, I knew they would be together. But to see it on paper and imagine her walking down the aisle just caught me off guard. I wondered what we would say to each other on her wedding day. As I sat there sipping my coffee, a bit of sadness came over me. I admitted for the first time, to myself, that in many ways I had failed Ella as a mother; and despite my less than stellar performance when it came to being her mother, she still managed to turn out okay.

Wait 'til her father came home. I knew he would be overjoyed. I wasn't sure how to break the news to him? Should I just leave the invitation on the table, or should I wait up for him and tell him in person so I could see his reaction? As I was about to turn in for bed, I heard Lee Otis coming in. I decided I would show him the invite myself.

"Sadie, you still up?" he said as he made his way back to the kitchen.

"Yeah, I'm back here," I said as I put my coffee cup in the sink.

He came in the kitchen and said, "You the only person I know that can drink coffee all day and still go right to sleep at night. I don't know how you do it."

"Never mind all of that," I said trying to hold back my excitement. "Look at this." I handed him the invitation.

"What is this?"

"Open it and see."

He sat down at the table and carefully opened the envelope. There was no expression on his face. I sat there staring at him, waiting for some type of reaction.

None came. He finally put it down and said, "Did you put some dinner in the oven for me?"

"Yeah." I said. "Did you read the invitation?"

"Didn't you just sit here and watch me read it?"

"So, you ain't got nothing to say except, where's your dinner?" I said, trying to sound calm.

"What you want me to say? The girl is getting married. Look to me like everything's already been said." He made his way to the oven to get his plate of neck bones, black-eyed peas, cabbage and cornbread.

"Well, do you plan on attending?" I wanted him to share his thoughts and feelings with me.

"Of course I'm going. You?"

"Seeing as how the invitation was addressed to both of us, I guess I will attend."

Lee Otis sat back down at the table and began to suck the meat off the neck bone, I could tell just by his posture that he wasn't going to talk about the wedding right now. I decided to let it go - for now. Wasn't no sense in getting into an argument over this. Besides, I knew we would just start fussing about the same old stuff, it would just be dressed up in different clothes. I pushed my chair back and said, "I'm going to bed." I walked on back to the bedroom. He kept sucking on his neck bones and never looked up from his plate.

His reaction to the wedding invitation did surprise me. I thought he would have been overjoyed about his baby girl tying the knot with a college professor. Maybe he would want to talk about it on a full stomach. I got in the bed and waited for Lee Otis to join me. I figured he would be another twenty or thirty minutes. He sho' did fool me. The next thing I heard was the front door opening and then closing. "Lee Otis is that you?!" No reply. "Lee Otis?" Nothing. I went to the front door and heard footsteps going down the stairs. I turned my head and called his name again. No answer. Ain't that nothing? This man done walked out the house and ain't bothered to say a word to me. Where in the world was he going at 11 o'clock at night? Probably down to that bar. Guess that invitation upset him more than I thought. I would deal with his behind in the morning.

CHAPTER 40

LEE OTIS

Yeah, I had to get out of the house for a minute. I didn't want to say anything to Sadie, but that invitation really messed me up. One minute Ella was just a little girl. Then she was trying to get over what Do-Man did to her. After that, I was in jail and hadn't laid eyes on her for more than ten years. The next thing I know, she's a young woman dating an old man and now she's getting married. Man, it was too much. I needed a few stiff drinks to help me put my head around this whole thing. Even though I thought Mr. Buckley was a nice man, it was just hard to imagine my baby girl married. There was no natural progression of things when it came to Ella. We went from one to one hundred in a matter seconds. I had to hurry up and get to the bar. Those stiff drinks were calling my name.

Tuesdays were always slow at the bar. I was grateful. I didn't want to talk to nobody, I just wanted to drown my thoughts in a bottle of Old Grand-Dad. I slid onto my regular bar stool. Ironically, it was right across from where Do-Man used to sit his ass every night. The thought of Ella getting married just did something to me. I knew this should have been a joyous occasion, but I couldn't help thinking, Ella wasn't ready for marriage. She was too young. Plain and simple. She hadn't dealt with everything that happened to her the way she should have.

Maybe I was expecting too much from her. After all, she was doing good to have gotten this far in life with out having a complete breakdown. Maybe this was the best thing for her. What the hell did I know? Maxine was working the bar that night. She was my favorite barmaid. If I wasn't so in love with Sadie, I would have had me some Maxine. "Can I get you something else, Lee? We'll be closing up in about thirty minutes," she said as she gently leaned over the bar, giving me a full view of those pretty ass tits.

"Yeah, give me another highball. Heavy on the bourbon and easy on that 50/50."

Maxine laughed and said, "I hear you, Daddy."

She brought me my drink. I took a sip, and it was just the way I liked it. Bourbon found its way on my tongue and wanted to make a permanent home there. But the back of my throat was calling out to be watered. So I let the bourbon travel to the back of my mouth where it said a quick hello to the back of my throat and slid its way down to my stomach, warming every inch it touched along the way. My stomach was glad to see its old friend, it had been a whole five minutes since bourbon had been there to visit. My head was trying to say that we had seen enough of the bourbon for the night and that we should all go home. I gulped down the rest of bourbon's family and decided that my head was right.

I eased up from my stool and felt a little woozy. Maxine asked, "Hey, baby, you okay?"

"Yeah, I'm fine, sugah. I'm just gon' walk on home. I'll be okay." She looked at me for a moment, not knowing if she should take my word or not. Then she said, "You want me to call Sadie?" Before I knew it I yelled out, "Hell naw! You don't need to call no damn Sadie. I'm a grown man. I can make it home by myself!" I turned around and made my way to the door. I was a little high, but I would never admit it to Maxine. On the walk home, I kept seeing Ella in my head, she was walking around in a blue wedding gown. Why was she wearing blue? Was she pregnant? If that damn Buckley got my baby pregnant, I'll kill his old ass! I was going to call her as soon as I got back to the apartment, but first, I had to find her number.

By the time I got to the third floor and was about to open the door to my apartment, Sadie flung the door open. That damn Maxine. I told her not to call Sadie. The first thing out of her mouth was, "You're drunk!" I didn't even bother to argue. I walked right past her not in the mood to hear her nagging. I went back to the kitchen and found a pot of coffee on the stove. I poured myself a cup, skipping the cream and sugar. Unlike my bourbon, my coffee would be straight, strong and black. Sadie came in and sat down across from me. She knew I was hurting. I looked at her and was thankful that she didn't open her mouth. She reached out her hand to grab mine and we sat there, hand in hand, while I drank my coffee.

I woke up the next morning and Sadie was in my arms. Normally, when I came home drunk, she wouldn't have anything to do with me. She barely wanted to sleep in the same room with me. She would falsely accuse me of snoring and passing all sorts of foul gas in my sleep. One day she said the gas was so bad I must have been trying to kill her.

I eased out of the bed trying not to disturb her sleep. My first stop was the bathroom. My own morning breath almost made me sick. I couldn't find my toothbrush fast enough. Once my mouth was fresh and clean, I decided I could pee in peace. I took a quick hot shower and then went in the kitchen to put on a pot of coffee. Sadie finally drug herself out of the bed and made her way to the kitchen. I looked at her as she sat down at the table. She seemed to be glowing. I knew she was going to ask me about that damn wedding invitation. Sure enough, right before the coffee was ready, she asked, "So, have you given any more thought to Ella's wedding? Are you going, or what?"

I let out a sigh and sat down at the table with her. I took her by the hand and said, "No, I'm not going to the wedding. We are." The surprised look on her face was priceless. She didn't even bother to respond. She just sat there sipping her first of many cups of coffee for the day.

Before I gave my full attention to Ella's wedding, I had to finish up this rescue operation with Butch. We were scheduled to leave in two days. If everything went according to plan, we would be home in about three days.

CHAPTER 41

ELLA

After I finally agreed to marry Charles, he made me sit down and set a date. Although I knew I wanted to spend the rest of my life with him, the thought of actually saying "I do" was a bit overwhelming for me. I don't think it really hit me that I was getting married until I began to send out the invitations. At that point, it was no longer 'that something' that Charles and I just talked about, we were actually letting other people in on all of our plans. The mere thought of other people having an opinion about what I was doing scared the hell out of me. Charles couldn't understand why I felt the way I did. Truth be told, I didn't understand it myself.

We agreed to have the ceremony at the campus church and told the pastor that we wanted to keep it short and simple. Now, because we were getting married in six short weeks, the pastor came right out and asked if there was a reason for the quick wedding. In all the years I'd known Charles, I'd never seen him blush. His perfect brown skin turned a deep red the day we sat in the pastor's office preparing for our first of six pre-marital counseling sessions.

My mother finally called me. Really, she shouldn't

have. I almost laughed when she asked if there was anything she could do to help. What could she possibly do to help me? It took everything within me to include her name on the invitation. Had it been left up to me, she wouldn't be coming. Even after the invitations went out, I expected her to come up with some stupid excuse as to why she wouldn't be able to attend. Instead, I received a phone call asking what she could do to help. It was almost funny. Had I not still been so angry with her, I might have laughed. I politely told her that I didn't need any help and that we had everything under control.

Shortly after my mother called, Grandma Babe called and said she was coming to South Carolina to help with the wedding. That was the last thing I wanted. I tried to tell her that we had everything together, but she wouldn't hear of it. She told me she would be in town in exactly three weeks. Before I could even respond, she had hung up the phone and no doubt was packing her bags and calling Uncle Butch to tell him that they were making a road trip, real soon.

I could see right then and there that this whole thing was about to spiral out of control. I began to regret being talked into having an actual ceremony as opposed to a simple civil ceremony down at the court house. This whole ordeal was to be stress free and simple, but Grandma Babe had other plans.

The time seemed to fly by. Before I knew it, Grandma and Uncle Butch were ringing my doorbell. As soon as I heard the bell, the butterflies started causing havoc on my stomach. I began to have doubts about the whole thing. Maybe I should call the wedding off. I knew Charles would want children and I wasn't sure if I could continue this terrible cycle my family couldn't seem to break.

Grandma Babe blew into the apartment like a mighty wind. She started giving orders as soon as she crossed the threshold. I stood there feeling like I was ten years old again. When she saw that I hadn't moved, she stopped dead in her tracks and said, "Did you hear me, gal? I said let's git dis place in order. You gon' have people traipsing trough here like forty going north in just a few days. Now let's git a move on it."

The next thing I knew, I was running around in my own home doing chores like I was still living with Grandma Babe in East St. Louis. Everything had to be spic and span. She wouldn't rest until the apartment was literally sparkling. I tried to tell her that no one would be at the apartment; everything was taking place at the church and the hall that we had rented. Her reply was, "You never know when someone gon' stop by yo' place. Has you got any food in dis here 'partment?"

All I could do was laugh. I had to admit, I was glad to see my grandmother. I was glad to have someone actually there to help me prepare for my special day. Truth be told, I had no clue as to what I was doing, and because I didn't have any female friends to walk me through this, I welcomed my grandmother's help.

After Grandma had made out a list of all the chores that needed to be done, she sat me down at the kitchen table and asked, "Has you got yo' wedding gown all together?" Until that very moment, I hadn't given much thought to my dress. I figured I would just go downtown and buy a simple little dress and call it a day.

"Well, I figured I would just get a simple dress and

be done."

"What do you mean a simple dress? Dis is yo' wedding we talkin' 'bout," she said with her normal huff.

"Yes, Granny, I realize that this is my wedding, but I want to keep everything simple," I said, practically whining.

She went into the bedroom and returned with a garment bag draped across her arm. She quietly unzipped the bag and gently pulled out its contents. I couldn't believe my eyes. There in her arms laid the most beautiful white beaded gown I had ever seen. "Granny, you made this for me?" I said, with my hands covering my mouth, too afraid to touch the work of art.

"Ain't nobody else 'round here gittin' married, is dey?" All I could do was laugh. She handed me the dress and told me to try it on. I ran in the bedroom and could barely get the zipper down because my hands were shaking and my heart was racing out of control. Grandma must have known that I was nervous because she made her way in the room to help me try on the dress. Was the mirror playing tricks or was that really my reflection staring back at me in that beautiful white gown? I don't know how Grandma did it, but the dress fit like a perfect glove. I was so glad my grandmother had come.

Looking at myself in that gorgeous gown made me wish that I was going to have a huge wedding instead of the small intimate one that was already planned. Either way, I was glad that Grandma Babe was there. She was going to make sure that this was the best day of my life. She stood behind me as I looked at myself in the mirror and just held me from behind. The tears began to roll down my cheek. Grandma said, "Look here, gal, don't git yo' wedding dress all messed up wit' those tears. You have plenty of time to cry on yo' wedding day." We both laughed as she gently held me from behind and told me, "You gon' be da most beautiful bride dis town done ever seen."

My wedding day finally came. I woke up that morning in a cold sweat brought on by the nightmare dancing in my head. I dreamed that Charles and I were standing at the altar listening to the pastor ask if anyone saw just cause why the two of us should not be married. A hush fell over the room. All of a sudden, the front doors of the church flew open, and in comes Uncle Do-Man. Everyone in the church turned around to see what was going on. He stood at the opposite end of the aisle, and said in a demonically seductive voice, "She can't marry him because she's already married to me!" He stood there with his outstretched arms waiting for me to run and jump in them. I began to scream.

Grandma came into my room to find out what was going on. She sat down on my bed and began to rock me in her arms. In between the rocking and smoothing of my hair, she said, "It's gon' be okay, baby. You just got wedding jitters, that's all. Every bride has 'em before she walks down da aisle. You be okay."

Normally, her words and hugs would comfort me, but today they had absolutely no affect. I was still trembling when she finally left the room. I wasn't a drinker but I was wishing for one at 8 o'clock that Saturday morning. Then I remembered that Uncle Butch and Daddy had been drinking the night before. If I was lucky, there would be something left in one of those bottles that they were turning up like water. I just needed something to calm my nerves.

God was truly on my side. There was a little more than a corner in one of the Old-Granddad bottles. That was all I needed. I rushed for that bottle like it was the last drop of life on earth and ten men were behind me vying for the same drop. Just as I turned the bottle up, my grandmother walked into the kitchen. I damn near choked on that swig of alcohol. She said, "Gal, what in da hell is you in here doing?!"

I gulped down the brown liquor and put the bottle on the table. I wanted to speak but couldn't because of the fire that was making its way down my throat and into the pits of my stomach. My brain was telling the rest of my body that taking that swig wasn't such a good idea. I began to feel a tingling sensation in my arms and hands, and then it made its way down to my legs and feet. I had to sit down. My grandmother shouted her question to me once more. "Did you hear me, gal?! I said, what in the hell is you doing?!"

"Grandma, I had a terrible dream last night and I just needed something to take the edge off," I said as the alcohol rushed to my head.

She pulled a chair out from the table and sat down. Grandma looked at me.

"What kind of dream did you have?"

I told her about the dream and a sad look slowly walked across her face. She almost looked defeated. I didn't understand. Finally, she said, "Ella, let me talk to you fo' a minute." I scooted my chair as close to the table as I could. I wanted to hear every word she was about to say. Grandma wiped her mouth with her hand and said, "Listen, baby, I know you been through a lot, as far as yo' Uncle Do-Man is concerned. I just wants you to know that I am truly sorry for what happened to you. If I could take it all back, you knows I would. I never wanted to see any bad thang happen to you or any of my grandchildren. But sometimes bad thangs happen and deys out of our control."

"I don't blame you for what happened to me. I know it wasn't your fault. If anything, I blame my parents for not protecting me like they should have…" She cut me off before I could finish.

"Now, baby, I can't let you place all the blame on yo' Mama and Daddy. See, they really didn't know what type of person Do-Man was. But me, on the other hand, well, I knew when he was born. He just had a no-good spirit in him. I knew all along. Just ain't never wanted to admit it. But I'm telling you right here, right now, I'm sorry, baby, for all the pain you had to suffer because of my mistake." She grabbed me by both hands and held them in her hands as the tears fell from her eyes.

I don't know what scared me more, my dream or seeing Grandma cry. Never in all of my life, had I seen her shed a tear. Not even at funerals. Here she was, sitting at my kitchen table, allowing me to witness her vulnerability. Neither of us spoke. I wasn't even angry. The longer we sat there in silence, the more I began to understand. The tears began to flow from my eyes as well.

Uncle Butch came busting through the kitchen door and headed straight for the ice box. His head was half-way in the box before he realized that Grandma and I were even there. He eased back out of the box, turned to look at us and said, "What the hecks going on in here?" Grandma took her hands back and said,

"Boy, git whatever it is you gon' git from that there box and gon' git out of here. I'm trying to talk to Ella in private, if you don't mind."

The hangover that Uncle Butch was trying to nurse told him to listen to his mother and get out of her sight for now. That way he and the hangover could recover in peace. He found some lunch meat, grabbed some crackers and left the kitchen. The spell had been broken. Grandma was back to her normal self and she said to me, "Listen, baby, I meant what I said when I apologized to you. But like I always say, we can't harp on the past, we gots to move forward. Now Do-Man is dead and gon'. He can't hurt you no more. So somehow you has got to find a way to git over dis and move on wit yo' life. You hears what I'm telling you?" If only I could. I shook my head yes. "Baby," she continued, "You is 'bout to marry a mighty fine man. I know without a shadow of a doubt that he loves you mo' than you could ever 'magine. Now, you gon' have to separate what Do-Man did to you and what yo' husband is gon' be doing to you - it ain't the same. You see, baby, 'cause Charles loves you, he ain't gon' do nothing to hurt you. He gon' make love to you the way a woman should be made love to. And ain't nothing in the world wrong wit dat. It's the most beautiful thang a married couple could share." Never in a million years had I heard my grandmother talk like that. It made me blush, but I was glad she shared it with me.

"I know it's gon' take a little while fo' you to git used to the idea," she went on, "but after a while, you might even start to look forward to it. I know I did." Oh my God. I couldn't believe she was sharing her business with me like that. She saw the surprise on my face.

"Aw, gal, it ain't nothing to be ashamed of. If you just take yo' time and ease into it, you gon' be just fine. And because Charles knows you, I'm sure he gon' be very gentle when the time comes." I needed another drink.

I knew that Do-Man was dead and gone physically, but he still had a hold on me emotionally. I also realized that it was going to take more than a marriage and some motivational words to get over years of pain and struggle. I just prayed that somehow I would find my way through the past and begin to enjoy my present and look forward to my future.

The ceremony was beautiful. All of the relatives and friends that we invited were there. My mother sat right on the front row with my father. She appeared to be genuinely happy for me. I tried real hard to concentrate on the ceremony and the festivities of the day and not let my mind wander back to when I was a little girl. This was a joyous day, I kept telling myself.

My father walked me down the aisle and gave me away to the most wonderful man in the world. At that very moment, I looked at him and realized that not only was I marrying a very handsome man, but he was my soul mate. He was the epitome of love: kind, patient, giving, caring, forgiving and understanding. Had he not come into my life when he did, I don't know where I would have wound up, probably in an insane asylum.

The ceremony itself lasted about thirty minutes, followed by the reception. We danced, ate good food and drank a lot of champagne. Of course, my daddy and Uncle Butch had their own drink. But it was okay. Even Grandma didn't mind them having their own bottles that day.

Towards the end of the evening, my mother came up to me and tried to give me a hug. I almost didn't know how to respond. I hugged her like you would hug a stranger, the polite pat on the back and lots of space in between. In many ways she was a stranger. She told me that I was a beautiful bride and she was very proud of me. I smiled and graciously said, "Thank you."

My sister Cora was there. She looked like she was coming down from a bad high. Maybe they should have left her at home. I briefly overheard Daddy and Uncle Butch talking about what they went through in order to bring Cora home. I didn't get all of the details, but from what I did hear, it wasn't a pretty scene. Hell, she's lucky that the three of them made it out of there alive. Anyway, I didn't want to spend my wedding day thinking about Cora's issues. So I made sure that I kept a smile plastered on my face, and the thought of my honeymoon in my mind.

I couldn't wait to get out of there and head straight to the hotel to start my married life with my new husband. The next morning, Charles and I were catching a 7 o'clock train to New York City, my first ever, real vacation.

CHAPTER 42

SADIE

I was nervous about going to Ella's wedding. I hadn't seen her since her high school graduation, three years earlier. I wasn't even sure that I knew what to say to her. The day finally came and Lee Otis and I decided that we would drive down to South Carolina and make a nice little trip out of the whole thing. Cora even agreed to go with us.

When we got there, Lee Otis wanted to go straight to Ella's apartment. I wanted to go to the hotel and freshen up a little bit. Thank God he understood and agreed with me. Once we were checked in our rooms, I told Lee Otis to go on over there without me and that I would just see Ella a little later. He gave me a look but decided he would go on without me. Besides, Cora was in her room so I could always go and talk to her if I just wanted to talk to someone. What I really wanted to do was take a long nap. I'd see how I felt once I had gotten some rest.

Lee Otis didn't get back to the hotel until 1 or 2 o'clock the next morning. He smelled like he had been drinking for forty days and forty nights. I should have known. He got over to Ella's, hooked up with Butch, and that's all she wrote. It was just as well, that way I wouldn't have to face Ella until the next day, her wedding day. Hopefully, Lee Otis would be sober enough to even go to the wedding the next afternoon. Luckily, for Lee Otis and Butch, the wedding wasn't until 2 o'clock the next day. So they each had plenty of time to sleep off their high and still look some what fresh for the wedding. Some things never change.

I called Ella that morning to see if she needed, or wanted, me to do anything for her. She politely told me that her grandmother was helping her with everything she needed, and that all I had to worry about was getting to the wedding on time and making sure that her father was there to walk her down the aisle. I told her if she changed her mind to call me at the hotel; I would be there until 1 p.m. Maybe once she got to the church, she would need me to help her with something. I knew in my heart that as long as she had her Grandma Babe helping her, she wouldn't need my help in a million years, but I kept hoping.

I thought we would be the first people to arrive at the church, but to my surprise, there were about ten other people already there sitting in pews, all on the groom's side of the church. I wasn't sure if I was going to be escorted down the aisle, or not, so I walked right in and took a seat in the middle row of the pews. Cora followed closely behind me. Lee Otis disappeared to God knows where. Cora and I sat there in our seats, stiff as boards. We didn't say a word to each other, nor to the other people that were making their way into the place. I don't even know if we remembered to breathe.

After sitting there for about forty five minutes, Butch came upstairs and told me that I was to be escorted down the aisle by one of the ushers. I was grateful to be included, even if it was just to walk down the aisle. At least she was acknowledging me as her mother. When I made my way to the back, I saw this gorgeous woman standing in the middle of the floor with a few people gathered around her. When our eyes met, I couldn't believe how stunning she was. A wave of emotion swept across my face and through my mind, all at once. I didn't know what to say, so I just stood there staring at the beautiful young woman in front of me.

Ella made her way over to me and gave me a polite hug and said, "I'm glad you were able to make it." I wanted to throw both my arms around her and tell her how sorry I was for all of the things that had happened to her, and for all of the things that happened between the two of us. But I thought it best if I just politely hugged her back and kept it moving. She introduced me to Mr. Buckley's parents and then told me that I should line up behind Ms. Babe. Lee Otis' younger brother, Sonny, was going to escort me down the aisle when the time came.

Standing there waiting to walk down the aisle, I realized that Ella was probably the only one of my three daughters that would ever have a beautiful church wedding like this. Poor Cora was such a head case that I'm sure it was going to take years for her to get back to normal. And Mattie was so far gone it would take a real miracle to bring her back.

The ceremony was absolutely beautiful. She was a striking bride, and the dress that Babe made her looked more spectacular than any of those gowns in the bridal books; and it fit her to a tee. We had a great time at the reception, also. I guess I was caught up in the festivities of everything because, I began to look back over our lives and guilt tried to take over. I did everything I could not to cry. I didn't want people thinking that I was sad about the wedding. Nothing could have been further from the truth. In fact, I was glad that Ella was able to move on with her life and actually found someone to love and cherish for all eternity. I secretly prayed that the cycle would stop with her.

After the reception was over, we all went back to the hotel for an impromptu after-party. I really wasn't in the mood to party, but the whole Boxx clan was there, and they insisted on having a party. So we all gathered in Lil' Sonny's room and the party began. I don't think I left from down there until 2 the next morning. I know Lee Otis didn't come back to our room until 5 a.m.

Luckily for us, we weren't leaving until the next morning, so Lee Otis had the whole day to sleep off his hangover.

CHAPTER 43

LEE OTIS

Yeah, my baby's wedding was something to behold. Even though it was small and intimate as she and my mother put it, it was really classy. My baby got good taste. I was so proud to walk her down that aisle and give her away. I do believe I gave her away to a real good man.

When we first got the invitation to the wedding, I didn't know how I was going to do what I had to do with the wedding, and handle the situation with Cora. But me and Butch figured out the whole thang. See, we had to fly all the way out to California to get Cora. At first she and her sister were right here in Chicago with those Black Hebrew Israelites. Then we found out that she went out to California with one of the other leaders, and that's when she realized that she needed to get out of there.

Well, we went on out there and tried to talk to the so-called leader of the group. But he wanted to try and tell me and Butch that it was "Abaja's" decision to be there, and she could leave whenever she wanted. However, he didn't believe that she was ready to leave at this time. Then he turned and looked at Cora and said, "Isn't that right, Sister Abaja?" She stood there afraid to open her sunken-in mouth, so I spoke for her. "Look here, Brother YaYa, or whatever the hell your name is. I didn't come all this way just to hear you talk all this jive. I came down here to take my daughter home and that's just what I'm gon' do. Now I suggest you step aside and let *'Cora'* go head on and get her things so we can be on our way."

That's when brother YaYa made his second mistake of the day. He looked me dead in my eye and said, "Sister Abaja, ain't going nowhere, except for where I tell her she can go. See, what you fail to realize is that she belongs to me now. And the one true God, YHWH, wants her to stay right here." Well, that's when my true and living God told me to whip his natural black ass. And that's exactly what I did. I beat that nigger to within an inch of his life. Butch was standing there with two pistols drawn at his side just in case any of YaYa's flunkies wanted to jump bad.

Once I finished beating his ass, I grabbed Cora by her frail arm and we walked right up out of that joint. We brought her crazy tail home with just the clothes on her back. It was a long quiet flight all the way back to East St. Louis where we dropped off Butch and picked up my car.

On the drive back to Chicago, I finally asked Cora, "What in the hell made you and your sister join up with some crazy ass niggers like that, anyway?" She didn't say anything she just kept looking out of the window. "Cora, look at me." She slowly turned her face from up against the window to look at me. I quickly glanced at her and realized for the first time how much she looked like my mother. She had that same reddish brown skin, just like Mama, the same keen nose and a beautiful pair of almond shaped eyes that were so dark you would think they were black. When Cora was a little girl, she had long jet black wavy hair and everyone thought she was the most beautiful child to ever grace this earth. You would never know it to look at her now. She had cut off all of her beautiful hair, and what was left of it was all matted up like it hadn't been combed in months. Her eyes were vacant, almost void of life. I was really afraid of how Sadie would react when we walked through that door.

"Cora, what was it about those people that made you want to join up with them?" I said as calmly as I could. We were approaching a rest stop and I decided to pull in so we could talk face to face.

She was crying so hard by the time she finished telling me her story, that she could barely see straight. I wanted to turn that car around and drive straight back to California and kill that son-of-a-bitch with my bare hands. Instead, I sat there speechless, trying to calm my own nerves while trying to figure out what I should say to my child. There were no words. We got out of the car and walked around for a minute. After we stretched our legs, we got back in the car and hit the road. I drove the next four and a half hours to Chicago in complete silence.

CHAPTER 44

CORA

To tell you the truth, I never did want to join them. It was all Mattie's idea. I just did it because of her. From the beginning, I thought they were all crazy, but I was too afraid to say anything, so I went along with it, even though I knew it was wrong.

Mattie started dating this fellow named Bobby Carson. He worked at some plant way out in Indiana. I'm not exactly sure what he did for a living; all I know is, I didn't like him. Mama always made me tag along with them on their dates because she really didn't know him or any of his people. We really didn't know where he came from. It was like he just appeared out of thin air. He was always talking about black people taking their rightful place in the world and how we was the true Jews. It all sounded weird to me, but Mattie was buying it hook, line and sinker.

He started dragging us to all of those meetings with those other crazy people. During the meetings, he would pump our heads with all kinds of nonsense about us moving to Israel to take our rightful places in our true native land. He would talk about how our men were really princes and our women princesses, and how the government over there couldn't wait for us to "come home." The biggest problem for me was when he told us that we would have to start adopting the Israelite customs and traditions. That meant that the men would start taking on as many wives as they wanted. Now initially, Bobby said that he only wanted Mattie. But after he got total control of her mind, he decided that he needed three additional wives. He said he needed to get all of his wives together before we made the voyage to Israel.

He tried to force me into marrying one of his lieutenants. When I refused, he beat me and then told the other man to rape me. The beatings and rapes were nothing compared to the prostitution that most of us girls were forced into. They told us that that was our way of financing the move to Israel. The more money we made, the faster we could all make the journey. This all happened once we moved the operation to California. I knew then that I had to get out, but I didn't know how. The beatings and raping continued right up until Daddy and Uncle Butch came to get me. That's just a couple of the ways they got the girls to do whatever they said to do. They used all kinds of mind controlling methods, including drugs, to get you to submit. It wasn't that difficult to do because the majority of the girls came from broken homes where they were either physically, mentally or sexually abused, (if not all three,) or had some type of mental problem. We all had self esteem issues.

I guess Mattie and I were no different than any of the other girls there. We had our own set of issues. Daddy was locked up, Mama worked two and three jobs at a time, and Ella was off in East St. Louis, living the good life, or so we thought.

CHAPTER 45

ELLA

Charles and I didn't get to see much of New York. We spent most of our time in bed. Grandma Babe was right on the money. He was extremely gentle with me. Our train pulled into New York around 5 o'clock in the evening. In the cab ride over to the hotel, we were awe-struck by the beautiful sights around Manhattan. There was an energy in the air that was unbelievable. The cab pulled up in front of the most beautiful 30-story hotel I'd ever seen. I looked at Charles and said, "You sure they let black people stay in a place like this?"

The cabbie stepped out to retrieve our bags, and the doorman came to help us out of the cab. I couldn't believe it. Where in the world was I? As Charles and I walked through the front door of that magnificent hotel and on to the front desk, the smiling white desk clerk cheerfully said, "Welcome to the St. George's Hotel. How can I help you today?" Charles did all of the talking. After we were checked in, the woman behind the desk gave Charles the key to a honeymoon suite and told us to enjoy our stay.

The bellhop opened the door to the most spectacular thing I had ever seen. I was expecting a room with one king size bed. Instead, the door opened up to a beautifully decorated living room with a television, a fully stocked bar, and a great view of the city. Then the bellhop led us up to the bedroom. When I saw that round, pink, plush bed, I just wanted to take off all my clothes and run and jump up and down on it. The bellhop sat our bags down and waited by the door for his tip. Charles and I were so out-done by the suite, that we almost forgot the man was even there, that is until he cleared his throat to remind us. Charles gave him $2.00, thanked him for his help and then walked him to the door. When he came back in the room, I was still standing there staring at the bed. He whispered in my ear, "Think you might want to try it out?" I immediately began to tense up, then I remembered Grandma's words, 'just ease into it.'

He must have felt me tense up, so he took me by the hand and led me out of the bedroom and onto the couch in the living room. We sat down and he began to softly touch my face. He told me how beautiful I was and that I was his one dream come true. He began to gently kiss my face in between the words he was now whispering in my ear. I could feel my shoulders relaxing inch by inch. My heart was starting to do its own dance and there was this tingling in between my legs that I had never felt before. Charles kept kissing my face and whispering in my ear. He didn't touch me. After about ten minutes of teasing me, I tried to put his arm around me, but he wouldn't cooperate. He told me he had something much better in store for me.

We got up from the couch and he led me to the bedroom and stood me in front of the bed. He whispered in my ear, "Unbutton your blouse." I did as I was told.

Then he whispered, "Take off your skirt." Again, I did as I was told. Before I realized it, I was completely naked. He ran his hands over my body, just inches from actually touching me. Then he told me to do the unthinkable. He said, "Touch your breasts." I was so caught up in what he was whispering in my ear that I readily obeyed.

I began to touch my own breasts and it felt so good that I slowly slid my hands down my stomach and over my hips. My eyes were closed and my mouth slightly opened. I felt his lips gently touch mine and I let out a slight moan. Then he told me to touch myself 'down there' and the spell he had on me was almost broken. I opened my eyes because I was afraid. He told me to close them, and touch myself so I could finally know what real pleasure feels like. He gently licked my breast. I was under his spell again. I touched myself and was glad I did. I had found a new jewel whose beauty and worth no man could measure.

Charles and I made love all evening and into the morning. We stopped long enough to order room service, eat, take a bath and then back to bed.

By the time we got back to South Carolina, I could barely walk. That was the sweetest pain I'd ever experienced. I have to admit, I was real nervous about the honeymoon. I wasn't sure that I would be able to perform my wifely duties. And even though Grandma Babe had a long talk with me, I was still scared.

CHAPTER 46

ELLA

Charles and I had been home from New York for just over a month and were settling into married life pretty good. One evening we had just sat down to dinner when the phone rang. "Hello," I said, trying not to sound upset that someone was intruding on our dinner. "Hello, may I speak with Mrs. Buckley please?" the woman on the other end said.

"This is she."

"Hi, Mrs. Buckley, this is Nurse Tucker from Dr. Bailey's office, and I'm calling to give you the test results from your pregnancy test."

My heart almost dropped. I had been waiting a whole week for the results and now they call in the middle of my dinner to give me the results. Please, God, be merciful.

"Mrs. Buckley, are you there?"

"Yes, I'm here," I said almost unable to speak.

"Congratulations. You're about four weeks pregnant. Now Dr. Bailey wants you to come in one day next week so he can get you started on your pre-natal care. Would you like to set up your appointment now, or call me later?"

I told her that I would call her later and hung up the phone without saying goodbye. Charles finally looked up from his dinner plate and asked, "Who was that?" I didn't know if I should tell him then or wait until I figured out what I was going to do. Who was I kidding? I knew exactly what I was going to do. I would have this baby and try to move on with life.

I sat down at the table and told him about my brief conversation with Nurse what's her name, and all he could do was smile from ear to ear. Good thing one of us was excited. I just kept thinking that this couldn't have come at a worse time. I only had one year of undergrad to complete, and then I was going to work on my masters. But with a baby on the way, all of my dreams would have to be put on hold.

The first three months of the pregnancy were terrible. I threw up every day, and most nights. I wanted to eat everything in sight. But once I put it in my mouth, it made me gag. The only thing I could keep down was pork-n-beans. I had gas so bad that I thought I was going to blow up the apartment.

By the grace of God, I was able to finish the entire spring semester with all A's and B's. Unfortunately, by the time summer break was over I started having really bad cramps and I was spotting. The first thing I did was call Grandma Babe and told her what was going on. She told me that I should get off of my feet for at least a week and stay in bed. I should only get up to use the bathroom.

The first couple of days, I did just as she instructed, by the third day, I was about to lose my mind. So I would walk from the bedroom to the living room just to have a change of scenery. One day while I was sitting in Charles' big recliner, I felt this gush of something ooze from in between my legs. I looked down and saw a big puddle of blood on the chair. When I stood up, a huge blood clot slid from my vagina onto the cream colored carpet. I almost passed out. I made my way over to the phone and called the operator and told her to send an ambulance.

Charles and the ambulance made it to the apartment at the exact same time. I was in the bedroom lying across the bed on top of a mountain of towels, praying that I didn't bleed to death. I was rushed to the University Hospital only to be told what I already knew. I had lost the baby. They did a D&C on me to clean out whatever was left of the baby and to make sure that no infection set up.

I left the hospital three days later with an empty womb and empty handed. As much as I didn't want to have a baby at that time, I was grief stricken. The doctor told Charles and me that sometimes these things just happened. It was just nature saying that, for whatever reason, this particular child wasn't ready for this world. His words did little to ease my mind. The doctor also told us that we were young enough to try again and again. When I heard him speak those words, something inside of me said that was the one and only chance we had to have a child. Never again would I subject myself to such pain. Besides that, I never wanted to have kids. I shook my head yes when the doctor said we could try again in about six months and everything should be fine. Inside of that agreeing head was a voice screaming out, "Not in this life time will I ever have a child!"

After six weeks of healing, and no sex with my

husband, I should have been all over him. I wasn't. He couldn't understand why I no longer desired him. I didn't know how to tell him that I equated having sex with getting pregnant, and that just couldn't happen again.

He was so frustrated that there were times when he wouldn't talk to me for days, sometimes weeks. I didn't care. The one big problem with my no sex, no pregnancy philosophy was that it was about to lead to no marriage. That's when Charles suggested that I go to counseling. I agreed. Our first appointment was set for the following Tuesday.

We waited in that cold lobby for at least twenty minutes before the middle aged blond woman poked her head out to tell us to come in and have a seat. Charles and I did as we were told and followed her into the intimate office behind the door and took our seats. I was surprised that I immediately felt comfortable when we sat down. Her spirit was warm and inviting. She had a way of putting you at ease right away. I looked around her office and was most impressed by the beautiful view of the ocean and the art work on the walls. The one that really struck me was the one entitled Motherless Child. Most people would have looked at that painting and thought it was hideous, but I guess I could relate because that's exactly how I felt.

Charles couldn't stand looking at that painting. It unnerved him to the point that he found it difficult to keep going to counseling. But I convinced him to keep going. However, after about three weeks of therapy, Dr. Free suggested that I start individual therapy because all of our issues were stemming from my past.

With little coaxing, I agreed to the one-on-one therapy. I told her all about my childhood, and to my surprise she shared some things that happened to her while growing up as well. She too had been molested as a child and that is why she went into psychology, so she could help other men and women who experienced the same things as she did as a child.

There were days when I wanted to quit therapy because she made me dig deeper than I had ever allowed myself to do; and some days it was just too painful to face. The thought of losing my marriage was a great motivator to keep going.

I went through counseling for an entire year before I felt comfortable enough to confront certain members of my family. Dr. Free pushed me beyond my comfort zone and made me deal with different aspects of my childhood; the molestation, the nine year old Ella, my school experiences, my lack of friends, feelings about my father killing on my behalf. At the end of our first year together, Dr. Free felt I was ready to deal with the people we had spent the last twelve months talking about - even my Uncle Do-Man. She told me I would know how to deal with each person at the appropriate time, and that there was no wrong or right way to handle it. I just had to be willing.

The first person was my father. After I spoke openly and honestly with him about how I felt, I was able to truly forgive him in my mind and heart. I didn't realize it, but I was holding him responsible for the family falling apart. Had he not gone to prison, the family would have at least stayed together. Even though I called myself having a close relationship with him, I never shared my real feelings about him, the molestation or his brother.

I took the train from South Carolina to East St. Louis to talk to my Grandma Babe. I felt that I needed to thank her face to face for all she did for me while I was growing up. She was really my first therapist. It took me paying a whole lot of money and spending a whole lot of time on a stranger's couch for me to realize that my grandmother had been telling me the same things all my life. Sometimes during a session, Dr. Free would say something and I would jump up and say, "My grandmother used to say the same thing!" She would laugh and get back to the session.

Grandma Babe used to always tell me that in order to move on with my life I had to, "Forgive other people for all they mess, 'cause just as sho' as time is marching on, somebody, somewhere, is gon' have to forgive you fo' all of yo' mess." Sometimes that statement would make me so angry. I couldn't imagine ever having any mess to be forgiven of, after all, I was the victim, wasn't I? Sure enough, I had to ask my husband to forgive me for all of this mess that I was carrying around, not willing to release.

When I got to East St. Louis, Grandma responded just like I thought she would. I told her thanks for all that she had done and taught me over the years, and that I didn't know where I would be if she hadn't stepped in and saved me from what I thought was a sho' nuff hell. She said, "I don't deserve no thanks for doing what any grandmother worth her weight in salt would have done; 'sides that, you might have turned out a whole lot better had somebody else come along and rescued you," she said with a big smile.

I didn't know it at the time, but Grandma had just been diagnosed with breast cancer. She fought it until the end. She lived two years after she was diagnosed. She refused to get any type of treatment, and certainly wasn't going to have a mastectomy. She would always say, "Those damn doctors must be out of they cotton-pickin' minds if they thank for one minute I'm gon' let them take what the good Lawd done blessed me wit. Oh, hell naw! They ain't cutting nothing off me. I'm going back to the earth with everythang I done come here wit."

All of her children begged her to have the mastectomy. Grandma's mind was made up. She died just like she lived - her way.

Since I had purchased a round trip train ticket from South Carolina to East St. Louis, I decided to borrow one of Uncle Butch's cars and drove up to Chicago to talk to my mother, face-to-face. My therapist said that it would be better if I talked to my parents individually and in person. My dad just so happened to be coming to South Carolina when I got up the courage to talk to everyone. So by the time I went to Chicago, my dad and I had already spoken.

When I pulled up to the apartment, I was almost afraid to get out of the car. All of the memories began to flood my mind. I wasn't sure that I could make it up the stairs. Dr. Free told me I might feel that way. I just didn't know I would be overcome with such emotion at the sight of that old building. I wondered why they never moved. The neighborhood had changed – and not for the better. Where there was once an empty lot full of grass and a safe place for the neighborhood kids to play and hangout, looked more like an abandoned lot for wino's, gang bangers and drug addicts. I couldn't believe my parents were still living in this neighborhood. I had to shrug that off. That was not the purpose of my visit. I was there to release myself from a mental and emotional hell that I had been held captive for far too many years.

I got up the courage to take the key out of the ignition and open the door. At that moment, my legs froze and I couldn't move. I took several deep breaths and quickly asked the Lord to give me strength. He must have been looking right at me that day, because as soon as the thought left my mind, I got a burst of energy.

I made my way to the front step and had to stop again. 'Okay, Lord, I need some more strength. As a matter of fact, You gon' have to just carry me on up these stairs, otherwise I ain't gon' make it.' It was as if the Lord spoke to me Himself and said, "I'm always with you, but I want you to make the first step, then let Me do the rest. I promise you'll get stronger with each step." I told the Lord I didn't know about that. I wouldn't have been surprised if my legs would have given out on me the minute I touched that first step. Well, you know the Lord was right. I held on to that banister as if my life depended on it. I put my right foot on that first step and pulled myself up to the next.

My heart was pounding so loud and hard, I heard and felt it in my head, arms and legs. A little sweat broke out on my forehead. I tried not to think about where I was, but instead where I wanted to be - in my parent's apartment talking face-to-face with my mother. Before I knew it, I was standing in front of the apartment door. I couldn't bring myself to look up to the next floor where Uncle Do-Man lived. I just wanted someone to hurry up and open the door.

I knocked and stood there moving from side to side like a child does when they have to pee. My mother finally answered the door after I knocked for the second time. The last time I looked at my mother standing on the inside of the apartment, I must have been about 4 feet tall. She seemed like a giant back then. Now, I stood on the outside of the door and saw a woman who was no longer a giant, but someone I could now look eye to eye. She had also aged quite a bit since the last time I saw her.

She gave me a nervous smile and stood back and said, "Come in," as she opened the door wider for me and my purse. I could tell she was expecting to see at least one suitcase. I walked in to the apartment expecting to find things exactly like they were when I was nine years old. To my surprise, everything was different. There was new living room and dining room furniture, a big color Television with a remote control, new paint on the walls, and even wall-to-wall carpet instead of the hardwood floors we had when I was last there.

My instincts told me to go straight to the kitchen, but my legs couldn't seem to make it past the front hallway. I stood there for a moment trying not to panic. My mother saw the anguish on my face and said, "Why don't you have a seat up there in the living room? I'll go and get some coffee." She walked away before I could answer. The several deep breaths I took must have unlocked my legs because once I started breathing, I was able to make my way to the new couch in the living room.

I sat there not knowing what to do with myself while

I waited for her to bring the coffee. The apartment was so quiet that I figured we must be alone. For that I was grateful, but scared. During the long drive from East St. Louis to Chicago, I had rehearsed everything I was going to say when I saw her. But when she opened that door, I was nine years old once again.

I had to find my courage and my voice before she returned with that hot java. She had to know the pain I suffered all those years, and she had to know the part she played in that suffering. My resolve to stand up, be an adult and confront my mother, began to dissolve like a snowball in hell. I heard the flip-flap of her house shoes as she approached the living room with the coffee. Clearing my throat, hoping to conjure up some semblance of a voice before she returned proved to be a waste of time. Maybe once I took a sip of coffee the words would start flying out of my mouth.

She walked into the living room with a serving tray that held her grandmother's silver coffee pot and two cups from her grandmother's china. I remember the set from when I was a little girl. It was one of the only things she ever got from her grandmother after she died. My mother didn't receive her inheritance until her stepmother finally died, and her father gave her the coffee and china sets.

My mother carefully placed the tray on the coffee table and then stepped back and sat down on the edge of the loveseat behind her. She didn't know what to do with her hands, so she began to smooth out her skirt over her knees. I sat there looking at the woman who gave birth to me, that I should have referred to as mother, but all I could see was Sadie, the woman who never protected me. Then I had to remember that I wasn't there to place anymore blame. I was there to give forgiveness. But while I was there, I would have to ask the question, why?

She sat there for a moment, nervously fidgeting with her skirt and her hands. Finally, she offered to pour us each a cup of coffee. After we each had our cups in hand, she sat all the way back in her seat and crossed her legs. I took a sip of the hot Maxwell House and put my cup back on the tray. I wasn't sure how to start our conversation, especially since we rarely spoke. She must have felt the same way because she said absolutely nothing. I figured if I didn't want to be sitting there until tomorrow I better say something.

I leaned forward on the couch and said, "Well, as you know, I came up here so that the two of us could talk." I was beginning to lose my voice. I cleared my throat and continued. "I've been seeing a therapist for the past year and she feels that it's time I speak to you honestly about what happened to me as a child and how I felt and feel about what happened." My mother began to squirm in her seat like a child does when being scolded by a parent.

"Trust me, this is just as uncomfortable for me as it is for you. I struggled for weeks with the idea of talking to you." I wasn't sure what to say next. I really wanted my mother to say something but it was obvious that she, like me, didn't know what to say. I took another sip of coffee and tried to continue. "My therapist said that I should just come right out and tell you that I didn't feel you protected me like you did Cora and Mattie, and that I should ask you why you didn't protect me like you did the others. So I'm asking, why?" Dr. Free was right. I did feel a sense of relief after I asked the question. Now

I was nervous about the answer.

She sat on that loveseat staring at me as if she had seen a ghost. I waited for at least two minutes for her to answer. Maybe the Maxwell House had burned her tongue because for the longest time, she did not open her mouth. I was starting to think that something was wrong with her. I leaned forward again and asked her if she heard what I said. She continued to look at me with that frightened look on her face. My nervousness was turning into anger. How dare her not answer me. I asked again, "Did you hear me?" with more force than before.

Still no answer, just more staring. She just kept looking at me with those big green/grey eyes of hers. I didn't know if I should be nervous or angry. I began to fidget again. Why wouldn't she answer? She, of all people knew the answers to all of the questions I asked. Frozen like a statue is how she appeared. Two hundred and fifty nine miles from East St. Louis to Chicago in 90 degree heat and this is what I get; a grown woman too afraid to answer her daughter's questions. This was just great. I was expecting some closure but all I got was more frustration. Why did she agree to see me? She knew it wasn't a social call.

I decided to give her one more chance. "Why did you let Uncle Do-Man do those awful things to me?" She cleared her throat and said, "Would you care for more coffee?" Okay, that was it. I slammed my cup and saucer on the table, grabbed my purse from the cocktail table and stood to leave. As I made my way to the door, I heard her say, "Ella, wait." I stopped but didn't turn around. I waited for her to say something. She never did. I shook my head and walked out of the door.

On my way down the stairs, I heard Dr. Free telling me during our last session that I shouldn't expect too much from my mother. I had to remember, I was the one who had gone through counseling, not her. So while I was ready to confront my demons, she on the other hand probably was not.

By the time I reached the bottom of the stairs, I had a good mind to turn around and go back to the apartment and go off on my mother. But the longer I stood there, I realized that that type of behavior wouldn't accomplish anything. Instead, I went to the five and dime store and bought some stationary. I sat at the lunch counter in the store, ordered a Fresca and began to write my mother a letter. By the time I finished, I had fifteen pages.

When I put the last period on the last sentence, my heart began to beat at a normal rate again and my mind felt as light as it did when I was about seven years old. Years and years of anger, hurt and shame rushed up from the pit of my stomach, burned through my chest, only to meet up with the craziness from my head. And it all slid down my arm to my fingers and out to the pen and paper. I felt like I had lost about 15 pounds by the time I folded the letter and shoved it in the envelope.

I walked back to my parent's apartment and slid the fat envelope in the mailbox that hung on the wall in the front lobby. I turned and walked out of 5419 S. Indiana and never looked back. I got in to Uncle Butch's car, started up the engine, and headed for the expressway. As I got on the road, I remembered what Grandma Babe used to always say: "Sometimes when you going through, you start wondering if the Lawd is gon' work that thang out the way you want Him to. More than likely, He won't. That's when yo' faith got to kick in and you just got to believe that the Lawd know just what He doing. It's at times like these, baby, that you got to relax and let the Lawd move you, and everythang will work out just the way it's suppose to."

EPILOGUE

When I hit the city limits of East St. Louis, I decided I needed to talk to one more person before I headed back to South Carolina. Before I even realized it, the car was heading in the direction of the local cemetery. It was time for me to confront Do-Man. The only reason I knew where his gravesite was is because Grandma Babe had purchased a family plot and I remembered going with her to visit Grandpa Cleveland's grave when I was a little girl.

I drove to the side of the cemetery where the family plot was, but I couldn't drive up to the plot right away because there was a long line of cars slowly pulling away. Once they were out of sight, I pulled up to the gravesite and got out of my car to make my way to Do-man. As I made my approach, my legs decided to lock up on me, forcing me to stop dead in my tracks. I took a few deep breaths to try and calm my nerves. The grave diggers were lowering a casket into the ground right next to the family plot. I decided to stand by the big weeping willow tree that was just off to the side. I wanted to wait for them to finish so I could have some privacy. They didn't seem to notice me standing there.

Once the casket was in the ground, the men picked up their shovels and began to fill in the hole. One of the workers stopped, turned and looked at me and said, "Hey, wasn't Do-Man your uncle?" I shook my head yes and he said, "I thought so." And they went back to filling the hole. I stood back and watched and waited for the men to finish their work.

Once they were gone, I stepped up to Do-Man's grave and a tear rolled down my cheek. At the time, I didn't understand why I would shed even one tear for such a vile and evil man. It wasn't until years later that I realized the tears I shed at Do-Man's grave were not tears of sadness, but tears of anger, bitterness and eventually, forgiveness.

As I stood over his grave, I kept asking the question, why? Why would my own uncle do such horrible and disgusting things to me? What did I do to deserve such treatment? Why did he choose me and not one or both of my sisters? Why didn't that little girl's mother have him arrested when she found out what he did to her daughter? Maybe then he wouldn't have been able to hurt anyone else. I then began to question how my own mother could have allowed this to happen to her own baby. Why couldn't she just stay home and not work like Daddy wanted, then all of this could have been avoided.

The longer I stood there looking at that headstone, the angrier I became. Before I knew it, I was jumping up and down screaming, "I hate you! I hate you! I hate you!" The last time I jumped up and down on that grave, a snake crawled from underneath the ground and hissed at me. I screamed to the top of my lungs and took off running through the cemetery and didn't stop until I reached the main road.

I stood there trying to catch my breath when I saw a familiar figure walking towards me. It was a small-framed woman wearing a lady's brown, felt hat with a chocolate brown wool coat that was worn and tattered. She wore thick, brown stockings that sagged in the ankles, and dusty black run-over shoes. It was strange attire for the middle of summer in 90 degree heat. I couldn't quite make out her face until she was about ten feet in front of me. That's when I noticed the big black Bible underneath her arm. Then it came to me who this strange looking woman was. She was the woman that roamed through town, stopping at street corners, yelling out Bible verses to sinners and saints alike. This was the same woman who appeared in the courtroom when my father was being sentenced for killing his brother. Now, she was standing in my face about to shout one of those Bible verses at me.

"No need in you being 'fraid of me, chile. I ain't gon' do nothin' to hurt you. But I do have a word from the Lawd just for you." She stuck out her hand and gently grabbed my face. Terrified, I looked at her with tear-filled eyes. She said, "The Lawd wants you to know dat He loves you and dat you is very special to Him; and just 'cause some terrible thangs don happened to you, it don't mean dat He's forsaken you. He has great thangs in store for you, but you gots to trust and believe His word. Right now it seems like da pain is too much to bear and the hurt is too deep to heal. But believe me, chile, when I say, you won't feel like dis always. The Lawd is gon' take special care of you."

The tears were now running down my face as the woman spoke. I could feel the power of God emanating from her entire being. Before I knew it, I was on my knees weeping. She stood over me and prayed. When she finished, she said, "The Lord is saying it's time for you to stop asking why and move on with your life." She turned around and walked away.

When I left East St. Louis that summer, I never returned. Not once did I ever feel the need to look or go back. But in the back of my mind the question remained, "WHY?"

Statistics on Child Molestation

It is estimated that at least two out of every ten girls and one out of every ten boys are sexually abused by the end of their 13th year.

-Child Molestation Research
and Prevention Institute

There are 400,000 registered sex offenders in the United States, and an estimated 80 to 100,000 of them are missing.

-The National Center for
Missing and Exploited Children.

89% of child sexual assault cases involve persons known to the child, such as a caretaker or family acquaintance.

-Diana Russell Survey, 1978

The average child molester will molest fifty girls before being caught and convicted.

-Stats on Child Molestation
- Registered Sex offender News

¾ of the violent victimizations of children took place in either the victim's home or the offender's home.

-BJS Survey of State Prison Inmates, 1991

All but 3% of offenders who committed violent crimes against children were male.

-BJS Survey of State Prison Inmates, 1991

The typical offender is male, begins molesting by age 15, engages in a variety of deviant behavior, and molests an average of 117 youngsters, most of whom do not report the offense.

-Dr. Gene Abel
National Institute of Mental Health Study

Like rape, child molestation is one of the most underreported crimes: only 1 - 10% are ever disclosed.

-FBI Law Enforcement Bulletin

The behavior is highly repetitive, to the point of compulsion, rather than resulting from a lack of judgment.

-Dr. Ann Burges, Dr. Nicholas Groth, et al.
in a study of imprisoned offenders

If you or someone you know is a victim of child molestation call 1800-799-SAFE, or **go to**
www.darkness2light.org
for more information.